Thrall Conspiracy Genesis

Genesis

A Polaris Effect, Twin Helix Chronicle, Book 2

Case ID: 1-13320117601

ISBN: 978-1-957459-04-2

Dedication

This book, like all Thrall Conspiracy chronicles, is dedicated to the future of Greta Thunberg. She relentlessly reminds humanity of its vulnerability to the weight of human inertia.

Once "reminded," individuals remain responsible to carry through with action. This book is also dedicated to readers who go beyond their personal frames of reference and consider the bigger picture.

We have one chance in 10,000 to survive the next thousand years.

So, let's do it.

Acknowledgment

I gratefully acknowledge the wonderful assistance of Darshana Parekh of Mumbai, India, in writing this novel of gestation, giving birth, and raising very alert children with gobs of love and hope.

Her experience as a mother of two great kids, a girl and a boy, plus living in Mumbai, makes the pages glow with authenticity and power. Thank you, Darshana, for expressing those feelings in your prose and poetic touches throughout the story.

I also gratefully acknowledge the daily encouragement of my best partner in life (and wife), Theresa M. Olson. I look forward to seeing her book *Paws for Enlightenment*, which Darshana also pushed to fruition.

Also, for the record, this story taps into archetypal forms and motives that I didn't know existed when outlining the plot. Identical twins, anyone? It turns out that Artemis and Apollo carry a psychological message in Greek myth, just as they do today. The idea of "identical twins" was *required* when I outlined this novel, but my conscious mind did not know why. (We'll hear more about DNA hybrids and psychic moms later.)

But today, at the end of this publishing journey, the notion of identical twins (OK, *doppelgangers*)—and, importantly, of different genders, represents the undercurrents of life we all must reconcile: the *anima* and the *animus*. Check Google search, or better, ChatGPT or whatever near-sentient (or post-sentient?) AI tool exists now to see how the anima and animus of our shadow selves seek manifestation so that they can dissolve in resolution.

The idea of "complementarity" attempts to explain wave/particle duality to satisfy our curiosity about "physics." Similarly, the idea of "wholeness" attempts to explain male/female duality to satisfy our quest for understanding "metaphysics." That's the story of anima and animus. Write an essay on the topic with pros and cons.

It was interesting that just yesterday, the feelings generated by reading the end of this story pulled my own imagination towards that wholeness more than I had ever experienced before in print. Ha, and I (a part of me, anyway) invented that story. So, *that* was quite a day.

I hope you experience similar revelations.

Epigraph

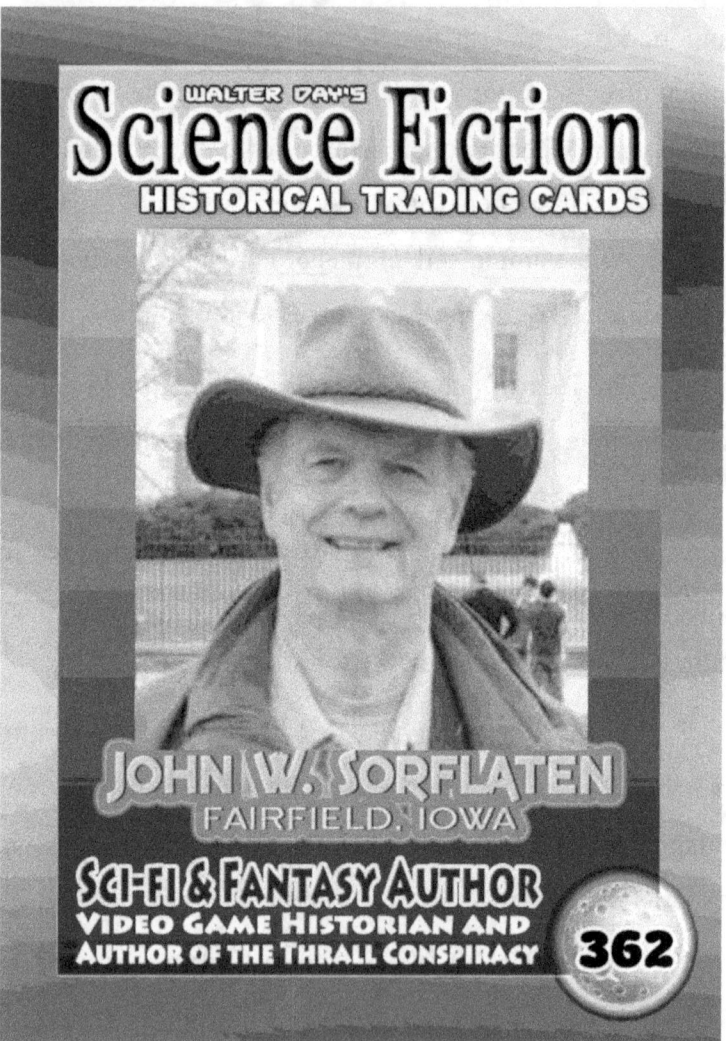

Walter Day's Science Fiction
HISTORICAL TRADING CARDS

JOHN W. SORFLATEN
Author of the *Thrall Conspiracy* Novels

John Sorflaten's mythic sci-fi series of "Thrall Conspiracy" novels hit the discerning public in 2023. This was the conjunction of successful GPT-3 Artificial Intelligence Story Generators and the story of death and destruction by Global Warming (now playing in Act II at your neighborhood continent). It all began during John's own origin story: a 30+ year career, during which he provided "user-friendly design" consulting and training to Fortune 500 companies as well as the National Security Agency (NSA). He hopes for a "user-friendly earth" now. As luck would have it, he also directed Louis Wilson's great video camera work of the Twin Galaxies 1982 Video Game Olympics and the famous 1983 Life Magazine Video Game Champions photo shoot. That footage appeared in films like *Chasing Ghosts: Beyond the Arcade* and *King of Kong: Fistful of Quarters* (both 2007) as well as *Frag* (2008) and CNN's documentary "*The Eighties*". John's telluric myth-building centers around Pole Star radiation influencing DNA during the first breath of identical twins–a girl Sacha and a boy Isaac, Jr. The driving question is, how will the boy accomplish his destiny to save the world after his dying mother tells him he was "born outside of time"? So put on your detective hats, grab your sugar cane and walk to the nearest Amazon webpage to find out. Search John Sorflaten-*Thrall Conspiracy*. If you don't see it, then you are one of the chosen few invited to return in a few weeks.

Image Credit: ©2022 John Sorflaten **Source:** John Sorflaten

© 2022 The Walter Day Collection, LLC
600 North Third Street, Fairfield, Iowa 52556
TheWalterDayCollection.com

362

Table of Contents

Chapter 1:

Seven Months Only

I have a gift, a capacity - a delusion if you will - called 'psychic. I have been called many things, from a charlatan to a miracle woman. I am, at least, neither of these.

On a hot summer evening in 1956, Nancy Clark, the top US and international psychic in New York, closed her journal in a fastidiously decorated pale-gray suite taking up the entire floor. She looked at the old grandfather clock on one of the least pretentious walls of her office. Isaac was going to take her sailing tomorrow. She should be on her way home now.

But something stopped her from winding up. She quickly ran a check through the article that she was writing for 'Tomorrow', her monthly magazine of literary and public affairs. But her eyes went back to the telephone on her desk with the feelings she had not known before.

Time was ticking, and despite knowing it, Nancy rolled the sleeve of her shirt. Maybe today would again be one of those long days at work. Of course, she didn't mind it.

It was exactly ten minutes later when the telephone rang.

Psychic experiences were a part of her life from childhood. She was always searching for more information concerning the secrets behind consciousness and the mind

"Hello," she picked it up at the first ring.

"Can you participate in a remote viewing program?" The voice at the other end was full of static.

Her blue eyes narrowed as she stood up now. Although she was 5 ft, 7 inches, her petite and feminine frame made her look younger than a 29-year-old woman.

"And who you would be?" She asked as she bent and swiftly opened the notepad on her desk. Her clear, patient, but authoritative voice vibrated in the silent air.

"President's office," the man replied, "We are located somewhere between New York City and Menlo Park, California. We will shortly go to a target that we would like you to be described."

Nancy pulled her chair over and sat down. It was six p.m.

"Call me back at seven," was all she said.

2

As the caller hung up after agreeing, Nancy gauged his anxiety. As a psychic researcher, she recognized the need for a scientific and open-minded investigation of paranormal phenomena and didn't mind using her psychic abilities. Although Nancy mostly used it for volunteer work, like finding the biological parents of an adopted child, as an author, lecturer, and publisher, she sought to share her ideas and experiences with the public.

She dimmed the lights, carefully tied her long, blond hair into the bun at the nape, and closed her eyes. She needed to forget about everything else and concentrate on the task. She channeled her spirit to the work at hand, erasing all the distractions from her mind.

Beyond the horizon, the sun illuminated the shimmering glow, stretching the orange hue wide and far. Unaware of the glorious sepia tones, Nancy's face underwent many expressions, and finally, after a couple of minutes, she opened her eyes. There were some drops of sweat on her forehead despite the cool air conditioning.

Right now, she only cared to note what she had just seen.

Nancy hastily opened her journal and started to jot down her thoughts.

As a government observer, she was talking to the subject again after an hour, dictating the place's details.

"I saw a wide flat area—a ragged mountain range in the background—something to do with the earth's arteries— a mine…" Nancy paused as her eyes went back to the paper she was holding. After a couple of seconds, she continued.

No light–no movement of air–some machine humming through the deserted area–no lights–no warmth–possible secret installation–mustiness–sudden dampness–like visiting a whole underground town–don't like it at all–6.30 PM–walking along on the old tracks with a flashlight–passing through the arch leading to a glass dome–crossing many crates left behind by the giant mining machines–walking through them feels like I am returning to the core of the earth–walking on her hollow bones–now a brightly lit passage–sudden change–like a manmade steel wall..

Nancy stopped to breathe and then peered in her journal for more.

My lungs burn from the dust—my muscles ache—I trip and then see a lot of metal glow all over—at last pass through the long claustrophobic stone tunnel, finally relieved to see the other widening end of the tunnel welcoming me back to the evening light.

Until now, the man at the other end had yet to speak a single word.

It was as if Nancy was talking to herself.

Now, suddenly, the phone receiver came to life.

"President Eisenhower's team would like to meet you," the man stopped midway and added. "at ten sharp tomorrow morning. Let's keep this between us. I'd rather you not even mention this call to anyone."

Nancy got up. Her wish to spend a perfect day with her husband again went for a toss. But she knew he wouldn't mind.

Nancy murmured a few words of assurance. If she was asked to keep this confidential, there must be a good reason.

As she took a cab, all her mind could think about was what tomorrow would bring.

§§§§§§§§§

Once home, Nancy ran a bath and started to check the contents of her fridge when Isaac called. It was difficult to hide why she was canceling their date, Nancy perfectly remembered how she had to keep her meeting confidential.

§§§§§§§§§

The next morning, dressed in a stylishly cut navy blue dress and a feathery hat, Nancy, a smartly coiffed woman in powerfully constructed clothes, took a cab to the White House. She went through the security routine at the gate, and then a uniformed guard escorted her to the Office of the Vice President.

After the quick pleasantries, she lowered herself onto the white leather upholstery before the large walnut desk as the Vice President's voice turned low to the confidential level. His face wore a grave expression.

"You must have heard about Sputnik, how the Soviet Union led the world into the Space age."

She silently nodded.

"The Soviet Union appears to have an edge in the technology race. We will need to take immediate action to counteract them, especially to show the strength of our scientific advancement."

Nancy shifted a bit in the chair. Her eyes were fixed on the large map covering the wall behind the desk. She sat up straight and looked at him.

He said, "We need to use psychic means to find the source of the leak on American rocketry that made Sputnik a success."

Nancy opened her mouth to speak when the Vice President added. "We have to find out the Soviet intentions about Sputnik." He paused and then continued. "The US is planning an ocean-to-ocean voyage, under the ice, crossing the entire Arctic Ocean, through the North Pole."

"North Pole?" Her eyes narrowed now.

"Yes. This trip is more important than merely reaching the destination. President Eisenhower's team is selecting you to do the psychic detective work on the Nautilus."

She uttered. "Yes, sir!"

"We don't have much time. It sails next week."

As Nancy hailed the cab back and rode towards her office, she wondered if the Nautilus crew should be notified that she was seven months pregnant!

Chapter 2:

The Test

Two years back

As the phone rang that morning for what seemed like an eternity, Isaac stifled an urge to take the receiver off the instrument. Instead, he thought of an article he had read last week about a psychic detective's first psychic project.

As a psychic researcher working as a university student, what he found in the article was quite interesting. For the hundredth time, he wondered how Nancy Clark helped at the crime scene. His friend had informed him that a security agency invited her as a parapsychologist to make the police aware of her work.

In those days, nobody knew what or how a psychic detective operated. Isaac's friend, John, was in the police service, and he had asked Isaac to join him. He thought of all the work he had to do yet, the pending research, and he sighed. There was no way he would be able to attend the seminar. And yet, when his friend called him at five that evening, Isaac was ready to go, as his curious nature got the better of him.

The small auditorium was packed when Isaac and John entered the back row. He could sense the apprehension running high in the air. His eyes narrowed as he looked at the faces of policemen around. This was a matter of science versus mysticism. Or about having an open mind against the closed ones. Isaac didn't know yet.

But many of them were there to rip her apart. He supported his hands on the wooden bench and bent forward to look at the lady sitting on the stage. She was the only woman in a room full of cops, and Isaac couldn't help admiring her guts. On the stage, an officer explained how psychic detectives are far from new in their field and why law enforcement planned to educate their officers about this investigation tool.

Isaac had his own doubts. But for a couple of hours, he was ready to keep them aside. His heart beat faster as he scrunched his eyes to see the dynamic, good-looking woman with an immense stage presence and commendable personality. She was wearing a plaid button-down shirt with a pair of comfortable trousers. Nancy's elegant but professionally cut hair and rigid posture declared that she was a woman who considered herself equal to all men and was not intimidated easily by any.

Isaac spotted two empty seats ahead and tapped John's shoulder. He didn't want to miss what would happen in this auditorium today. Two minutes later, his eyes met hers, and Isaac didn't know why, but it stirred something in him, drawing him closer to her, perhaps an urge to know more. His sense of detachment and high intelligence quickly surfaced, urging him to break eye contact immediately.

And yet he kept staring into those ocean-blue eyes, the swirling whirlpool of emotions hidden in the depths, passion on the ice, and Isaac blinked.

After a few minutes, it was Nancy's turn, and Isaac's breath hitched higher unknowingly.

"I saw a son of my close friend get into a car accident." Nancy's clear, patient voice echoed.

"The only problem was – it had not happened yet!" She paused and stressed each word, now speaking at the intellectual level of the listeners, "I always chalked it up to *déjà vu*. Over the next few years, I didn't pay much attention to my intuition, my gift. Two years back, after an intense soul searching, I realized it was my calling. Until then, I had never admitted I had psychic abilities."

"What happened to your friend's son?"

Someone from the dais asked her.

"I told my friend her son had to be careful. The crash happened as I had seen. Luckily, no one was injured, and he escaped with few bruises."

"Do you connect with a medium, or perhaps consult an oracle, or employ various other forms of divination, including astrology?"

"Some call it psychometry; others name it remote viewing or clairvoyance. I see it as a God's gift to me."

"So, how do you connect with the crime or the victim?" Someone from the first row asked.

"Where is your divining rod or the spiritual medium," asked another skeptic voice, and Isaac swallowed the anger. He clenched his fist closely while his mind was focused entirely on what Nancy would reply.

"I get contacted by families all around the world. You know, I get psychic impressions from objects connected with a particular person." Her authoritative voice was music to his ears. "They show me pictures and tell me what happened."

"Can you exhibit your psychic abilities?"

Nancy ran a hand through her hair and smiled for the first time. "I believe that's why I am here!"

The officer gave her a few wallets he had gathered before. "By touching them, can you describe who they belong to?" He added.

Nancy nodded in response.

Isaac almost forgot to breathe as his eyes went to the stage, observing Nancy's even minute movements. She took one wallet in her hand and closed her eyes. She was now touching it, feeling the texture, the design, the stitches running on the edge.

And Isaac would never understand in his entire life why he wanted her to succeed at any cost.

The tension ran thick through the auditorium and in the silence, he was able to hear his own heartbeat. He was not sure what turn the frenetic evening was going to take now. He scanned the audience for their reaction. Most of the faces were eager to see Nancy's failure.

Despite the cold air, sweat trickled down Isaac's back. A few drops beaded on his forehead as well, and his hand went to his pocket.

"Can a person with the initials I. O. stand up, please?" Nancy rotated her head, scanning the audience from one end to another. But no one stood up.

Isaac could see her scared interior behind the tough exterior. She was on the verge of crying. Perhaps a tear or two were already threatening to burst out as she was standing against a large volume of people, and he felt bad for her.

People had started to whisper by now. Some had stood up, wanting to leave the auditorium, not wanting to be part of this whole circus anymore, when Nancy touched the wallet again. "Mr. I.O., you have thick brown hair and hazel eyes. You are five feet ten inches with an academic build. You have a Harvard Ph.D. degree and write academic books regarding your experiences." She rubbed her hand against the wallet now. A soft panic grew in her belly as she breathed slowly.

The inky darkness of the hall grew more intense as silence lingered in the air. The slow hum of rotating fans filled and vibrated in the air.

"You are from the upper middle class." Her desperate voice came peering through again. "You hold a US government diplomatic position; government administrators and university high-level faculties are your colleagues." She stopped to breathe as she clutched the wallet tightly. "Are you somewhere sitting in this audience, Mr. I. O.?"

A muscle twitched involuntarily at the corner of his right eye as Isaac searched his jacket pocket for the handkerchief again.

It was different from where he usually kept it.

And then it dawned on him!

Nancy's smile grew wider as Isaac slowly rose from his seat, cursing himself for what he had put her through!

"Isaac Oldfield, Naval War College."

"How'd I do?" She asked immediately.

Isaac nodded in affirmation, not knowing how his handkerchief had ended in her hands. But that was the least of his problems right now.

The first and foremost thing was to contact this enigmatic lady. Being a serious and academic guy, he knew his intellectual achievements and rational nature were quite opposite to her clairvoyance and mystic personality.

And yet he could feel it in his bones that this might be their first meeting, but this was definitely not their last.

Chapter 3:

New Friendship

Two years back

There were days when Nancy wondered if her mind was an engine, an exhaust, or perhaps both. And she was feeling that way after meeting Isaac Oldfield that day. The constant ringing of the telephone added more to Nancy's already frayed nerves.

The telephone was still buzzing, and Nancy put a stop to her thoughts and picked it up.

"Hello, Nancy here."

"My daughter took off with her boyfriend. Can you find her?"

Nancy rubbed her forehead and grimaced.

Before she could speak a single word, the mother at the other end added, "She is twenty-two!"

It was so difficult to make parents see that she could do nothing in such cases.

After some conversation, she made the mom see her point that she didn't handle such issues.

And Nancy sighed. When would that one person call, for whom she was waiting and silently willing the phone to buzz?

She couldn't put a finger on her feelings yet, not in this case, anyway. But she could still not ignore that emotion in the pit of her stomach that her life would take a turn. Damn, she wished it would be better. Being a psychic detective was hard, especially regarding the hunches about her own self. She still remembered every detail of Isaac Oldfield. What had he said, how confident he looked from the way he stood that evening, his slow yet steady voice vibrating through the auditorium air. Was she dreaming, or did he really exist?

She was not new when it came to the affairs of her heart, yet there was some enigma about that man who had put a sweet smile on otherwise stern Nancy's face.

It was a clear day and almost noon when she heard a knock on her office door.

"Come in," she replied without lifting her head from the file.

But when an unknown but undoubtedly masculine spice cologne filled her nostrils, she had no choice but to look up.

Isaac Oldfield was standing in front of her desk. From inside, she shuddered, from outside, she acted cool.

"Hi," she cleared her throat.

"Hi, how are you?"

"Good!" Nancy gestured towards the chair. "Please sit."

"Thanks," Isaac slipped in and asked. "I hope I've not come at the wrong time."

Nancy looked at him, a little puzzled. "Of course not!" She replied at once, although she was dying to know who gave her address to Isaac.

"Well, a retired naval officer has gone missing from his apartment, and police have been trying to locate him for days." He looked into her eyes. "They don't have any leads until now."

"I see." She frowned and then took out her notebook fast. She had never thought they would meet again, not under the given context! But here he was! In front of her eyes.

"So how did you come to know about the case? I mean.., she opened her hands in a gesture, and Isaac smiled a little. "I am a naval officer and well-connected with the government." He paused. Then, hesitating, he added, "Actually, the police sergeant, Captain Morgan, is my friend.

We talked a couple of days ago, and he said he was planning to contact a psychic detective. I thought about you.

"Hmm," she started to write.

"Where was the body located?"

"Near a large forest."

"Any idea when and where he was last seen?"

"Nope! Although one of the neighbors said they had seen him ten days before."

"How old he was?"

"Sixty!"

Her gaze went to the far horizon, although she was equally aware of this enigmatic man sitting in front of her now. She had been a psychic detective before she even knew the term. Nancy trusted her instincts very much, although there had been instances of being deceived or scammed.

As she didn't speak, Isaac cleared his throat again. "Ahem, I have brought the map. Perhaps you would like to see."

"Sure."

Isaac passed her the map and she spread it on the table.

Isaac stood up. "Here is the place where Mark lived." He pointed towards a location.

Nancy took a deep breath and flapped the sleeve of her shirt, which was drenched from perspiration now.

He peered at her for a good five seconds before again sitting down.

Nancy focused on the map again. Beads of sweat now started to form on her forehead as well.

Sometimes, she got vision after hearing about the person or the incident.

At other times, the picture of the victim triggered his/her whereabouts.

As if Isaac was able to read her mind, he spoke. "Perhaps looking at Mark's picture might help."

She nodded.

Her heart sank as she looked at the fine young man smiling at the camera. From the depth of his eyes to the gentle expression of his face, Mark was extremely handsome. It was not as if his was the face that stopped you in your tracks. And yet, something in him pulled people towards him. Nancy winced and then closed her eyes tightly.

She was having difficulty breathing, and some unknown anxiety had taken hold of her.

"Mark never married." He spoke suddenly. "Wanted to live his life his way."

Nancy didn't react to his words.

Isaac squirmed a little but still waited patiently for her to say anything.

"A few of us wonder if he took his own life. But he was not that kind of person, you know!"

Now she opened her eyes and looked at the tall, lanky officer who was so hopeful to find his colleague and perhaps his best friend. He looked perplexed yet hopeful, awaiting what he wanted to hear.

This was the worst part of her job and something Nancy extremely hated from time to time. But she had no choice.

"I am sorry." Her voice was gentle. "But your friend is no more!"

"What," he almost got up from the chair. "I am sure you are making some mistake, detective."

Nancy's eyes went to this young man. When she found her voice again, she noticed it was dry and hoarse from the pain of experiencing many emotions simultaneously.

"He didn't kill himself." Nancy hated to tear up his hopes. She now circled a small spot on the map. "He struggled for a breath and fought hard before losing the battle."

She turned quiet, letting Isaac digest the news, and offered him a glass of water, searching for a way to explain herself. "Not only was Mark a smooth and successful naval officer, but he also led an enviable life due to his inheritance. And that was what ultimately led him to death!"

Isaac opened his mouth to speak, but nothing came out.

Evidently, he was still struggling to accept what she had just revealed.

"Who killed him?"

"A distant relative who wanted his money!"

They both exchanged some looks, and Nancy pointed towards the map again. "Get a search dog and scan the area."

"Police have already surfed that area; they found nothing!"

Although she never got involved personally, Nancy couldn't stop expressing her feelings.

"It breaks my heart to say that Mark experienced a very tragic death."

Isaac gulped as he looked at her. She quickly continued. "The suspect has a construction job and probably buried Mark in a concrete wall."

Isaac squinted his eyes; he was visibly agitated now.

There was a silence between them now.

"Detective," Isaac spoke after pondering for a few seconds. "I will initiate the new search with the help of a search dog as you have suggested.

By the end of the next day, with the help of a search dog, police managed to pull out Marl's body from the precise spot Nancy had suggested. While the body had deteriorated, there was clear evidence that he had been attacked and brutally killed before getting buried in the wall.

That was the day Isaac and Nancy's friendship began. But neither of them knew when it turned into romance.

Chapter 4:

Unknown Origin

1958

The dark, sleek hull of the Nautilus bobbed on the surface to welcome their visitors.

"I still can't believe we are on the world's first operational nuclear-powered submarine," Eileithyia whispered to her sister Nancy.

Despite being older than Nancy by six years, she outshone anyone. This tall, willowy woman was not beautiful in a classic way. But she had a kind of understated beauty that can be felt at once but could be hard to describe. Perhaps it was because she was so unaware of her good looks.

Nancy and Eileithyia were close from their childhood. Although Eileithyia had her own life and responsibilities, she had left everything to make things easy for Nancy and to help her relax on the voyage, considering Nancy's pregnancy.

"Hmm, yeah," replied Nancy.

"Do you think she really stays submerged for an unlimited amount of time?" Eileithyia murmured and then smiled. Her inner beauty lit her eyes and made her skin glow.

"Yes, I guess so. We will see." Nancy spoke slowly as she fought hard to control the bile rising from her stomach. At times, wondered why it was called 'morning sickness.' She felt sick throughout the day, like she had the most terrible hangover. She was nauseous and liable to vomit at the slightest provocation. She hoped against hope that this sea journey would be uneventful.

One look at her pale face and Eileithyia was alarmed. "You okay?"

"Kind of, Eile." Nancy flashed a smile. "Forget the ship. All I care about right now is some food and a clean bed to sleep."

"But we will have to wait before we get that," Eileithyia replied. "The commander should be here any minute to show us around."

"I wonder where Isaac is," Nancy spoke.

"Keeping two women in private quarters, even on a submarine this big, is a tough task, Nan!"

"Whatever, but I must say, I have never seen such a beautiful vessel. Look at the interior. Until now, all I have seen are traditional dull navy gray ships." She ran a hand through the intricate panel of wood. "It looks like an interior decorator was hired to result in this attractive color scheme."

Eileithyia opened her mouth to reply when a man came running towards them. Dressed smartly in his navy uniform, Isaac leaned slightly and kissed Nancy gently.

"Hey, how was the trip to Hawaii?"

"Good but tiring." Nancy sighed as she rubbed her belly. The pregnancy took a lot of her energy, and she often felt tired.

Isaac nodded. He turned towards Eileithyia and waved.

"On top of that, I didn't have much time to think or to pack properly. One week is very little time to prepare for such a voyage. I hope we will be back soon." Nancy spoke without pausing. Right now, she sounded less like a psychic detective and more like a weary pregnant woman, but she didn't care.

Isaac nodded. "Yes. Before the delivery."

"Remember, I eat like a horse nowadays!" Nancy smiled, and her happiness was reflected in her eyes.

"Don't worry. The food is the best in the navy!"

"What about our travel gear?" Eileithyia asked Isaac in a soft voice.

"Had a tough time disguising it as scientific equipment, but all taken care of now. We can discuss it later, first, let me get you settled."

They passed through a nuclear laboratory, a tiny but well-equipped machine shop, and a library.

"I was stunned when I was invited onboard, you know!" Nancy added as if she was still not sure about the journey. "I have no clue what they have in mind or what they are looking for by getting me on the sub."

"Hmm." He kept walking.

"Is it safe?" Nancy suspiciously looked around.

"Trust me. They have the best crew. Each man is carefully chosen. They are already experienced sailors. The safety and the wellbeing of every man and now 2 women is the most important thing here."

"This is going to be one of the greatest adventures of our lives," Eileithyia spoke and beamed at Isaac.

"You bet," he replied. But their small banter did nothing to ease the worry lines on Nancy's forehead. Everything seemed perfect, yet she couldn't wipe out the panic that had settled low in the pit of her stomach.

As they made their way, the great ship again submerged in the water, destination: the North Pole. Isaac led the women to a two-bunk suite. Nancy's eyes shone when she noticed their luggage near the small desk.

"It's not huge," Isaac glanced around. "But the mattress is comfortable."

While Nancy pulled off her heels and lay on the bed, Eileithyia opened a small stainless steel drawer and unpacked.

"Why don't you rest?" Isaac ran a hand through Nancy's hair. "I will send somebody with food."

With that, he left, and Nancy got up.

"Let's refresh and have our dinner. Then we can call it an early night and start working tomorrow."

Eileithyia nodded.

The suite was small yet had all the basic amenities. There was a small wash basin and a desk in the other corner. The yellow light bulb had bathed the whole place in a soft glow. The air was damp and relatively cool. And yet she noticed a few beads of sweat on Nancy's forehead.

Eileithyia fetched a glass of water at once.

"Are you hungry?" Her voice was laced with concern. "Why don't you sit down?"

Nancy strained her vocal cords to reply, but nothing came out. She quickly grabbed the bedpost and steadied herself.

A dog barked somewhere far away in other quarters. Nancy turned her head towards the direction. She closed her eyes and then quickly opened them.

"Where is Isaac?"

"Umm, I don't know." Eileithyia shrugged. "Why, what happened?"

"I don't know." Nancy sat on the bed now. Her eyes were widened now, and her pupils dilated. "Get him at once. Something is not right here."

"But he just left us..."

The dog's bark filled the air again, and Nancy got up. "Are you scared as well, little one?"

"Scared? Wait? What's happening here?"

"I can feel it in my bones!" Nancy looked at Eileithyia. "They want to kill me!"

Her sister's eyes widened now. Nancy's chest was heaving; she breathed hard as if her heart was racing fast in her rib cage.

Eileithyia pulled out a paper towel and started to wipe Nancy's forehead. The dog's barking was getting uncontrollable with each passing minute now.

"Even he can sense!"

"What's going on? Can you hear me?" Nan?"

"Have you ever feared for your life, Eile?" Nancy's deep voice vibrated in the small space.

"I say we leave this ship and go back," Eileithyia spoke in a frightened voice.

"We can't." Nancy continued. "This is my destiny, and no one can ever escape theirs."

"Which destiny are you talking about?" Eileithyia slipped near and almost shook her.

"They're coming to kill me. I intercepted a transmission from an unknown origin."

"What transmission?" Isaac, who had returned with the food, placed the tray on one of the beds.

"Nancy, you are shaking."

"Lock the door!" she said.

"Okay, if you say so." Isaac took her in his arms. "Don't worry."

She supported her head on his military chest and tried to take a few calming breaths, but it didn't work. Finally, Nancy lifted her head and looked into his eyes. "My instinct tells me to run."

"You are completely safe here, Nancy." Isaac touched her face. "We are under the sea, remember? No one can reach us."

"Then, why do I feel so strange? Something is going on!"

Isaac and Eileithyia looked at each other, not knowing what to do.

And suddenly Nancy screamed as she clutched her forehead in her hands, and the light went off on its own!

Chapter 5:
Promises, Promises

A purple swirling streak, out of nowhere, took over the night sky as the dark, purplish clouds dominated this part of the sky. The light in the cabin was back now, but Nancy was still sleeping. Isaac dimmed it and sat down in the nearby chair. Although it was late, sleep was hard to come by tonight.

Isaac was not traveling on the sub for the first time. He had seen each corner and nook of the ship. Most of the time, the sub remained submerged in the water. No one could reach them. Then, what was the reason behind Nancy's agitation? Why was she repeatedly mentioning that someone was trying to kill her?

Unable to calm his disturbed mind, Isaac decided to discuss the incident with the captain in the morning and closed his eyes.

After a few hours, he opened his eyes and stretched his body.

He didn't realize that the storm that had overtaken the sky last night had subsided. Instead of depressing dark clouds, the sky had a bright, sunny light. He was about to leave the cabin when Nancy stirred a little. Isaac moved near her at once.

"Relax," he said. "How are you feeling now?"

Trying to smile at him, she sat down on the bed. "I'm good."

Isaac looked into her pale face, blood-shot eyes, and ruffled hair. He pressed the galley button on the intercom and asked for three breakfasts.

Nancy gripped his hand. "The dog?"

"He was found dead this morning!"

Isaac sighed inwardly. He was a little concerned about the incident and quite a lot about Nancy.

"Whose dog was it?"

"Captains! A captain can bend the rules."

"What happened to him?"

"Nobody knows the exact reason yet. But they found him whimpering with pain, and before they could do anything, it just gave up."

Eileithyia, who was dozing off on the upper bed, opened her eyes. "That's strange!"

"The ship is getting crowded, what with the crew and their clothing, equipment, etc. When the cooks started to store the grocery supply, one of them saw him in the galley last night."

Isaac stopped suddenly and then spoke slowly. "But I recall hearing one of the crew members that the captain had found a burned mark on the dog's body.

Nancy got up now. "Burned mark? Isn't it strange?"

"Yeah, it is. We conducted a detailed tour of the whole ship, guaranteeing no fire hazards. No one has noticed the slightest fire threat, yet this mark...!"

"Weird things are going on!" Nancy rubbed her eyes and then said in a low voice. "I clearly remember the sudden penetrating pain in my head. I have never experienced such kind of awful discomfort. Not even while solving my toughest cases."

She lifted the picture of her parents at their wedding ceremony from the nearby table and ran her hand over it. "It was as if a strange kind of doom had taken over. It was as if someone just wanted to make sure I was not alive. I shouldn't be happy." Her brows furrowed. "I wonder if it has to do something with what I do!"

She closed her eyes. Outside, there was no sign of anything out of place. The world was as it should be. The sun loomed large in the distance, tinting the sky with radiant pinks, purples, and oranges. Of course, Nancy couldn't see it. But she could feel it. Until yesterday, she was totally in control of her surroundings. And suddenly, she was finding herself in a world she didn't know. All she knew was that there was a missing piece of a puzzle that she had to find. Was Isaac hiding something?

Nancy opened her eyes and cleared her throat. The silence on the sub was deafening. Her gaze now turned to Isaac. She folded her hands in front of her chest and asked. "Do you know something that I don't? Your connections with the government, academia, and international people should give you easy access to the latest information."

Skimming his finger up and down the bed rail, he stared into the distance and then turned to her after some time.

"The Nautilus is going to the North Pole with a special purpose."

Her eyes scrunched. "This nuclear-powered submarine is a recent phenomenon itself. I thought it was an ideal platform to explore the Arctic region."

Isaac inhaled and then opened his mouth. There was a hesitation in his voice. "Actually, we are carrying a UFO that the Nautilus will deposit at the North Pole!"

She got up, her forehead wrinkled. She seemed to be at a loss for words for a fraction of a second. Her eyes and mouth were frozen wide open in stunned surprise. Then she spoke. "What are you talking about?"

"Yes, we will lower the UFO onto the ocean floor at the North Pole."

"But it's a big risk. Too many things can go wrong!" she spoke again. "I mean, the sea bottom is almost a new territory, and we hardly know about the depth and form of the ice. On top of that, we are carrying a UFO. Imagine the radiation…"

"Nancy, we are sailing on a top-rated nuclear submarine. Everything has been taken care of."

"But why the North Pole?" Eileithyia asked.

"During World War II, the Commander of the Army had declared that if World War III should come, the North Pole would be the strategic center." Isaac looked at her now. "After Russia sent up the Sputnik satellite and got a lot of international recognition, the U.S. was under pressure to reestablish its technological power. Therefore, we are on this voyage." He added.

"Whatever, but why was I not told so before I joined the ship? Did they think that it was not important for me to know?"

"Actually, the whole thing is a secret affair. I wonder myself how many on the ship know about it. While most of the crew think this voyage will cover a lot of territory and get more information about the Arctic ice and the ocean floor, the actual purpose is hidden. President Eisenhower wanted to make sure there would be no issues during the transfer of our cargo. The government expects you to detect issues with the attached UFO during the placement of the UFO at the bottom of the ocean at the North Pole."

"I see!" She replied.

"Yes. So getting you onboard was to detect any problems with the UFO."

"And they didn't think I should know so that they can prevent unconscious bias forming in my psychic practices of remote viewing and telepathy?" She connected the dots quickly.

"Yes!" Isaac agreed.

"But if we succeed in planting the UFO at the North Pole, it will then emanate any radiation like a transponder or homing beacon from a unique spot on the earth – the Pole– where there is no Earth rotation."

"Right!" He nodded.

"And alert other aliens that Earth now has control of a UFO," she stated, as a matter of course.

"Well, you are not new to the fact that aliens exist on Earth, and they can communicate with humans," said Isaac.

"So, the government's ulterior motive is to get psychic insight into where the UFO communicates to!" She stated it as a matter of fact. "I wish I would have known this before." She paused as if she was trying to catch up with her thoughts. Then she placed a hand on his shoulder. "No wonder greater forces are at play when we are aboard a ship carrying a UFO."

He took her hand in his. "It will be okay, I promise!"

This time, Nancy's eyes locked on the man she loved and trusted wholeheartedly, but her eyes were as immobile as the rest of her face. "Why do I feel that you will have a hard time keeping this promise?"

Chapter 6:

The Transponder

While Isaac got busy with his technical work on the sub, Nancy started to dig around and get whatever information was available about the North Pole and the UFO they were carrying. When she was lost in her own world, trying to find a delicate balance between her research and the pregnancy, the rest of the crew, including Isaac, were attending films, lectures, and briefings on the voyage.

She couldn't point to it yet, but Nancy was able to catch the drifting anxiety in the air. However, with that, there was also a feeling of excitement among the crew members as they would do something that no one had dared to do before.

Eileithyia thanked the crewman who daily carried their breakfast to their rooms. She passed one tray to Nancy.

"Nah, not again, Eile. I can't keep anything inside at such an early hour."

"You know you have to eat, right?" Her sister brought a glass of water and the premed pills. "Maybe you can try the brown bread toast!"

Nancy hesitantly started to butter the brown toast, hoping against hope that she could keep it down this time. Although the voyage was going to end soon, she could hardly wait to get done with it. Still, two months were left before she could finally hold her baby in her arms. She grinned. Those two months seemed too much to her. She wished she could zip ahead, getting rid of this exhausting lethargy while her heart banged loudly against her chest.

After somehow finishing the breakfast, Nancy sat at the desk, peering at her notes again when the ship shook violently.

"What's going on?" Eileithyia asked.

Nancy shrugged in response when there was a loud knock on the cabin door, and Isaac entered at once without waiting for their response.

"The ship has suddenly taken a dive angle, and the captain and the crew are working hard to avoid hitting whatever lies in our way."

"Should we be worried?" Eileithyia still looked relaxed, but her voice was filled with concern.

"Of course not!" Isaac smiled. "Didn't I tell you we are in good hands?"

"Our ship doesn't have any windows, unlike other ships." Nancy's tone was calm yet firm. "We must be alert for unseen icebergs, uncharted undersea peaks, or other obstacles."

"The ship has the absolute best sonar system. The officers keep constant vigil, looking for anything out of the ordinary."

"You can't rely on the sonar itself. Remember, this part of the sea is an unchartered territory until now." Nancy got up and went to Isaac. "Life at sea can bring any kind of unexpected twists and turns."

With that, she again sat on the bunk bed, her gaze focused away.

"Was that your research speaking or your psychic intuition?"

She smiled a little. "You can take it any way you want, but do get a word to the captain."

Isaac sat beside her now and took her hand into his.

"Are you worried about the pregnancy?"

She minimized her concerns. "Yeah. Not much, but imagine what happens if I go into early labor?"

Eileithyia cut into the middle of their exchange. "But it's never going to happen. Why should you think that?"

"We are practically in the middle of the Pacific Ocean, Eile. With almost no medical help." Nancy replied to her sister.

"You keep worrying and fretting, no matter what," Eileithyia said sternly. "You are just imagining things. Try to relax."

Nancy was about to speak when Isaac intervened in the potentially heated arguments between the two sisters. "Don't worry. We are almost there. The captain mentioned we should reach the North Pole in just ten days."

"That's some relief." Eileithyia grinned. "I am fed up with sitting in this cabin the whole time listening to Nan's strange theories. It seems like a prison."

"Oh, but you don't have to do that." Isaac smiled at her. Then he got up and nudged Nancy's hand a little. "Come, I will show you a place where you can take a walk. You will feel better."

Nancy stole a look at her large belly. She was always on the slimmer side. But the pregnancy had obviously made some changes in her body. While her face and hair shined at their best, her ankles were swollen with water retention, and her back constantly ached, carrying the additional weight. However, it was little of her concern right now. This walk would give her a chance to look around, and she may be able to find out the reason behind her agitation.

"Walk sounds good," Nancy said as she got up slowly and took a few calming breaths. With an unknown feeling of apprehension that she couldn't get rid of, Nancy joined her sister and Isaac.

The fluidity of life far below the waves should have relaxed her. But Nancy was anything but that right now. Down here, her senses were altered as she carefully made her way under the influence of the neon light.

Day and night were the same here, and Nancy took in the undertone of male deodorant and the typical musty smell usually associated with a vessel spending weeks deep under the water. They were somewhere at the back end of the sub now. She imagined the water streaking off the silver casing as this oval steel whale gracefully glided through without any noise.

Isaac had left them now, and Eileithyia was a few steps behind when Nancy was suddenly filled with overwhelming nervousness and anxiety. She closed her eyes. Her body felt as if it was plugged into a wall socket.

She looked around and found nothing to sit on; she just sat on the floor. There was an urgency to follow the visions erupting on her mind's screen like pictures on a television.

Oh! The human-like creature was really in distress. His vessel was about to crash on the Earth. Time was running out. Nancy gasped for air. Perspiration beads started to gather on her forehead. He desperately looked around, touching every control he could, but nothing was helping.

His random actions sat a panic as the UFO started to vibrate heavily. Can't he see that big green button on the right side? Nancy mumbled. While he has tried everything he could, all he needed to do was to turn on the transponder.

Come on, Nancy murmured. It's just there in front. You can save yourself and this amazing vessel as well. Press that green button now!

As the pilot still fumbled with the other controls, hardly looking in the direction she was urging him to, a trickle started to run down her spine. She had to do something. She had to help this vessel and stop it from crashing.

Wait, don t panic. I am going to help you, she silently mouthed to the pilot. However, she was not sure if he was able to hear her. Nancy felt nauseous as she combed through many controls.

An unknown desperation took possession, and Nancy fought hard to find a solution. Focusing all her energies on the task, she finally reached the cockpit and pressed the button!

"There," she pointed towards it. "It was so easy. All you had to do was to press this green button to turn on the transponder…"

"Transponder?" Someone was shaking her. "Open your eyes, Nancy!"

As she did so, Nancy found Eileithyia's concerned face in the periphery of her vision.

"Green button? There is no green button where we are, Nan!"

Nancy got up, wondering what she had seen or done.

Chapter 7:

Contractions

All was well on the submarine except for the slight fog inside the ship, thanks to the condensed moisture on the recent transponder radiation. Nobody noticed it until now. However, the crew on the Nautilus had other issues. The Captain and Isaac conducted a detailed tour of the ship, along with some other officers.

"We need to test all our instruments," Isaac spoke, thinking of Nancy's recent experience. "Anything could happen once we are running under the ice."

They were standing on the bridge. It was mid-morning, and the sun filtered through the ice water, turning it into vivid shades.

"This ship is equipped with two high-quality compasses plus gyros." Oliver, the captain, replied. "We don't want to be caught unprepared if this boat gets into trouble near the magnetic Pole!"

"We can't take anything for granted because we will travel uncharted territory where compasses and gyroscopic navigation could give false readings." one of the other officers said. "The ice is much thicker than anticipated."

"And the water temperature is colder than expected," Isaac added.

"I know some crew members are somewhat doubtful and hesitant about this idea. And they are not wrong. Hell, we could easily get lost. We don't have any solid reference points, and we can drift in any direction." Oliver added, smiling," But I'm confident that our submarine's speed, the crew's expertise, and its maneuverability will help us reach our goal."

He stopped. "I have considered all extremes or emergencies with the ice, or getting stuck at the sea bottom, or wedged between two icebergs…but our men know what they are doing. Almost all of you are entirely familiar with the operation and the working of the ship. I know we'll complete our mission."

"Yes sir," smiled Isaac. The Captain was right. Everything seemed to be in order. There was nothing they had not thought of or imagined. And yet, Nancy's words were not going away from his mind. Was she just being cautious, or was it something she had seen with her psychic abilities and intuition?

They dispersed and started to do their duties. The ship was now almost on the last leg of the trip. Nautilus nosed under.

After ten days.

The sea floor looked nothing like what they had seen on the charts. Isaac sighed. Of course, they had some accurate charts showing the ocean depth at different places. But they didn't cover all the routes. Due to heavy icebergs closing the navigable gap between the ocean floor and ice, Nautilus took uncharted paths.

He finished his cup of coffee and proceeded to check on Nancy. Although her health looked stable, Isaac's mind was churning with thoughts about her well-being. He was still worried about her and happy that their voyage would end sooner than later.

They had been underwater for ten days, their longest continuous submerged run while going to the North Pole, carefully navigating under the floating ice.

"All hands, this is the Captain speaking," his sturdy voice echoed from the microphone. Isaac stopped walking. "We are on a route where no man or vessel has ever succeeded."

He paused, took a deep breath, and then continued. "And I want to thank all of you. This nationally strategic task would never have been possible. We would never have achieved it without your hard work, courage, and support. I appreciate what you are doing to bring this mission to success. Continue as we make our way to the North Pole."

There was an uproar on the boat as the crew congratulated each other. Some raised their cups of coffee in the crew's mess, and others stopped whatever they were doing to hear what their skipper had to say.

Isaac smiled. They were almost there. He couldn't believe he and Nancy were part of such a big mission. He started walking again when Eileithyia came running from the opposite direction and almost bumped into him.

His smile vanished at once.

"What's up, Eileithyia? What brings you here?"

Her breathing was accelerated, and she was drenched in sweat. His eyes took in her face, and a sweat trickled down the back of his neck. Unseen by Isaac or the crew outside, a heavy fog had solidly overcast the horizon, turning the outside visibility to almost zero.

Eileithyia was almost as white as chalk. "It's Nancy."

Isaac got alarmed now. Eileithyia was standing as if in shock.

This was not a time to panic. However, it was challenging to make Eileithyia see that. Isaac inhaled slowly.

"I can't think straight," she added.

"Let's go!" Isaac spoke and then almost ran in the direction of the cabin. All thoughts of celebration were forgotten now; all he could think of was Nancy. He hoped that it was not as bad as he had imagined. Eileithyia followed him.

When he reached the cabin, Nancy was whimpering with pain. Her eyes were closed, and although she made no significant sound from her mouth, one look at her face and Isaac knew something was wrong.

"Nancy?" Isaac lifted the towel and wiped her forehead, which was drenched with sweat. "I am here."

She opened her eyes and tried to smile. "So Eile finally found you!"

"Yes! How are you?"

"My water just burst, Isaac!"

"Gosh!" This was even worse than what he had thought. Although they were prepared to deal with every kind of emergency, this was not one of the anticipated ones.

"Don't worry. It will be alright," was all he could mutter at first. But his voice revealed a lack of confidence.

"We are in the middle of the sea, Isaac, and we're submerged, almost on the sea bottom," Eileithyia said. "Is it possible to go back to the surface?"

Isaac looked at his watch. It was evening. They would be hovering over the ocean floor any minute now, and the crew had to lower the UFO to the bottom. This mission was finally going to be successful. But he didn't know how to tell this to Eileithyia.

"Don't be silly, Eile." Nancy chided her sister and saved him from replying. "This mission can't be aborted like that." Isaac drew in a breath of relief.

Her sister nodded. "I get it. And even if we resurface on the water, we would still be in the middle of nowhere!"

"Exactly," Nancy spoke and winced as another contraction sliced through her body and shook her. Right now, the contractions were low intensity, but, given how they came, Nancy knew it would catch up with her soon.

"First delivery takes longer, Nan," Eileithyia spoke in a low voice. "We will find a way." She fetched a glass of water and urged Nancy to drink it.

Then she turned to Isaac. "What are we going to do?"

This is so early," Isaac found his voice again. "I mean, the baby…we can't stop the labor."

"You're right,." Eileithyia grasped Nancy's hand reassuringly. "It has already started."

He paused. Going through labor in the middle of the Arctic Circle seemed like a daunting task. But, well, the moment was here now. And he had to do something.

Nancy's presence on the ship was still kept a secret from the crew. And right now, Isaac didn't know where to go.

As if she could read his mind, Nancy took a deep breath, trying to ride one more piercing contraction, and once done, she spoke. "Go to Captain Oliver. He will know what to do."

This was not the time to burden the captain with one more task. But they didn't have a choice.

Isaac nodded.

"We would need water. Lots of it," Eileithyia added.

"Luckily, we have adequate water on the ship, thanks to nuclear power."

He was about to explain more when a guttural sound escaped Nancy's throat, and Isaac ran. The unseen, outside fog above the ice decided to sit on the water, hanging a dark blanket over the surroundings.

Eileithyia led Nancy to her bed, slipped a few pillows behind her back, and arranged a few cotton sheets underneath. Now, she sat aside her sister, slowly rubbing her back. "Don't worry. I am here."

Nancy looked at her sister's calm face. Her elder sister was a real hero at such critical moments, keeping every throbbing nerve under control to deal with the crisis. Nancy closed her eyes. Eileithyia took her sister's pulse and counted the elapsed time between contractions. The way things were going, time was paramount, and Eileithyia's eyes went to the door again. It was about time Isaac returned with some help.

Chapter 8:

Water Breaks

It was an ordinary evening like any other on Earth.

But for Isaac, this would be the most memorable day of his life.

He was on his legs, almost running in the ship corridor, desperately wanting to find help for Nancy.

The evening sun slowly descended to the horizon, and they were near their mission goal. But no one saw that.

Who would have known that far from the Earth, somewhere the hallowed pool of subtle light had adorned itself with the diamonds of a thousand moons? Physical beings, rather shadows resembling shorter, agile humans, were operating their kingdom and watching the Earth intensely.

Their dull, grayish-blue skin glistened in the waning twilight, showcasing distinctive markings on their faces, necks, and bodies. Their intelligent eyes and ears almost resembled the humans. However, their spindly arms and giant bald heads separated them apart from the people on Earth.

One such creature, Aundrid, was sitting behind what looked like a desk, assessing the data displayed on arrays of computers. These aliens had an advanced, complex, intelligent technology that was far from what people on Earth used.

The ash-filled sky and the cutting wind created dust storms covering this planet when Commander Esnine stretched out his antennae and tuned into the emotions of the planet. And what he felt was almost good enough to jolt him.

As more and more data began to roll out on his computer like a snowfall, Aundrid signaled others, and soon, a group of aliens was summoned. Aundrid's thin lips pursed in a thin line, resembling a drawing made by a child. He pointed towards the screen, showcasing the intercepting signal he had received from a ship called 'Nautilus. '

At any other place, such news might have brought its share of chaos and confusion. But not here! After a few minutes, a bunch of them sat inside the meeting room, discussing their next strategy.

§§§§§§§§§

Eileithyia's anxiety mounted with each passing minute. It was difficult to sit here and watch her sister writhe in agony. The cabin was too small, and Eileithyia wished it had more space so she could have paced or walked a little to calm her mind.

Although she was a bundle of jittery nerves, Eileithyia hid her true feelings. With each contraction, intense pain started to dominate the entire being of Nancy. But she made no sound.

When the pain came rushing, slicing her belly in two, Nancy took a deep breath, riding the wave of throbbing heat and feverish agony, hoping it was the last one. But that was not the case. And Nancy and Eileithyia both knew it.

Another contraction came, almost doubling Nancy over.

Eileithyia clutched her hand fiercely, hoping to give her much-needed strength.

Seconds turned to minutes, and minutes seemed like an eternity, but Isaac was not back yet.

Stealing a look at her sister, Eileithyia spoke. "Should I go and find out where he is?"

Nancy rolled her head in denial. "No, I want you here."

Eileithyia started to rub her back. "This is going to help."

Her gentle yet firm touch soothed Nancy, and Nancy's face relaxed a bit.

"Try to breathe in through your nose and breathe out through your mouth." Eileithyia demonstrated, and within a few minutes, both sisters practiced calm, rhythmic breathing.

The cabin with practically zero space was not the right place to give birth, and Eileithyia wished they could have moved her to a bigger room at least. But she was not going to tell that to Nancy right now. It was essential to keep a check on her insecurities.

She sat beside Nancy, holding her hand and giving her silent support.

After a few tense moments, Isaac finally returned with two men and the Captain.

Nancy looked as if she was caught in a storm. Her hair was plastered on her cheeks like a second skin.

"Babe, how are you feeling?" Isaac wiped the drops of sweat from her forehead and tucked in a fat lock of curl behind her ears.

"Surviving!" She replied and then gasped when her eyes went to the people standing at the door.

She hissed. "Who are these men, Isaac?"

"Male nurses!"

"I am absolutely not letting them help me!"

He clutched her hand and looked at her helplessly.

"This is the best we can do, Nan."

"Even a thought of these strangers being in my delivery room disgusts me. How can you do this to me?"

Her voice was full of hurt, pain, and accusation.

Eileithyia overheard their conversation and sighed. It was going to be more difficult than she had assumed.

"But I will be there! I am not going to go through it alone, Nan." Isaac added.

Nancy's face was clinched, her body taut and her mouth pressed in a line. When she didn't say a single word, Isaac again spoke. "Do you have any better idea?"

Nancy breathed slowly as one more contraction hit her belly, passing a burning heat in her middle. She let Isaac's words sink. One look at Isaac's worrisome eyes, and she knew what to do.

She clasped his fingers. "You are right. We don't have a choice. I will have to go ahead with the labor. Not as planned, but to serve the inevitable."

He pressed her hand a little. "Thanks. We are going to find you a room. I will be back soon."

Nancy nodded.

Considering the limitations of the submarine, finding her a bigger room was going to be difficult. But what to do?

Nancy was not a woman who believed in limitations. So, what if she couldn't go to her calm and composed gynecologist, who literally had a troop of doctors ready at the snapping of her fingers if anything went wrong with the delivery? Her doctor had also discussed the labor procedure with Nancy, making her aware of what was going to happen and how she would still succeed in the process.

Nancy concentrated on what was in front of her—the birth of her baby. However, in her slightly confused state owing to the pregnancy hormones, Nancy had almost forgotten that apart from the birth of her baby, one more event would take place in the submarine that evening.

By late afternoon, Nautilus had crossed the open ocean and was ambling towards the north, the last leg of their trip. Many contour features at the bottom of the sea that were not on the charts had started to be visible. The ship proceeded slowly through the cold waters, carefully steering clear of the floating ice packs. It would be the first ship to reach the pole.

After an hour, Isaac and Nancy's sister led her towards the other room. The captain had managed to move around some furniture to make space.

Soon, Nancy was passed a hot water bottle for comfort and some painkillers, which she refused to take at this stage.

Seeing her settle down a little, Isaac whispered. "We are going to make it. Don't worry at all."

"No, I am not worried."

Nancy's lips curled in a little smile for the first time that evening. "I can't wait to meet our baby."

Isaac wrapped his hands around her and kissed her forehead. "Me too!"

"I can try to take a nap. The contractions have calmed down a bit."

"That's good." His eyes glistened. "You look exhausted. Maybe the rest will recharge your batteries."

"Yeah."

"I will be up on the deck with the captain."

"Don't worry, I will send you a message if we need you here." Eileithyia stepped forward.

And as Isaac proceeded to leave the room, suddenly, the lights in the cabin started to flicker.

"Oh God, what's going on?" Nancy fought hard to hide the tremor in her voice, but she couldn't. She got up from the bed at once. Her chest heaved as she breathed faster now. Her heart started to beat faster now.

A pulse throbbed at Isaac's neck as he quickened his pace to reach her. "Nothing is going to happen."

As if someone was mocking those words, the flickering electricity stopped, enveloping the room in complete darkness, and Isaac's eyes roamed around, wanting to find the faint silhouette of Nancy.

Chapter 9:

Fire

They were about to reach the North Pole, scaling a new height of naval achievement and succeeding in their unique mission. And here they were, without electricity.

Eileithyia quickly turned on her flashlight, greatly relieving her sister and Isaac. However, her eyes narrowed when she noticed Nancy was sweating profusely and breathing heavily.

Quickly moving, she flew to the nearest door, gesturing for Isaac to follow her.

Standing in a secluded corner, she blurted out. "This is not going to help. Nancy has started getting the contractions again."

He rubbed his forehead. "Yeah, I know. "How much time before she goes into labor?"

Eileithyia folded her hands in front, eyeing Isaac from head to toe. "She is already in it!"

"Damn! Enough to reach the North Pole, huh?"

She mumbled, "I don't know. The first delivery usually takes time."

"There is nothing usual about this delivery!"

Nancy was standing behind their back in the glow of the flashlight. "This whole thing is totally unpredictable and…"

She was right. Who would have wanted to give birth to her first child, away from the comforts of her gynecologist and hospital at the seventh month, and that too, in the stark darkness of a submarine, about to reach the place called 'No land'?

Nancy had not signed up for this.

"Let me find the reason behind this darkness." That was all Isaac spoke before leaving the cabin.

"Smart man," Nancy grumbled behind his back. "Hurry, we don't have much time!"

As Nancy's face once again clouded with uncertainty, Eileithyia coughed and marched inside one more time. This was a time to take whatever measures she could. Looking at Nancy's petrified face, she confessed she was such a lousy sister. She was here to provide help and support and bring Nancy back safely before she went into labor. She had already taken leave from her job to be with her younger sister. She had learned meditation and massage and even helped Nancy assemble the nursery. But clearly, her luck wouldn't have any of it.

"I hate this silent lethargy, the waiting…" Nancy stammered. "I feel trapped."

One look at her taut, big stomach, and Eileithyia gulped. After their father's early demise, she became a mom to Nancy. It was not because they didn't have a mom, but because she had felt so protective about her younger sister even at that young age.

Nancy was practically a kid, and Eileithyia walked her to school, helped her with her homework, and put her to bed when their mom was out at work. For most of her life, Eileithyia had worked hard to make Nancy happy. So, what if the tables were turned now, jolting them to the reality? She was not giving up now.

Eileithyia bolted to her sister at once. "So, have you thought about a name yet?"

"No, that thought hadn't crossed my mind yet."

"So want to get started?" Eileithyia seized the pad and pen. "Well, how about Randell?"

"Hey, come on Elie, you can do better than that!"

§§§§§§§§§§

Captain Oliver could be somewhere in his late forties. But in the harsher darkness and dim candlelight, he looked closer to fifty or even more than that. Matured, wise, and vigilant. Behind his spectacles, his eyes quickly read the documents while his sharp mind focused on what could have gone wrong.

The reason behind this sudden darkness implied a breakdown of critical machinery. Or it could be his worst fear and a nightmare – fire. He ran a hand through his hair when sweat fell from his forehead. Everything seemed to be going well. Things were finally coming together. He knew how much was at stake here. But they could be immobilized beneath the ice, out of reach for anyone.

Before Oliver's mind could find out the reason behind this trouble, Isaac entered the cabin.

"The men in the engine room are experiencing smoke.."

Oliver was on his legs at once.

"If there is smoke, there could be fire."

"They had seen smoke," Isaac added as they walked towards the engine room.

"Did you call the engineer?"

"Already passed the word." Tears from irritating. particles washed over Isaac's eyes as he spoke. "They reported a lot of smoke there."

As the men strode towards the room, the smoke billowed black, filling their lungs.

"God, this heat! It's suffocating."

"I didn't hear any alarm." Isaac's voice was now filled with concern.

"The first thing to do is to find the location of this smoke."

"Some engineers are already down the ladder to the pumps." A blast of smoke choked Isaac. His eyes watered. "With their masks on."

As they neared the pump room, the smoke thickened, enveloping the whole space.

"This looks more serious than I thought." Oliver pulled out his spectacles and wiped his face. "If we can't contain the fire, I must return the sub to the surface."

Chapter 10:
Outside of Time

The daylight had almost dwindled and Isaac peered in the periscope – all he could see was the vast amount of ice. Not very thick. Instead, chunks of ice. He removed his head from the lens and looked at Captain Oliver. "There appears to be a massive ridge of ice laid directly ahead. We might have to forget the whole idea if we are not careful. We don't want to be trapped behind a wall of ice."

"They are called 'ice keels. 'But this one looks deeper and denser than the normal ones." Oliver clarified as he sipped his coffee. "Thank God, we see it in advance."

Isaac sighed. "We have had enough for a day."

"Mm, we are not out of the woods yet." Captain chuckled. "For some reason, I keep thinking there is something about this day that I can't pinpoint yet."

"Well, then let's be prepared." Isaac got up from the desk. "I should return to Nancy as soon as possible."

"Isaac," Captain Oliver's concerned voice stopped him. "We have done our best under the given circumstances. I hope things go smoothly."

"Hope so," Isaac replied. He tried to smile; however the lines on his forehead had their own tale to tell.

When the last rays of the sun kissed the calm sea, greens and purples melted into the gray. Before the fire event, Isaac thought he might accompany Captain Oliver when lowering the UFO at the North Pole. But now, he was not taking the chance. Nancy was exhausted from the constant labor pain and the psychic agony of finding the source of the fire.

And Isaac wondered if he had done the right thing in consulting her. Anyway, the deed was done. And all he could expect was to see Nancy putting in the same energy in the birth process. While she was going through it, he had to be with her.

The sub made its way past the northernmost part of Alaska. Outside, the sea was calm. The dense fog that had accompanied them for a few hours was still there. But it didn't hinder the moonlight. So, visibility was not much of an issue. As Captain Oliver steered the submarine safely to its destination, Isaac's thoughts remained on the impending birth.

While he was on his way to the cabin, Captain Oliver got the message that the water was getting deeper. They had managed to locate their destination. He instructed the crew to follow the sea valley as the ocean floor gradually deepened and widened.

They were finally in the Arctic Ocean, and the sub increased the speed. The captain slowed his breath, waiting to reach the right spot.

As the submarine went closer to the North Pole, the tension of the crew also grew. The captain instructed one of the crew members to be prepared.

As the sub sank lower and lower on the ocean bed, the unseen moon rays shone on the surface like a searchlight, bathing the snow in the silvery glow, illuminating it. The crew members painstakingly activated the pulley controls and opened the cargo bay where the UFO was kept.

Lowering such a large UFO onto the ocean floor was difficult. Special machinery had been brought on board, and skillful people were trained for this mission. Of course, the whole crew needed to be informed about the event. Many were still unaware of the actual mission of the sub's travel to the North Pole.

The UFO was a saucer-like thing, made of something that looked like wood, of twenty-twenty-five feet. The material couldn't be either broken or burned. There was not a single electronic equipment or instrument inside it. However, it had a great number of small pieces of metal, like tin foil, making up the bottom surface. Small beams with some hieroglyphics supported it. Pink and purple symbols on the top looked as if they were painted.

Eileithyia played recorded calming music; its relaxing notes soon spread in the space as she helped Nancy walk around.

"Eile, the contractions have become longer and stronger."

"Don't worry. We have got a support team." Eileithyia spoke. "The labor gets more regular from here. Listen to your body and be prepared for the hard work ahead."

"What if it does not go as we thought?"

Nancy's elder sister pressed her hand gently. "Let's not send any negative energy to the baby. We have gone through a lot lately. I am sure the baby will slide out of your body without more issues."

When Isaac returned to them, Nancy was sitting now. Her face was pale with pain, and Eileithyia was holding her hand.

Isaac looked into her eyes as Nancy's body shook with one more strong contraction. "It's easy to feel overwhelmed. But don't let yourself go. Just concentrate on one contraction at a time, and things will be fine."

Nancy nodded and took a deep, calming breath, relaxing and restoring her energy.

Eileithyia applied a warm compress, lending her quiet support to her system.

"We are reaching the geographic North Pole to achieve our goal." Captain Oliver's calm yet upbeat voice echoed in the sub.

There was an air of jubilation and festivities as the sub made its way to the North Pole, expertly navigating around the icebergs and within irregular depths of water.

Emotions ran high as the Nautilus became the first ship in history to be 'underway at the North Pole on nuclear power.'

Just as the ship touched the North Pole, the crew trained to handle the UFO slowly lowered the UFO towards the ocean floor. Above the surface, the dense fog again wrapped around the ice and snow like a blanket, but nobody knew its real reason.

Nancy began pushing,.

"How are you feeling, Nan?" Isaac asked again.

"Well, quite clearheaded and determined now," Nancy spoke between the grunts.

As the crew started to lower the UFO on the floor, Nancy's labor reached the last stage. And a baby's strong healthy cries filled the cabin.

"It's a boy!" Eileithyia smiled at her sister. Her voice showcased excitement, joy, awe, and relief.

Nancy smiled through her pale lips, finally taking a breath of relief when one more contraction jerked her body again.

Simultaneously, a slip of the cable allowed the UFO to free-fall for several yards before stopping with a severe jerk to the sub above. The sudden stop triggered the UFO's transponder—the homing beacon telling its home world that it landed hard. The transponder radiation suddenly beamed upward through the Nautilus towards the Pole Star, meeting the star's downward radiation directly above the earth's North Pole. The upward and downward-moving streams of energy-laden particles collided as they ripped through the crew and Nancy's twin miracles of birth. The two beams joined to create a glow barely visible in the submarine's air.

"What is happening, Eile?"

And to their utter amazement, a second baby was born before they could think or speak.

"My God, look at them. A boy and a girl – each so perfect even though they are premature." Eileithyia's voice was filled with awe this time.

"What's the time Eileithyia?" Isaac asked at once. "We need to record it!"

"11:15 PM New York time," Eile replied.

"Oh, these babies are born outside of time, Isaac," Nancy murmured. "At the North Pole."

"You are right, Nan," Eileithyia added. "A place where all the time zones converge. I know how hard it is going to be. Raising two kids at one time together. I wonder what kind of future they are going to have."

"My children are going to be a game changer for sure," Nancy replied with élan.

Isaac cut the umbilical cord for both the babies and looked at Nancy with pride when the twins started breathing simultaneously, no spanking required, their lives forever intertwined by their inheritance of identical DNA.

Soon, the babies were dried, wrapped in clean clothes, and brought to their mother. Nancy draped her protective arms around them, looking at their cute little faces and robust bodies.

Chapter 11:

Solving Problems

Tiny fingers curled around Nancy's finger as she watched her newborn babies with awe and joy. She felt their soft breath on the back of her hand and sighed.

"Aren't they beautiful?" Eileithyia eyed them as she draped their tiny bodies in a blanket.

"The most beautiful human beings I have ever seen..." Nancy's eyes traveled to their perfect bodies and contented faces. "They feel so light and yet so perfect, so divine. It's a shame I don't have any of the beautiful clothes we bought or that fabulous nursery you had designed so painstakingly."

"Nan, dear, we will be home soon." Eileithyia patted her sister's head. "Look at you. Who would believe that you were crying in pain two days ago?"

"More for feeling helpless at that moment," Nancy stated as a matter of fact and then beamed at her sister. "I can't thank God enough that the births happened properly." Nancy held one of the babies near her.

"And how are you feeling now?" Eileithyia's voice was full of concern.

"Fit as a fiddler on the roof."

Eileithyia's eyes looked at her sister's glossy eyes, pale but happy face, and she cringed inward.

"You just gave birth to two babies. It's not an easy thing. I am going to fetch some more painkillers for you."

"I already got them," said Isaac as he entered the cabin. "Aren't they the angels?"

"They are perfect!"

"Just like you." Isaac kissed her forehead.

"Wait 'till they grow!" Nancy smiled at him. "You know, you are so soft-hearted. I am sure I'll be the bad guy in disciplining them."

Isaac leaned and kissed the babies. Then he turned to Nancy. "What are we calling them?"

Nancy wet her lips. "Um, I don't know. I haven't thought much about it."

"How does Sacha sound to you?" Isaac passed her a glass of water and medicine. "It suits our little girl." It means "defender or protector of mankind."

Nancy gulped the pill in one go and smiled. "I like it. And I will call the boy Isaac, Jr."

"That's amazing." Isaac took Nancy's hand in his own. "You need rest. It won't take long to reach home now."

"Provided we don't face any more problems." Nancy ran a hand through Sacha's mop of hair.

Isaac's eyes narrowed. "Wait, what are you saying? Is it one more of your prophecies or what?"

Nancy's eyes danced in merriment. "Prophecy, huh? Forget that I said anything."

"Well, you know what, it's just that I have started taking your words so seriously. Listen, Captain Oliver called me."

"Nothing serious, I guess."

Isaac, who was standing at the door, turned his head. "No, the sub's garbage mechanism has become blocked."

"Wait, what exactly does that mean?"

Isaac walked back to Nancy and sat. "The Nautilus has a vertical ten-inch tube. It extends from the scullery through the bottom of the ship and reaches the sea."

"Okay. So where is the issue?"

"When the outside door of the tube is closed, the cooks open the inside door and fill the tube with the trash. Once the inside door is closed, and the outside door is open, this garbage gets discharged to the sea when we pump the water into the top of the tube."

"Hmm, I get it. There can be an issue if both the doors are opened at the same time."

"You are right," replied Isaac. "Sturdy interlocks keep both ends protected."

"I can imagine the amount of garbage the sub creates, with a hundred and sixteen men on board."

"Right. And this is the only way to dispose of all of that. Now, here is the problem. The outer door lock has been damaged. It is not locking properly."

Nancy got up from the bed. "That means, if it's not locked in time. It could create a serious problem."

"The Lieutenant and Captain are already at work. The repair gang has done everything they could. However, the water has started to enter the tube, and so far, the inner door is holding up. But it has started to leak through the seals."

"Oh my god, so what is the crew doing?" Nancy asked.

"They are trying to stop this leaking by welding the leaking parts to close them."

"But they can't. The leaking water prevents the welding area from getting hot enough to melt the welding metal!"

"Exactly." Isaac stood up. "It's a small area. But dangerous if not stopped. We need to do something about it."

Nancy nodded. "I get it."

He pressed her shoulder in reassurance. "Don't worry. I am sure things will be under control by now. The crew knows their way around."

With that, Isaac left, but the assurance in his voice did nothing to soothe her mind. Nancy looked around. Her sister was sleeping calmly after the maddening night. The twins were sleeping as well. Their tiny faces reflected the peace they felt within. She wished she could even sleep peacefully like them. But not tonight.

She foresaw the necessity not to underestimate this problem.

But what could she do? She was not a technician or a crew member with knowledge of the inner intricacies of the sub.

But that didn't mean she should leave the issue to them. What if the repair gang couldn't solve the problem?

The whole ship might be flooded!

Nancy's eyes went to her childrens 'faces again.

No. She can't let it happen.

She sat down on her berth and closed her eyes again. There, she had found the solution. She would use her psychic power to send a distress call, a Mayday call to the universe.

The wrinkle on her forehead became smaller as she concentrated hard. Vivid pictures about the problem started to erupt on her mind's screen as she thought harder about what the crew was doing and how trapped they were. They would be flooded, submerged entirely at the bottom of the Arctic Ocean if the issue wasn't resolved.

Perspiration beads gathered on her forehead as Nancy silently focused on the task. Usually, one passes the Mayday distress signal via radio communications. But she didn't have one. She finally thought of sending the intense signal to the universe.

Mayday! Mayday! Mayday! She repeated it three times and followed it with all the relevant information potential rescuers would need. She started to describe the type and identity of the Nautilus, the nature of the emergency, the location, the number of people on board, and the current weather.

Her eyes burned, and her chest heaved as she made her distress call intense, hoping someone somewhere would catch the signal's wave and help them.

Once done, feeling a little relieved, she took a calming breath and opened her eyes.

What was this? She blinked. Was she dreaming? No, it couldn't be true.

There was an aura of blue around the babies 'heads, which she had never seen before. And what was more, the aura was expanding with every passing second, creating a shape like a giant bubble.

Nancy rubbed her face in disbelief and drew in closer. Was she imagining things? This couldn't be true. But she had to find out what this meant. There was no time to call Isaac, but Nancy shook her sister, who woke up immediately.

"What happened, Nan? Did any of the babies wake up?" Eile rubbed her eyes as she spoke.

"Shh, just look at that. Are you also seeing what I am seeing?"

And Eileithyia's mouth remained open in awe as she gasped and watched the bubble getting enlarged. Its edges were glowing with blue in the dark of the night.

"What the hell?" Eileithyia whispered back to her sister.

"I don't know." She murmured back. "I have never seen such a thing before."

And before they both could add anything more, the "thought bubble" showed Nancy an image of the kitchen compartment being sealed off and the air pressure there being raised enough to prevent further leaking...

"Oh my gosh! Look at it." This time, Nancy almost screamed. "Go, get Isaac. We have found the way to stop the calamity."

By the time Eileithyia left, after demonstrating the solution to the issue, the "thought bubble" had vanished.

And both the children were sleeping as peacefully as ever.

Soon, the repair gang sealed off the kitchen, the galley, and the chief petty officers 'quarters and increased the air pressure. Once it was high enough, they opened the inner garbage ejector door and removed some trash bags that had jammed the outside door.

Once the significant danger was averted, everyone on the ship slept peacefully that night except Nancy and Isaac. It was evident that their kids were not like other normal children.

Chapter 12:
Earth Seeks Help

They were nearing the land now, and Isaac couldn't help but wonder what they would do about their twins, who were quite different from the normal babies their age. He and Nancy had talked about it several times. But none of them could still figure out the thought bubble that had illuminated over the twins 'heads that day.

Frankly, when Nancy informed him about what she had seen, Isaac was a little worried. The twins were premature babies, although they hardly looked or sounded like one. While he counted it as a blessing, being a scientist, he gauged some higher forces were already at play at the birth of his children. While he tried to shake off that feeling, he could not. He felt it would be even more intense in the future.

However, Isaac knew he could sleep peacefully, knowing full well that if there was anything amiss, Nancy's intuitive mind would soon resolve it.

As he went to see Captain Oliver tonight, Isaac was informed that the captain was in the mess compartment. So, Isaac walked towards that area now.

After averting the big crisis, everybody on the sub was in high spirits. And why wouldn't they? The twins have saved them all from a big danger. However, not many on the ship knew about the babies.

When Isaac entered, the mess compartment looked different. It was turned into a movie hall. A few chairs were arranged in front of a big white screen. A low light illuminated the otherwise dark room, and he found the Captain sitting in one of the front rows.

The atmosphere was relaxed, and Isaac didn't mind this little entertainment.

"I was just planning to watch a movie. Care to join?" the Captain asked him when he saw Isaac.

"Of course. God knows he has had a few bad days." Isaac spoke as he slipped into one of the chairs. "What's the name of the movie?"

"The Goddess Unchained. It's about global warming."

"Global warming?"

Isaac raised an eyebrow.

"Yes," the captain nodded. "Knowingly or unknowingly, humans are changing the world's climate, and we have no idea what the future will bring."

"I had read that our factories and automobile industries release more than 6 billion tons of carbon dioxide in the atmosphere," said Isaac.

"True, and as a result, the earth's atmosphere is getting warmer and warmer with each passing day. If even the planet's temperature rises a few degrees, the polar ice caps will melt."

"And the sea levels would rise undeniably."

"Well, yes, and we still have time to do something about it before the damage gets irreversible." With that, Captain Oliver gestured to start the movie, which was over in an hour. But what they discussed was on Isaac's mind as he went to see the babies that night afterward.

When he reached, the twins were sleeping peacefully, and looking at their calm faces, nobody would ever imagine them having a special power.

"Hey, any more incidents that I should know about?" He asked Nancy.

"No. I haven't seen that bubble thing after that day." She replied.

"You know, I just watched a movie on global warming, and I thought it would be a big issue soon."

"I know what you mean. Mankind has taken the Mother Nature for granted. And I am sure we are going to pay for it someday." Nancy sighed and dropped her head on his chest. "How many days before we reach home?"

He wrapped his arms around her. "Tired? We are just a week away."

"Hmm, I don't know how I will manage them." She gestured towards the twins. "Maybe I'll ask my sister to stay some more days."

"Hasn't she already done too much for us?" Isaac whispered.

"You are right. But why do I feel these children will be a handful?" Her voice told Isaac that perhaps Nancy was hesitant to be alone.

Isaac's eyes flicked to her face. He tucked a bunch of her hair behind her ear. "Don't you have a trust in your abilities?"

She took his hands in her own hands. "It's not like that. But I still cannot forget that aura around the kids 'heads. I don't know how difficult it is going to raise them."

"We will find a way, don't worry," Isaac spoke confidently. "You see, the movie has set the wheels of my mind turning. Can you recall the UFO crash? Remember how you had psychically investigated the crash? Set off the Mayday thought amplifier?"

"Of course I do."

"Why did the UFO crash? What went wrong?"

A knot formed in Nancy's stomach as she recalled how she had made her way through the Mayday thought amplifier. It was one incident that she would not forget in this life.

"Well, the ship didn't crash normally. All the systems were working perfectly." She stated.

"There was no system failure? Then how did it go down?"

She got up now and folded her hands at her chest. "The UFO was actively attacked."

"Attacked? By our US military?" Isaac asked.

Nancy said. "Of course not. Our forces didn't have a single clue about how to approach it. The UFO was attacked by other aliens who want Earth for their purposes."

Isaac scratched his head. "Other aliens? What do they want the earth for?"

Nancy sighed. Now, she sat up near him. "There are many things that are still not known or explained. However, you must know that all aliens are not good and kind. Some of them do have their selfish motive. They want to possess our earth and turn the remaining population into slaves!"

"What do you mean by 'remaining'"?

"Well, as you know, melting the polar ice caps will raise the oceans around the earth. This will create chaos, especially for those millions living in the low-lying cities next to the oceans. It will be a big task to relocate them once this happens..."

"I get it," said Isaac. "Then, we must somehow stop them from taking possession of our planet. I can see why they would love to increase the global warming."

"Hmm, but how do we stop it? We are just two people and can't fight against someone so powerful."

"We will have to find a way." With that, Isaac kissed the top of her head and started to walk towards his cabin. However, what they had discussed didn't let him sleep that night. And while everyone on the ship was sound asleep, unaware of the turmoil in his mind, Isaac recalled how Nancy had accessed the UFO system.

He had now found a way to beam a signal to the good aliens by using that captive UFO as a transmitter. The UFO transponder beam carried a vital message: "Earth seeks help against the thralls."

The message consisted of a human psychic transmission radiating in a single direction into space. The UFO transponder beam amplified the psychic transmission. The beam emanated from the most stable spot on Earth—the North Pole—to ensure the alien home world knew it was purposeful.

If the transponder faded in and out because of Earth's rotation, the home world would assume an accidental crash occurred and thus would ignore it.

He had done his job. Now, all he had to do was wait for the help.

Chapter 13:

Love Tugs

Washington DC, Bethesda. One week later.

"Look at him," said Eileithyia as she put Isaac Jr. in the crib. "Doesn't he look big for his age?"

"Shh, now stop hovering over my little one." Nancy smiled when her son's blue eyes found hers, and he laughed the way only a baby can laugh. His delightful voice lit her from inside, and her eyes widened when his miniature fingers clasped hers. "I had heard mothers complaining about how their kids didn't sleep, or how they kept crying through the night or never slept. Sacha and Isaac nurse every four hours, don't cry, and have slept throughout the night since we returned home."

"Mine were not this easy to raise," Eileithyia spoke. "You are lucky."

OK, I'll bite. Maybe after going through that unexpected birth on the sub, God finally answered my prayers." Nancy spoke as she ran a hand through her son's soft hair. "I can't believe my overpowering love for my children." Then she went to her sister and pressed her hand. "And the thing is, you are still here with me, even after going through all that. I know your work is suffering, but just so that you know, I am grateful for what you are doing for us."

Eileithyia eyed the sleeping babies. "They are worth all the sacrifices."

"Did you remind Isaac about the ticket? I am going to miss you big time once you go."

"We still have a week. I am glad we are past those adventures now, and you all are settling down here."

"Yes. I am glad you had completed this beautiful nursery before we went on that trip. What would I have done otherwise?" Nancy spoke as she placed a pale pink blanket on her daughter's tiny body. She and Eileithyia had done the nursery in the shades of pink and blue, not knowing whether she would have a girl or a boy.

"We could have done better, you know. I still want to add a few things to make your life easy once I am gone."

"Don't you think you deserve a break after all this?" Nancy's lips curled in a smile as she led her sister out of the nursery and to the kitchen. "I will just make some coffee for us while they sleep."

Eileithyia nodded, and as Nancy got busy in the kitchen, Eileithyia suddenly spoke. "Don't you think you should make a 'psychic inquiry 'into the twins 'destiny? I have still not forgotten that incident."

"You know, even I think about that," Nancy kept the mugs on the table and sat in front of her sister. "One day, while I was changing diapers for Sacha, Isaac woke up and started to cry."

"Oh, why didn't you call me?"

Nancy took a sip of her coffee. "Think nothing of that. Also, I need to see how I will do alone once you leave."

"That's true. So, what happened?"

"Isaac won't stop crying. First, I tried to soothe him by talking to him, mentioning I would attend to him. But he wouldn't listen. And before I knew it, the aura at his head was back, and this time, it was bright red."

"Hmm, probably for anger!" Eileithyia wrapped her hands around the coffee mug. "That's not a desirable outcome."

"And the thing is, once he started crying, even Sacha caught it up and started to match him at the top of her voice.

"What did you do to calm them?"

"I picked Isaac first, noticing the bubble disappeared once I had him in my arms. Then I put him down and carried

Sacha, wanting to feed her. But a strange thing happened. When the twins were close together, I felt the things in the room were floating." Nancy threw her hands in the air in desperation. "I wonder if I imagined it, or maybe I had not slept properly, so I was dreaming it, but I saw the things moving around."

"Well, I don't know what to say." Eileithyia kept her cup down and rubbed her forehead. "So, what did you do?"

"Can you believe it? I moved Sacha apart at the farthest corner of the room and things returned to normal."

"OK. Now, this has made me wonder. I'd guessed your life with these twins will never be dull."

"Never." Nancy grabbed a biscuit.

"Nan, I don't want to get you all worked up. Probably, we are just imagining things. But on the safer side..,. have you told this to Isaac?"

"Of course, I have. He keeps on telling me there is nothing wrong with our babies."

"Maybe they have developed some psychic power, and you need to find out how they do that."

"If I tell a single soul, they would think I am crazy. Nobody has heard about such a thing before!"

"I am just saying maybe you analyze the circumstances of the birth and see if you can come up with some explanation."

Nancy was about to answer her sister when the telephone started to ring.

"Just a second, Eile." Nancy got up and received the call.

"Hello."

"Is it Nancy Newfield?" Someone spoke from the other end.

"Speaking."

"I am calling from the president's office."

"Okay, I hope everything is alright."

"Yes, they are. Thanks. The President appreciates your performance on the sub: giving the psychic assistance and helping avert the crisis."

"Really?"

"You will get a 'secret citation', a kind of medal for your performance." The man paused and then continued, "Congratulations. You will be informed about the date and the venue."

"Oh, thanks. I was glad to be of help."

"Good day." And the line went blank.

With a big smile, Nancy was returning to her sister when she heard a cry from the nursery. They had put both the babies to sleep only a few minutes ago. She quickly walked towards the room. And once there, she gasped at the site.

Isaac Jr. clutched Sacha's hand in his tiny hand, and she had stopped crying.

As Nancy looked into her children's big, innocent eyes, love tugged at her heartstrings. Born with a superpower or not, her children had become her whole life, and she would do everything in her power to ensure nothing ever harmed her babies.

Chapter 14:

Very Hungry Caterpillar

The room was pitch black; Nancy could hardly see anything, as if she was blind. Her cheeks were wet, and her body was bathed in a cold sweat.

"Sacha, the voice boomed out in the space. "Surrender yourself. You can't escape us!" That voice was like iron nails dragged over a rock. At first, it was distant, too far away, but it came steadily closer and closer, all the while becoming more forceful, more distressed, until the owner of that scary voice was somewhere in the house itself.

Tears burned in Nancy's eyes as she cried out, trying to gauge the source of the sound and failing miserably to locate the person threatening her. She swallowed and once again turned to see the endless darkness of her room. But she couldn't see anything. She felt someone was in her house, checking each room, wanting to harm her children.

Sweat dripped from her forehead as Nancy looked at the tiny figure of her daughter sleeping on the bed. She shook her.

"What's that matter, mom?"

"Run, Sacha," Nancy's worried voice was hardly understandable. It was as if she was having difficulty in speaking. "They are after you. I know you can beat them."

Sacha grimaced. Her small, innocent face hardly registered what her mom was saying.

"Sacha," the scary voice rose again, deep, grainy, thrusting for blood. "It won't take me long to find you."

And a scream escaped Sacha's thought. She was now sweating profusely as she shook her head in denial. "I can't. Isaac is still in his room. They are going to catch him."

"I will take care of him." Nancy's chest heaved as she drew deep breaths, hoping to calm her panic. "Help, help..." Her room felt more like a coffin as she tried to find her voice and ask for somebody to save her children. But she wouldn't give up. Taking a step forward, she shouted at the top of her voice.

"Come on, Sacha, we don't have much time."

Suddenly, everything turned eerily silent. Had they gone? Fear flooded her belly now as she was unable to understand the reason behind this unnatural silence. She took one more step as her eyes hovered from one corner of the room to another, checking if anything was out of place. Yet, nothing was awry, and then a scream escaped her throat when she realized Sacha was not on the bed.

"Sacha…. Isaac…."

The lights of mother's love on top of her head bathed the whole room in light. It streamed across the room.

"Nancy, Nancy, what happened? Are you alright?" Her husband's tall frame came before her eyes, and Nancy opened her eyes after a visible struggle.

And she got up and sat down on the bed at once. She panted. "Go save our babies. They are going to kill them."

Isaac Sr. glanced over his shoulders as he took in his wife's large, fearful eyes, the shuddering and sweating figure of his wife, and wrapped his arms around her.

"Nobody is going to harm our children, Nancy."

She curled up in his chest and hid her face as a sob muffled and shook her entire body. "I heard them. They are going to do whatever it takes to tear them apart."

"No, no, you were dreaming, hon. They are sleeping peacefully in the nursery.

Her eyes widened as she inspected the face of her reassuring husband and grabbed his hand. "The beast had the scariest, most penetrating, deep voice I have ever heard."

"Trust me, there is no one here."

"And you're looking at me like I'm crazy, but I swear it seemed too real."

Isaac kissed the top of her head as Nancy still struggled to draw in her breath. "Of course, you are not."

"Then promise me, you won't neglect this. You have to help me. You must do something about the babies," she cried out. "Come with me," Isaac begged her. "You see it yourself."

As he led his wife to their children's room, Isaac swore he had never seen his wife in so much distress. His heart went to her. Was it just a simple nightmare or a warning for something bigger coming their way? He had no way to know it, right?

§§§§§§§§§

Sacha bounced in her high chair like she was on a jumping castle having the time of her life. Her head and arms went up and down while her face was a picture of pure joy. Breakfast was a serious business with two children for Nancy.

"Look here, sweetie," she urged her daughter to open a mouth as she opened the book Sacha loved. "The Very Hungry Caterpillar went deep in the forest and...."

Wham, the sound was not subtle, and the book fell from her hand at once. Annoyed by this sudden action, Nancy swore under her breath. The toll of managing twins on her own was making her weak. Perhaps so weak that she could not even hold a small children's book alone. She lifted the book from the floor and filled the spoon again.

Sacha was a non-fussy eater. She loved almost everything her mom made and devoured each spoonful until the bowl was clear. "The Very Hungry Caterpillar went deep in the forest..." Nancy repeated, concentrating on her daughter's open and eager, hungry mouth when the book slipped from her hand again with a thud.

She groaned. "Perhaps I am getting too old for this." She hastily fed Sacha, and as she bent down to pick up the book, her eyes went to her son sitting next to Sacha in his chair. He was eyeing the book eagerly. Was she dreaming, or was her son pointing a finger at the book her daughter cherished so much?

She had an idea. Nancy fed Sacha without getting the storybook, and once done, she turned to her son after grabbing the book from the floor again. She filled the spoon as she spoke to him. "On Tuesday, the caterpillar ate through two pears but was still hungry. On Wednesday, he ate through three plums, but his hunger didn't go away..."

As her story progressed to Sunday, day after day, Nancy noticed that the book didn't fall from her hand this time. Was it just her imagination, or when her son wanted something his sister desired, he had the power to make it happen? She didn't know. But the thought made her shudder as this was not something she could neglect anymore.

Nancy sighed as she focused on feeding her children. Her life was getting more weird each day, and she had no clue – why?

Chapter 15:

Ice Cream Freezer

Two years later, when the twins are two years old.

"Hey honey, I'm going to be home late tonight." Isaac Sr. called Nancy on Friday evening. "My director wants a bunch of us out for drinks."

"Oh, that's a bit disappointing. The kids are waiting for you, and so am I!" she replied on her phone.

Isaac Sr. sighed. "I know. This has been a difficult time for you. What with kids just turning two and …"

Nancy smiled. "Don't get me started. They are a handful."

"I know. Raising them has been quite difficult. And what with my travel and all that…"

Nancy ran a hand through her hair. "Forget about the travel. I wanted to talk to you about something."

"Nancy, what's that? Why do you sound so serious?"

"It's nothing. It's just that I have been observing some strange behavior lately."

"Oh boy. Honey, can we talk later? I gotta go."

There was nothing she could say then. Isaac's working hours were getting longer now, and she was afraid he was not spending enough time with the children.

"Oh, I see. Do you remember you had promised to take them out for ice cream?"

When there was no sound at the other end, Nancy ended the call and folded her hands to her chest. She wanted to tell him how Isaac Jr. could maneuver the things he wanted. She wanted to talk about how little Sacha was so strong when it came to the battle of wills and how she always won. She wanted to say that while she was excited to discover the kids' superpower, she was scared as hell, too. She didn't want to think about what would happen when the kids were grown up.

She blinked. No. She was not going to think about the future again.

"You know what? I will take them out myself!" Nancy spoke to no one in particular as she started to fetch her jacket. Going out for an ice cream was always fun as the twins loved it. And she didn't want to disappoint them although she had to come back soon to put them to sleep.

After running a comb through her hair, Nancy went to their room. "Isaac, Sacha, we are going out."

"Daddy?" They both spoke together, and Nancy shook her head.

"Your father will be late tonight. I could get you some ice cream."

If it was possible for a two-year-old to show disappointment, Nancy knew the look on her children's faces resembled the one. "OK, children. It's seven o'clock, and we will return in half an hour. It's time for bed, then."

"Not sleeping," Sacha pouted as her small mouth trembled.

Nancy went to her and picked her up. "Mmm, now what do you want to get?"

"Chocolate!" Isaac Jr. screamed in delight.

"Berry.." his sister didn't believe in imitating him all the time, and Nancy laughed as she looked at their little delightful faces.

Buckling them in their stroller, she started to walk towards the ice cream parlor around the corner. They would go to a mall or somewhere else when Isaac was around. But she was uncomfortable taking them both very far yet on her own.

As they walked into the black and white tiled parlor, Sacha clapped in delight. It was obviously her favorite place.

With her tiny hands, Sacha started to tug at Nancy's hand, urging her to get her down.

Nancy's mouth fell open when she looked In front. There was a line of customers, and now she was considering her decision to come here. As she unbuckled Isaac Jr., he ran to the chilled ice cream freezer at once. His hands spread over the glass.

"Isaac, let's get back to the line." Nancy urged her son gently.

"I want ice cream." He turned around to her now.

"Yes, but we can't get it directly from the freezer. We need to stand in the line..." Nancy patiently repeated her words.

"Want now…" suddenly Isaac screamed.

"Yes, but we need to wait our turn."

Isaac Jr. went to the freezer, now wanting to pull it open.

"No, no, you can't take it yourself. Wait, Isaac."

However, Isaac Jr. was not in the mood to listen to her. He started to cry at the top of his voice, and others looked at Nancy, which suggested she could not control her child.

Nancy tried again. "Look at Sacha. Your sister is waiting to get her ice cream."

But Isaac Jr. stomped his feet as if he had become deaf to his mother's soothing words. She offered him a long stare next, hoping to control his temper. But he was gone by now, and it was irreversible. She had seconds before his anger erupted.

He was screaming like she was hitting him with a stick. All she had said was 'No 'when he wanted to open the freezer. He stared at her with a sullen look as Nancy looked around and finally found a small, secluded corner. She lifted Isaac, holding Sacha's hand with the other hand as she led them towards the corner.

"Look, sweetheart," she looked into Isaac's eye as she spoke calmly. "I understand that you want to fetch the ice cream yourself. But you can't do it unless we have paid for it."

Isaac Jr.'s eyes went longingly to the freezer once again.

"We have two choices – either we stand in that queue and wait for our turn or go back home without ice cream. What would you prefer?"

Isaac Jr.'s chin jutted, and his little body trembled slightly, but ultimately he got her message. As he looked at his mom with big, innocent eyes, she kissed his head. "You know what, I love you. But there are certain rules we follow no matter what."

Isaac Jr. nodded and then smiled. "Want chocolate waffle."

"Alright then. Sure, tell me exactly, and we can get it. Meanwhile, will you take care of this teddy bear for me?"

Nancy pulled out Isaac Jr.'s favorite toy and gave it to him. Once his sobs died, she again led her kids to the queue. However, as they waited for their turn, Nancy's sharp eyes couldn't help but notice the small crack in the corner of the freezer.

Was it before there, or had her son caused it?

She had no way to know!

Chapter 16:

Daughter Emerald

After the twins 'birth, Nancy let Isaac care for both of them for the first time. It had been a few months since she had met with her sister, and Nancy missed her. Also, she wanted a little time for herself, away from the kids to think about their future. And then there were all those weird incidents around children, which were hard to ignore now. Maybe Eile could give her some pointers.

Eileithyia was more than happy when Nancy called and said she would drive down to her place that weekend.

"Well, why don't you spend the night here?" Eileithyia had suggested. "That way, you won't have to drive home in the evening hours."

"I would love that. It has been ages since I was on my own. I miss our long night chats, too."

"Then what are you waiting for? We can even go to your favorite spa if you wish."

"Won't it be heaven?" Nancy sighed. "But I am afraid it would have to wait. Because I don't know if I can leave my babies alone at night with that husband of mine yet..."

Nancy laughed. "You have to believe me. They are a handful."

"I do believe you. Won't I know?" Eileithyia laughed. "I have still not forgotten the latest ice cream incident. But Isaac is a capable man. I am sure the three of them can be happy together."

"Yes, he is very good with them when he is around. He has been under much pressure lately, and the kids hardly see him."

"The perils of hard work." Eileithyia drew in a breath. "I get it. Maybe we can do the weekend thing some other time. Now, do me a favor and start early. We have a lot of gossip to catch up with."

"I wouldn't miss it for anything in the world. Of course. I will be there soon. See you." With that, Nancy ended her call..

§§§§§§§§§

It was Friday evening, and after spending almost the whole day with her sister, Nancy was now returning home.

They had a lot of fun. And her sister knew how to unwind. However, as the day started to roll into the afternoon, Nancy became restless, saying she missed her kids.

And that was the reason she left earlier than planned. However, the country roads demanded more care driving in the rain, and she had to slow down. It would be some more hours before she reached her family, and Nancy didn't want to think about it.

Furthermore, they discussed the incidents of the ice cream parlor and the book. The issues had troubled Nancy.

"Does this happen when both of them want the same thing?"

"Most probably, yes."

"Do Isaac Jr. and Sacha get this extraordinary power in the same room, or does it work while they are on their own?" Eileithyia had asked.

"Umm," she thought, "I am sure they both have some individual strengths. But yes, I see that when they are together, it is something else."

"Why don't you separate them and check if it still works?" Eileithyia had suggested.

"We can definitely try that."

As she drove, softly splashing water droplets hit the car windows. The sky weighed down with a big blanket of gray. She could hardly tell the difference between the sky and clouds. *I shouldn't have driven in this weather.* She mumbled under her breath.

But it was of no use now. She was midway, and there was no point returning to her sister. At any other time, such rain would have excited Nancy. But not today. With each passing moment, her apprehension grew, and she didn't know if this weather was the sole reason behind it.

As the rain cascaded from the sky like white velvet, suddenly her eyes went to a strange light in the sky. It was not a flash of lightning, and she was sure this light seemed to follow her. Keeping her eye on the mirror, Nancy steadily and slowly drove through the bad weather, hoping the rain would stop soon. But it was not going to be.

However, the rain was the least of her problems now as she observed the strange light in the sky chasing her down the empty, winding roads. It looked like a falling star, she told herself. But as she added miles, the light became larger and brighter, and she knew that a falling star couldn't be so. She had read a lot about satellites, and perhaps this was one of them. But the thought did nothing to soothe her mind.

I could stop somewhere on the way, at a motel, she thought as she steered down the curving road. When finally, the light was no longer visible, Nancy regained the breath she had held for so long in relief. But she was sure she was not imagining things. Her mind saw things, and this was not one to be ignored.

She drove for a few more minutes with calm, only to find that the bizarre light was back and more visible than before. It was less of an illusion and more of a reality now. She had to know the answer. Nancy bit her lip and then pulled the car over to a halt, wanting a better look at it.

And what did she see?

It was not a strange light but a moving object indeed. It was now almost hovering on top of the place where she was standing, and the wheels in Nancy's brain started to spin at once. Oh God, was it really what she had thought? This can't be true. The big object was like an airplane in size but flat and circular.

I should go back to the car at once. She thought frantically as she looked at her wristwatch to see the time. But what was this? It had stopped working. This was not good. Something bizarre was happening.

Nancy ran towards her vehicle, opening the car window at once. She wouldn't remember what happened next except that she saw a glimpse of a blueish face with big, startling eyes before she lost consciousness.

When she opened her eyes, she was led to a long metallic ramp inside the disc that had been following her. A few wireless bulb-like objects floated in the air, illuminating the path. She leaned forward in part fear, part panic, and part excitement. She was sure she was stepping inside a UFO, but why was she brought here? She stole a look at the glistening shadow with distinctive markings on his face, neck, and body and asked. "Where am I?"

The alien's blue skin glistened in the dim light as he looked at her with intelligent eyes. "No question. Just move ahead."

His voice was deep and heavy, although she oddly didn't find it threatening. And it relieved her. It was apparent that they were sentient, intellectual beings. Whatever the reason behind her presence on the UFO, she guessed they would probably not harm her.

Nancy thought about her family as she took step after step. She couldn't remember being lifted from the ground. "Umm," she tried to talk with the alien with spindly arms and giant bald head, "why am I here?"

"Turn around now," the object replied in a clear voice.

They had reached a large hall-like structure now. She could see computer-like objects on several desks and some more aliens like the one who had brought her here. The metal vessel was surprisingly cool from the inside, and she could not know whether it was still floating and moving or paused in midair.

"Please, I need to go back to my family." She urged one of the aliens when a tall figure entered the hall from one of the doors.

"That's why you are here. Sit down, Nancy." His white eyes with a slight blue tint stood out against the darkness, and she knew that one was the leader. She looked hard into his eyes, wondering if they were peaceful beings or killers. But the eyes betrayed nothing.

Nancy's eyes went to the other corner of the room, hoping to get some clues. But there were none.

And then the alien ordered to another, "Bring Emerald."

"Sure Aundrid." And as the alien returned with a small child, Nancy's eyes widened.

"Who is this?"

Aundrid replied. "Emerald, your daughter."

"My daughter?" Nancy's eyes scrunched in disbelief now. "I only have one daughter, and she is at home."

"No, you have one more."

And as the alien returned back with a girl who oddly resembled Nancy in her childhood, Nancy didn't know what to say.

Chapter 17

Nordic Knowledge

"Emmy, meet Nancy," said Aundrid.

Nancy opened her mouth to speak and stopped as she looked at a small child standing before her. Gentle, soft brown curls like a color of pure earth surrounded that delicate face. Her green eyes gently reflected the glimmering color of emerald, every hue of the forest promising the beacon of hope in the dreariest of days. Next to the vivid brown shade of her hair, that deepest brown, those eyes revealed a light that showed strength to push into the things to make way.

Nancy looked deep into them and drew a deep breath. The little girl's aura was seeped in strength and courage like a wildfire: reckless, untamed, yet indisputably captivating.

Who was this girl?

Why had they introduced her as her daughter?

These questions flooded her belly like ice, and for a minute, Nancy didn't know what to say.

Is it possible they are lying? She thought. Perhaps they want something from me. Use my psychic power for their selfish purpose? But why? She looked around. The aliens were too advanced compared to humans. And she doubted it was her psychic power they were after.

Then, she thought, *were they the caretakers who wanted to save the Earth?*

Nancy had many questions, and she had to get the answers. But not in front of the child, named as her daughter. Holding her hands at her chest, Nancy turned to the leader. "Aundrid, can we talk?"

"Of course." With that, the chief gestured for another alien to take Emerald away.

Once she was gone, Nancy threw her hands in the air. "Why am I here? I don't get it. And how is Emerald…"

Aundrid smiled this time. "I get it. You have many questions. But why don't you have something to eat? We can talk while you are eating!"

"No." She rejected his proposal with dismay. "I am not hungry. And I must have the answers first."

Her eyes went to the far horizon, and they widened when she saw the azure sky hanging like a gigantic blue emerald. They were moving.

The realization sent a sudden shiver to her body, which Aundrid's expert eyes discerned with ease.

"Allow me to introduce myself formally. I am Aundrid, the chief director of Nordics. Now, what do you want to know?"

She narrowed her eyes. "Who are Nordics?"

"Well, you must know President Eisenhower was extremely interested in UFOs and ETs?"

"Yes." Her voice was calm and clear this time. "It was a secret, but President Eisenhower strongly believes in life on other planets."

"Very good," Aundrid said. "Let me give you more details." He clapped, and a giant screen appeared out of nowhere in front of their sitting area. Aundrid picked a calculator-like device, a small keypad, from the nearby table and started to tap on it.

Soon, the screen came to life!

"Check this," said Aundrid. "In February 1954, the president spent several days in Palm Springs on vacation. He disappeared for several hours one Saturday afternoon and even missed a public dinner. He was not seen again until late the following morning."

"But he had chipped a tooth." She spoke at once. "He had gone to see a dentist."

"Indeed not. Instead, he met me, including one of my colleagues."

"And what was the reason behind that meeting?"

"Don't you know?" Aundrid's heavy voice vibrated in the space. "The Earth is 'on a path of self-destruction, 'and we wanted to meet to help find a way to stop it."

"And could you reach any decision?"

"Well, Eisenhower wanted to form a treaty with us, but was unwilling to agree to our demand to cease testing nuclear weapons. We left with no treaty in place."

"I see." Nancy looked at Aundrid.

"It was so hard for us. We had traveled for so many years to give this message and help your planet. But it didn't work." Aundrid got up. "But we didn't want to give up. We tried to meet the president again, but our UFO crashed before we could do anything."

Nancy gasped for air now. "Crashed?" Was it the one she had seen in her vision on the sub?

"You are right," Aundrid spoke again. "The pilot tried hard to find a way to save the ship, but he couldn't."

"Oh my god!" Nancy didn't know whether she was shocked because now she could see where this led. Or was she shocked because the alien sitting in front could even read her mind?

"You are an intelligent woman, Nancy. And a great instrument between us and human beings. I know now you can see the whole picture. We wanted peace. We were trying to negotiate a positive settlement for Earth's problems. But we were unsuccessful."

Nancy nodded, still thinking about what Aundrid was saying, trying to figure out things. Although she knew little about the president's meeting with the Nordics, she had no option but to believe what he said.

She was lost in thoughts when, out of nowhere, loud voices and screams started to come from the adjoining space.

Nancy almost stood up when she heard Emerald's shouts and then some alien speaking in a language she could not understand. What was going on? However, she was in a strange place, and it was wise not to interfere.

"It is indeed what you are thinking." Aundrid sighed. "It is Emerald. She doesn't listen to us and starts throwing things when things don't go her way. And that's why you are here. To guide us about how to deal with her."

"Really?" Nancy scrunched her eyes this time.

"Yes. I admire the way you manage the twins."

"Twins?" She got up. "What do you know about them? How do you know about them?"

"Take it easy, Nancy. I have replies to all your questions, but it is late now."

"I don't care. I have all the time in the world right now." Her voice was firm now. "So first, tell me how Emerald is related to me."

"It's a long story. Do you recall your trip to the North Pole?"

Chapter 18:

Troubles 4 Nancy

"A VITAL ELEMENT in keeping the peace is our military establishment." The TV blared.

Isaac nodded silently as he finally let the Friday evening take over and sipped his beer. His favorite pastime, Sitting in front of the television after long, grueling working hours was his favorite pastime. And it was not different tonight. He would not miss watching President Dwight D. Eisenhower's farewell address to the nation.

Managing twins on his own without his wife's support was difficult. But he had done reasonably well. Maybe Nancy was overly worried or exaggerating about the twins 'superpowers. So far, he had not seen anything that would alarm him. Anyway, tonight Nancy was coming back. Maybe he can take the family out for lunch at her favorite restaurant tomorrow.

His mouth evolved to a smile at the thought as his fingers slid on the condensation of the glass. After a hearty meal, the kids sat at the kitchen table, scribbling to their hearts 'content. And Isaac Sr. was only too happy to let them be on their own for now.

"Our arms must be mighty, ready for instant action, so that no potential aggressor may be tempted to risk his own destruction."

Isaac slipped in the armchair, focusing on the president's words. The man sure knew his job.

"OUR MILITARY ORGANIZATION today bears little resemblance to that known by any of my predecessors in peacetime, or indeed by the fighting men of World War II or Korea. UNTIL THE LATEST of our world conflicts, the United States had no armaments industry. AMERICAN MAKERS of plowshares could, with time and as required, make swords as well.

But now we can no longer risk emergency improvisation of national defense; we have been compelled to create a permanent armaments industry of vast proportions. Added to this, three and a half million men and women are directly engaged in the defense establishment. WE ANNUALLY spend on military security more than the net income of all United States Corporations. THIS CONJUNCTION of an immense military establishment and a large arms industry is new in the American experience.

The total influence -- economic, political, even spiritual -- is felt in every city, every State house, every office of the Federal government. We recognize the imperative need for this development. Yet we must not fail to comprehend its grave implications. Our toil, resources and livelihood are all involved; so is the very structure of our society.

IN THE COUNCILS of government, we must guard against the acquisition of unwarranted influence, whether sought or unsought, by the military-industrial complex. The potential for the disastrous rise of misplaced power exists and will persist."

Isaac drew in a breath. Was he warning the nation about the corrupting influence? This was a big thing. He kept his beer on the side table and stood up to increase the volume.

"Dada!"

He heard Sacha's voice screaming at the top of her lungs.

"I am here." Isaac entered the adjoining room at once, knowing his son very well. Chaos greeted him there.

Multiple crayons were scattered on the floor, with many broken or on the verge of breaking.

"Dammit!"

The words escaped his mouth before he could even control them.

And Isaac Oldfield was right. Little Isaac Jr. tried to snatch one crayon from his sister's hand. Sacha was wincing in pain.

Wait, Isaac Jr. was not even touching her hand. Then why was she gasping?

In a rush to stop his son, Isaac smacked his toe against the table, and a moan floated briefly from his mouth.

Then Isaac Sr. went to peel his hand away from Sacha. But what was it? He was not even able to move it. Isaac Jr.'s grip on the crayon was like an iron clasp.

"No, no, you don't do that to your sister."

His son's big eyes widened. But he didn't give up.

Isaac Sr. then turned to his daughter.

"Let it go, Sacha. Let's pick up another crayon."

Sacha opened her mouth to speak when her father's eyes went to the wall behind her. It was covered with scribbles from a little child's imagination.

"No, no. That's wrong. You can't draw on a wall. Your mom would be furious." Isaac Sr. spoke immediately.

His children's faces fell a bit, and Isaac felt sorry. To appreciate their creativity, he took a look. *Whoa! What was it?*

A big drawing of a white star loomed on the wall. It was not exactly glistening, but it was an excellent try to create one.

The other drawing was what can be called a miniature replica of a flying saucer. And this time, it was very clear. From where he was standing, Isaac could see what it was.

Were two-year-olds this talented? he wondered. Isaac couldn't recall showing his children a picture of a UFO or telling them a story about one. Then how did they know about it?

"Who drew this picture?" Isaac pointed towards the star-like shape, hoping against hope it was not something he had imagined it to be.

There was no reply. The always bubbly Sacha and eager-to-reply Isaac Jr. were glued to their place like a statue.

Their eyes were focused on the sky visible from the window. What were they thinking? Was it their age or something else? He had to discuss this with his wife. And the thought led him to another idea.

Wasn't it about time she came home? What the hell happened? Did Nancy decide to spend one more day at her sister's place? Then why hadn't she called?

Taking one look at his children, who were still lost in thoughts as if they were focused on something, Isaac quickly called Eileithyia. Isaac knew something was wrong when she confirmed that Nancy had left early.

He knew his wife. She was punctual and organized and always stayed on her schedule.

Isaac Oldfield put his children to sleep first and then sat down to make a call.

"Hey, John."

"Hey there. Long time, buddy."

"Yeah," Isaac Sr. paused, thinking hard to explain his worry. He was uncertain and yet had to tell the police. It was eleven at night, and Nancy should have been home hours ago.

"Did you watch the president's address?" Unaware of his turmoil, John continued at the other end. "I know; the man got right to the point."

At any other time, Isaac Sr. would have loved to dissect every word of that speech.

Not tonight.

Isaac allowed his brain to let his doubts surface.

"Nancy had driven to Columbia, Maryland, yesterday to meet her sister."

The silence at the other end revealed John was all ears, like a true policeman.

"I just confirmed with my sister-in-law. Nancy left in the afternoon. But she is not home."

"That's about a 45-minute drive, maybe 1.5 to 2.5 hours during the rush hour," John added.

"Yes,"

Isaac had underestimated this cold night. Years later, he would recall it as one where his heart was a door left wide open to the icy wind, which was slamming against it.

"Her car might have run out of gas."

"She filled the tank before she left," said Isaac.

"Have the children gone to bed?"

"Yes, although I had a little explaining their mom's absence."

"Why don't you go to bed as well? I will call if I find anything."

Isaac grabbed the duvet from his bedroom, wanting to be near the telephone. While he could fit his rather large body on the living room couch, his mind was in bad shape and he counted each minute of that long night.

Many a time, he begged the telephone silently. *Please, please ring...*

Nancy can't disappear from the Earth's face overnight.

There had to be a reason behind her vanishing act.

Was it Russian agents?

Or someone else? A psychic had many enemies.

Isaac Sr. placed the receiver of his phone one more time on the cradle after checking the dial tone. Yes, it was working perfectly.

—two o'clock. No news!

His heart started to pound in his chest. Unable to sleep, Isaac Oldfield sat on the couch, pleading for the phone to ring.

And it did at 4 o'clock.

"John?" Isaac got it on the second ring.

"Isaac, I have some bad news to tell you."

"What?"

"I hate to say this, but a body has been found near the woods."

"What? What are you saying!"

"Isaac, listen. I am not sure the body is hers. Nancy is a psychic. She would know if she was in any danger. Are you listening?"

Isaac was in no position to reply to his friend by now. He buried his head into his hands.

"They found Nancy's car on the highway near Laurel. It was deserted. There was no clue of what could have happened to her. Whether she left it on her own or someone forced her to…"

Isaac's knees turned to rubber as the phone call continued.

"Can you name anyone who would want her dead?"

John's words evaporated in the cold night air.

Nancy was not abducted. She was dead.

Chapter 19:

It's Knot Nancy

After a few minutes, Isaac Oldfield tried to get up from the floor where he had been sitting. But it took some effort tonight. His heart pounded as he recalled what his friend had told him, and tears clouded his vision at the thought of going to the site to recognize the body. He thought of Nancy, their first meeting, all the years they had spent together, and a fresh bout of tears filled his eyes.

The pain skewered down to his guts when he thought of his children sleeping quietly upstairs. And he realized he couldn't leave them alone here.

He got up and put the phone back on the cradle.

He would have to call Nancy's sister at this ungodly hour, but he couldn't tell her what he had just learned from John.

Isaac somehow fetched a glass of water and gulped it all at once. Once he could think clearly, he picked up the receiver and dialed Eile's number.

Please, please, don t let it be Nancy, he silently prayed as he informed Eileithyia.

For a few minutes, there was silence at the other end.

Then her raspy, hardly audible voice spoke.

"This can't be true. Nancy can't be dead. It's all a big mistake."

Isaac swallowed the knot in his throat. His brain was still not functioning correctly.

Yet he knew –

The kids would be up soon, unaware of what was happening in their lives.

How is he going to explain the absence of their mother?

He didn't have any words for that.

He had to go to work in the morning.

But will he be able to?

"I need to go and check..." he couldn't finish the sentence.

"Isaac, look, I can imagine what you are going through right now. But don't lose hope. I have a feeling it's not Nancy!"

"Then where could she be?" Isaac gulped the weak tea which he had made hours prior. It had become cold and tasteless. Just like his life right now. "There is no message from her or anybody else."

Despite the fire in the fireplace, the cold had taken over the entire room, and Isaac thought of his wife once again. Nancy – she was out there somewhere on this dark night, and he had to find her.

"I am on my way. I will be there in an hour."

How had Eileithyia heard his unspoken words asking for help? Perhaps the grieving hearts understood the language of silence.

"The kids – what are we going to …"

She cut him in the middle. "Absolutely nothing. Not until we know what we are facing. I will take care of them."

"Thanks, Eile."

And as he ended the call, Isaac Oldfield once again thought of who could do such a thing to Nancy. Who had forced her to leave the car if it was not an accident?

The dark sky imparted the feeling of claustrophobia, and Isaac wanted nothing else but to leave the house right now.

And once Eile was there as promised, Isaac hardly exchanged words with her as he jumped into his car.

Bringing it to life, Isaac drove to the place John had spoken about.

While he was driving the vehicle carefully within the speed limit, the same couldn't be said about his brain, which was overworked, conjuring up horror stories.

After an hour, Isaac Oldfield had reached the spot he dreaded. The road was almost empty at this hour of the early morning.

After the blackness of the night, mellow blues and pinks blurred together in a pale blue sky to create another gorgeous morning. He might be grieving, but the sky remained as beautiful as ever.

John was already there.

He first led him to the car he had found.

Until now, Isaac was hopeful that John had made some mistake.

But when he looked at his wife's deserted car parked neatly at one side of the road, his gut lurched, and a churning mixture of digestive acids and tea filled his mouth.

It was impossible to evade the hurricane of thoughts now that what John had discovered was true.

He ran his hands over the vehicle, picturing his wife slipping behind the wheel. Her face was bright; her lips curled in a smile.

At that moment, Isaac wanted to be anywhere but here.

This whole thing seemed like a nightmare, and he waited for it to end.

But unfortunately, it wasn't.

"Yes, it's her car." Isaac painfully spoke the words, and John nodded, feeling the weight of those words. As he guided Isaac towards the nearby woods, every muscle of Isaac's body tightened.

This part of the wood was oddly quiet. Even the sound of his footfall sounded strange to Isaac as both the men walked. The old, yellow, and brown leaves hustled in the wind, and twigs snapped under their feet.

What was Nancy doing over here? The question was eating Isaac from the inside, and he had no answer yet.

"There were several fingerprints on the car. But they are all the same. So, I am assuming it must be Nancy's." John informed Isaac.

He nodded in response, not wanting to share the feelings of anxiety or dread with his friend.

Don t lose hope. I have a feeling it s not Nancy!

Isaac Oldfield remembered what Eileithyia had told. At this moment, he really wanted to believe in these words. Taking solace from those positive words, Isaac took the next step.

But when his eyes went to the corpse lying aside, all hope vanished, and his limbs felt rubbery. Although the dead body was covered, Isaac couldn't help but notice the structure and height.

No, he wanted to scream. This can't be happening. This can't be Nancy.

An unknown fear traveled in his veins, and a knot hit Isaac's stomach. He sighed, watching in horror as John started to lift the cloth from the body.

And when Isaac found the mop of blond hair, his legs buckled up under pressure. He didn't want to see John uncover that face. He fell to the ground on his knees, not knowing how to survive without Nancy.

Each second passed like an eternity, and when John lightly pressed Isaac's shoulder, cajoling him to lift his head and take a look, Isaac bit his lip and looked up.

A feeling of relief overtook his body.

It was not her.

Isaac slowly got up from the ground, wanting a closer look.

"This is not Nancy." He confirmed this to his friend, and his lips curled in a smile when his eyes noticed the dead body's uncanny resemblance to his wife.

Anybody would have mistaken the corpse for Nancy.

Chapter 20:

Twin Families

"Why don't I drop you off first?" John asked Isaac, and he made his way toward the highway again.

"It's okay. Don't worry." Isaac tried to laugh. "I can drive home on my own. Moreover, you also need to proceed with this case."

"Yes," sighed John. "Sometimes I really hate my job. Until now, this woman is just a dead body. But the minute I found out who she was, my job would become difficult. I must learn about her family and talk to those who love her. Watching them break down and mourn the loss is not easy."

"I understand," Isaac replied. "Especially when I am going through the same situation. Life's a bitch. It does things we never imagined."

"Keep me in the loop," said John. "If you get a phone call or hear anything about her."

"I will."

"And drive carefully," John shouted as Isaac opened his car door and slipped behind the steering wheel.

The drive back home was not long and not as dreary, and yet Isaac couldn't relax his tightened muscles.

The early morning sun was well risen by now, and Isaac found the light oddly bright this morning. The moonlit gray night had given way to the colors of the day. But their beautiful shades did nothing to lessen the burden of his soul.

It was a good thing that the woman was not Nancy.

But then, where did Nancy go?

Maybe he should contact his government contacts about Russian agents taking Nancy.

Lost in his thoughts, Isaac didn't even know when he had finished the journey. He parked his car in the garage and stepped into the drawing room.

What did he see?

Nancy and her sister were at the dining table serving breakfast to the kids.

"Nanny..." the words hardly came out as Isaac ran to his wife.

And within seconds, she was in his arms.

Isaac Sr. had never felt so blessed before.

He tightened his grip around her, never wanting to let her go.

But he had many questions.

"Why don't I take kids to the playground?" Eileithyia suggested. "It's a lovely day."

"Yes, it is indeed," Isaac replied. "Now." Then he loosened his grip on his wife and mouthed.

"Thanks, Eile."

She smiled knowingly, giving them both time to talk without the kids 'interruption.

Once they were gone, Nancy brought tea to the dining table and sat before her husband.

"You already have dark circles under your eyes." She chided.

"You don't know what I went through in just one night."

She sighed. "I know. It must have been difficult."

"Especially when I saw the woman lying on the ground resembling you." A shudder passed through Isaac's body. "Someone is definitely after you."

She nodded.

"So, where were you?"

She narrowed her eyes. "Will you believe me if I tell you that the aliens, the Nordics, abducted me?"

Isaac Sr. almost got up from his chair.

"It can't be true. Tell me you are joking."

"No. I wish it were a joke. But it's not." She kept the cup on the table, looking into her husband's eyes. "Some bad aliens wanted to kill me, and knowing that, the Nordics kidnapped me to save me."

"Bad aliens?" Isaac's forehead furrowed. "This doesn't make sense."

"The reason behind killing me is to hurt our children and break their morale, their superpower."

Isaac cradled his head in the palm of his hand as he recited the incident about Isaac Jr. and Sacha's drawing abilities.

"How could they come up with a star and a soccer ball?" He questioned. "They have never seen it."

And as if he had suddenly found the reply, he thrashed his hand on the table. "Oh my God, they knew where you were and were trying to tell me that."

She nodded.

"That's why they were so quiet last night." Isaac gulped.

"Yes, they silently heard the conversation between Nordics and me."

"I still don't get it. The thought of them having such superpower scares me. How come they are so different from the rest of the children?"

"That was one of the reasons the Nordics wanted to talk with me." Nancy took a breath and then continued. "Remember the circumstances of their birth?"

Isaac nodded. "Yeah, they were born on the Nautilus."

"Umm, not any normal sub," she added. "It was passing the North Pole with the Pole Star light not moving an inch. Add the radiation from the UFO transponder..."

"Oh my God," Isaac's voice raised a new octave. "The one we had to deposit at the Pole,"

She smiled, "Yes, the one which I had touched psychically to evoke the Mayday switch."

Isaac scratched his head now. "Why did I never think about it? The influence of the Pole Star and the radiation from the UFO transponder has blessed them with a superpower."

"Yes, and the Nordics mentioned that they must be raised separately as their combined power may get out of control."

"I have already seen what they can do when they join hands."

"Didn't I tell you how Isaac Jr. broke the ice cream box that day, creating chaos and panic?"

Isaac took a sip of his tea. "What are we going to do about this? I am sure as they grow, this power will increase."

"They are way ahead of other children their age. And that scares me." She looked at Isaac with concern. "The Nordics said the mental powers of another alien species have manipulated the weaker minds of the planet, numbering about a third in each country."

"What are you talking about?"

"Our kids will be instrumental in helping nations gain freedom from alien technology that distorts human judgment," said Nancy. "That technology encourages angry lashing out against human challenges instead of rational cooperation. Our kids will solidify humanity's fight against unchecked climate threats and autocratic rule ."

"And that was the reason they were after you?"

"Yes, Isaac. The lives of our children are in danger. We have to protect them."

"And how are we going to do that?" Isaac asked her. "Until this morning, I had no clue why somebody wanted to destroy you, and now this whole thing about superpowers...."

She pressed his hand lightly. "I am worried too. But at the same time, being a mother of such precious kids makes me happy and proud."

"But how will we manage? How will we raise them? It would be so difficult to separate them."

"I know Isaac. It's not going to be an easy journey. But we are not alone. The Nordics will help us."

"Huh? Can we even send our children to normal school? Will it be safe for other children?"

"Yes, if they are separated. And we have Emerald to help them, train them with the necessary skills."

Isaac's eyes scrunched. "Emerald?"

"Yes, my other daughter. Half human and half Nordic."

Chapter 21:

Emerald+Aundrid=?

"May I get you something to drink?" Nancy whispered to her husband.

She had a lot on her mind. There were too many things that even she had not grasped until now, and she didn't know how Isaac would react.

"No," said Isaac. "I'm already numbed by the events of these last two days." He looked at his wife with weary eyes. Nancy noticed a few lines on his forehead, which she had failed to see before, and sighed. She knew what he had endured.

"I am sorry for what I put you through."

"It wasn't your choice, Nanny."

Isaac stood up and went to the ceiling-to-floor window of the hall. The last sun's rays painted the sky in vivid hues of purple and orange before finally making way for the evening darkness.

Looking at his taut posture and rigid back, it was not difficult for Nancy to understand that her husband was trying to figure out the reasons behind Emerald's birth and how she was related to Nancy.

They had a lot to discuss!

Nancy breathed profoundly and then went to her husband. She tried to shut out the pain about their impending future. Whatever it was, they both would have to sort it out together.

"Do you want to hear about how Emerald was born?"

And Isaac was aside her, taller, gloomier, and thoughtful. She stared up at him as his dark eyes bore into hers. Nancy gulped. Meeting Emerald was not her plan, yet she was in their lives now.

He nodded. The air was filled with mystery, misery, and suspense as she took his hand and led him back to the couch.

A "Hey" behind her made Nancy turn to see the children with her sister. Eileithyia gauged the situation and mouthed that she was taking the kids out for dinner.

"Sometimes we feel that we know life. But then it takes us in another direction." She spoke softly. "And that's how I felt when I saw Emerald for the first time."

"I don't like the unpredictability either. But yeah, life does throw a curveball now and then." Isaac said.

"And what shook me completely was…" Nancy breathed heavily. "She looks exactly like I used to look at that age." She threw her hands in the air. "I mean, imagine what I went through when I saw the exact mini replica of my childhood. How is it even possible?"

"Well, that shows how absurd the Nordics are!"

"Well, yes, they are." Nancy paused and then turned her full attention to her husband.

"Do you recall how I operated the UFO while on the sub?"

"Yes, you were pregnant with the twins and not feeling well…"

"Exactly. I went for a stroll on the ship and accidentally ended up helping the UFO pilot through a psychic event. That was the time when the Nordics collected my DNA signature."

He scratched his head. "But you never mentioned about DNA."

"I think the 'thought amplifier 'uses the DNA signature to provide full identification of the person sending the signal," Nancy added. "And I didn't know their ship was scanning and storing my DNA."

"So, when you interacted with the UFO for the first time, they stored your DNA as a signature for future reference." Isaac relaxed a bit. "Well, who would have ever imagined such a technique existed??"

"Conceived using my DNA and a Nordic's DNA, Emerald is half human, half Nordic. Just our kids 'age. But I found her surprisingly mature for her age."

"Don't forget that she is a cross-breed humanoid. So, of course, she would develop faster than our children. But mainly, she is bi-cultural. She understands humans as well as Nordics! That's a win for both cultures," said Nancy.

Then she added, "But guess what, Aundrid wanted to know about the terrible twos!"

Isaac laughed a little now. "And before you tell me who Aundrid is, I bet there is no one better than you to advise him. Sacha and Isaac have put you through a lot."

"Well, yeah, I...., I mean, I'm happy that my tactics work with our children. But you know how they create chaos when they don't get what they want. And still, I love every minute spent with them." Nancy's voice lowered now. "By the way, Aundrid is the leader, or so I think. I met him on the UFO."

"So that settles it." Isaac's voice was relaxed and joyous now. "I hope the Nordics would at least inform me next time before abducting you for some child consultation!"

Nancy's lips smiled for a few seconds, and then she realized she was about to tense her husband again. The thought wiped out any trace of happiness from her face.

As her face paled, Isaac got alarmed. He slipped near his wife at once. "Are you hiding anything from me?"

She blushed; there was a hesitation as she opened her mouth and closed it.

Her eyes suddenly looked too big for her face. She let out an understated sigh and then spoke.

"Emerald was not the only reason the Nordics wanted to meet me." She told him quickly, determinedly.

A vein pulsated at his neck, and a mask of anxiety rose on Isaac's face. "What's wrong, Nancy?"

Nancy felt helpless as she finally spoke. "the Nordics mentioned that our kids 'combined power may get out of control."

He shook his head. "Well, I have seen what they can do when they join hands. But it was just a small thing. I mean, they are so young. What else can they do? It is not as if their actions can impact the world." There was a little amusement in his voice.

She knew her husband. She also knew how much he loved his family, and what she was about to tell would shatter him. But she had no choice.

"Of course, you are their father, so you look at them that way. And it's not your fault."

They were again sitting in front of each other, and now she got up and went to him.

"Why do you look so upset?" He asked. "The children will lose their power as they grow."

"And what makes you think that?" Nancy's voice was low now. "Did you know the mental powers of certain alien species have influenced almost one-third of the weaker minds of our planet?"

"What?" Isaac Oldfield almost screeched.

The tension which had left his body a few minutes before returned. And Nancy wanted to hug her husband then and there.

"Our kids will be instrumental in helping humans gain freedom from alien domination," she added. "But it will only happen after they are separated for a certain period. Because their combined power can be dangerous until they learn to harness it."

"And this is what those Nordics advised?" Isaac's eyes were red with a hint of anger. "What do they know about us? Hell, they can't be telling me what to do. I will not tear apart my family just because some alien fancies it."

Isaac had come from a traditional family where old values were still cherished.

For a minute, Nancy didn't speak. The Nordic's words were still echoing in her mind. This was a tough decision. Which parent would prefer to raise their twins separately? But after meeting the Nordics, she knew what was written in her children's destiny.

Nancy cleared her throat as she touched Isaac's face and compelled him to look at her. "I know what you are thinking. Our children have never been apart. We both have never lived separately…"

"And I never want to live separately." he broke her sentence in the middle. "For God's sake, Nanny, the kids are twins—identical twins, at that. There could be serious implications if they are separated."

"You are right. That thought has crossed my mind, too. But what are we going to do? On the one hand, we want to keep them together. On the other hand, if we raise them separately, they can save the world."

As she finished her sentence, Isaac looked into her eyes. His eyes were full of pain now. "I want both of these. While I don't want to tear our family apart, I don't want to be a boulder blocking our kids' destiny."

Unable to dull his pain, Nancy lowered her eyes as they glistened with watery tears. "Even I want that. But why don't you understand that we can't have both?"

Now, she sank to her knees, and a sobbing sound escaped her throat, tearing his heart apart. "I want us to be together. The thought of living without you scares the hell out of me. I don't want to be this intelligent psychic. I am a mom first and want my children to be raised together in a happy family environment."

Until now, she was the brave one, thinking about what the Nordics had told her. But, as everything came out in the open, Nancy's courage gave way to the pain she had somehow controlled until now. Her shoulders shook. She struggled hard to breathe against the crying. "Is it too much to ask? Can't I have a normal life like everyone?"

And Isaac's hand went to his wife's back, patting and solacing her silently. Once her sobs had died down a little, Isaac took her in his arms and lifted her chin. "We are educated people, Nanny. We can't be so selfish when it comes to the world."

"My children are my world." A fresh round of red-hot tears ran down her face. "I can't separate them, Isaac."

He ran his hand through her hair. "But don't forget the events of their birth and their unique destiny. They are made for bigger things. Do you want to keep them to yourself when the world needs them?"

Nancy clasped his shoulders when she didn't try to hide her grief. Her husband's words broke her heart as she knew he was right, and she cried and cried until no more tears came out.

Chapter 22:

DNA Mismatch

Nancy dreamt that Emerald told her their lives were in danger. Several times.

Thanks to this recurring dream, Nancy finally searched for her look-alike, who the thralls had killed.

She was never an insomniac, but for the past few days, Nancy had been restless and unable to sleep. Isaac's words about their children's true potential kept buzzing through her head. What mother in the world would ruin her family and tear them apart?

While happiness seemed quite far-fetched to her, Nancy would have given anything to bring back her peace of mind. But even that was not possible.

She tried everything she could to calm the chaos of her mind, to shush the monsters who were after her family and her joy. But something else worked. Tonight was also the same. In the dark oasis of her quiet bedroom, she was on the bed, floating in the pool of memories. How she had met Isaac, their marriage, and then the ultimate blessing of their lives together – the birth of the twins.

A gentle smile played on Nancy's lips when she remembered the extraordinary circumstances under which her children were born. Yes, they were unique in more than one way. But soon, that bliss turned to a grimace when she recalled what would happen to them.

She tossed and turned some more but couldn't find the correct position. A lingering fog of her desire to rest sat somewhere in the back recesses of her unconscious mind. But the future sat in her chest like an icy wind she could not get rid of, and Nancy fought hard to breathe as she urged herself to fall into a slumber.

"Don't struggle so much to balance."

Who was speaking this?

"Distance doesn't matter in the big scheme of time." This time, the voice was clear and crisp.

Nancy was sure she was asleep. But her consciousness told her that this was a dream. But it can't be. It looked so real.

Had not she heard this voice before?

And then, as if proving she was not wrong, Emerald's gleaming green eyes bore into hers. A white light created a calm aura around her. Nancy stole one look at her daughter, and her eyes scrunched in wonder. Was this the same girl she had met before just a couple of days ago? Emerald didn't only seem to have grown considerably in size, but there was also an air of maturity around her, which Nancy had yet to see in her kids.

"Emerald, what are you talking about?" Nancy's lips fluttered as she knew she was asleep yet awake deeply.

They are the Earth's soul, power source, force of action. They have a task at hand, and you are here to support them."

"But I do," defended Nancy as she stole a look at the girl. Emerald had worn a casual round-neck full-sleeved denim dress, pairing it with brown sneakers, and for a minute, Nancy couldn't take her eyes off.

Who took care of Emerald? At age two, the girl already had a unique dressing style with oodles of confidence. and that vocabulary!! How could a two-year-old use kinesthetic verbs without even blinking her eyes? No, Emerald was not an ordinary, average child. And Nancy sighed. She was a mother of three rare children, which had brought her ultimate bliss and a dose of chaos.

As if Emerald had noticed Nancy's gaze on her, she smiled. A brightening, innocent, child-like smile made

Nancy forget about Emerald's words for a fraction of a second. Emerald's light brown, straight hair framed her small face, enhancing her looks, and Nancy suddenly desired to run her hand on those lustrous locks and tuck them behind her daughter's ears. She remembered how Emerald always smelled like a wildflower and gulped. Will she ever be able to hold her in her arms like with Sacha and Isaac? What role was Emerald going to play in the tapestry of her life? These questions again fogged Nancy's brain, and she blinked to clear her vision.

Had Emerald left? No, she was still there.

Mom, Aundrid has given a message for you."

Nancy's thoughts vanished into thin air – maybe it was due to how Emerald had addressed her as her mother so quickly. Or maybe it was Aundrid's name.

Not only your life but even Sacha and Isaac s life are in danger. And you'd better prepare them to face their destiny."

Nancy's jaw muscles clenched, and her face wrinkled. "What are you talking about?"

Remember your lookalike who was killed?"

Her brain stuttered, and words left Nancy as she stared into those green eyes deep enough to hold a universe—those green eyes that promised to show you the way home even in the darkest times.

"But it was an accident." Nancy exclaimed.

A light laughter escaped Emerald's throat now. *That s what THEY wanted you to believe!"*

And the white light surrounding Emerald started to fade away.

"Wait," Nancy almost screamed. "Who are THEY? Why do they want me to believe it was an accident?"

As Emerald's shadow started to dim, all Nancy could hear was –

Look inside. You can find out what you are looking for!"

And with that, Emerald was gone just like that, stealing whatever sleep Nancy had planned to get that night.

Nancy snuggled deeper into the silken duvet and closed her eyes, thinking about what she had seen and heard. The soft eiderdown duvet caressed her cheeks, gently reminding her what was precious in her life. Nancy didn't know when she fell asleep again but found the answer when she woke up.

Yes, Emerald was not wrong when she suggested Nancy had the key to find out the answers. Why had Nancy forgotten she had a rare gift of psychic power to investigate the so-called accident?

And when her eyes opened, dawn's early light was touching the horizon, igniting her thoughts as darkness surrendered to the rising canopy of the sun. Nancy knew what she had to do now. She opened her table drawer and carefully took out the newspaper she had kept. Feeling determined to know more, she opened the newspaper, went to the required page, and then spread it on the table. Her eyes were now on the picture of a woman who looked like her carbon copy. Poor woman! Nancy felt bad for her and her family. God only knew what they were going through right now. She looked at the image for some more time, concentrating on it, and then closed her eyes. After half an hour, when Nancy opened her eyes, she had the answers she sought.

Isaac was in the kitchen when she joined him.

"Isaac, I was checking about my look-alike, Mary. Surprisingly, the woman lived nearby."

"What else could you find?" He asked as he passed a cup of coffee to her.

"That she was a happy human being."

Nancy paused. Her forehead was furrowed with lines.

"I still don't get who killed her and why."

"There is much more behind this than you think," Isaac said. Then he got up and brought a folder.

"The thralls were after you and used whatever information they had to find you."

"Me?" She looked at him.

"You are the great force behind our children's destiny. And they know it very well." Isaac paused. "Don't believe it? Check this report." He pulled out a report from the folder now. "Look at this."

"I will not let anything come between me and my family." She pursed her lips and looked at her husband.

"Using whatever DNA information they had to identify you, the thralls used the physical look component of DNA. Scanning thousands of people for a DNA match is not a joke. They got the best match in Mary."

"Oh my god, I can't believe it. My heart goes to the poor woman."

"Well, apparently, the Nordics are hard-working species. They have developed a better technology. So they were able to use a longer DNA identification string."

"And they got me spot on," added she.

And as Nancy read the report Isaac had given her, the hairs at the back of her neck stood up. And once she was done, Nancy said, "We can't let this happen. We can't give thralls the reins of our lives."

"There is only one way – let our children fight those monsters. It's their ultimate destiny."

And Nancy's eyes once again filled with water because, in her heart, she knew her husband was right.

Chapter 23:

Gosh, Mr. Ghosh?

After some years.

Sacha sighed as she looked at the giant palm trees surrounding the building. Yes, this was the right place. Dressed in her organic cotton clothes, albeit black, she resembled a Ninja. With a Bruce-Lee-like gait, she hurriedly climbed the steps and entered the big hall following the map app directions. In the sweltering heat of Mumbai, this sixteen-year-old girl was sweating and swearing under her breath. She was not enthusiastic like her dad Isaac and unhappily brought herself to the martial arts teacher's abnormally large house.

Two boys are fighting in the middle of the room. Their eyes focused on each other's moves. Their bodies are alert and agile to ward off the attack.

Where was she?

Sacha's eyes scanned the large hall. She was sure that she had not come to the wrong place. She opened her backpack and grabbed the juice bottle. There! She emptied it in one go. The cold, sweet-and-sour liquid calmed her.

Once done, she put her bag in one corner and looked at the boys again. They were not even aware of her presence.

Should she ask them about the teacher? She didn't know.

Her eyes went to a small white door at the side. It was ajar. She walked towards it and opened it. Sitting before a typewriter-kind-of-machine, she saw the most beautiful girl she had ever seen. Her very light, pale skin glistened in the dim light. She wore black leggings, a neutral top, and an olive jacket.

As if that much layering was not enough, she even had a camel-colored scarf wrapped around her neck. How could she look like a top-notch model despite so much heat? Another girl in Sacha's place might have wondered. But not her. Sacha was not jealous in any way.

"Excuse me."

"Sacha?" The girl's green eyes sparkled like emeralds as she got up. Her lithe body couldn't be hidden from Sacha's eyes. Despite its 5 ft. 9-inch height, Sacha was still short in comparison. All sorts of jewels glittered at the girl's wrists, fingers, even neck. Compared to her, Sacha had no jewelry or any bling, and she looked like a monk.

"Yeah," nodded Sacha, blinking her eyes and returning to reality. "I am here to learn martial arts."

"Emerald," the corners of her eyes crinkled, and her cheeks moved upward as she extended her hand, giving her name.

She was pleased to see her! But why?

As Emerald looked at her, Sacha felt she was redirecting instead of radiating positive, happy feelings towards her.

What was going on?

Was this fragile creature going to teach her this ancient art?

Did she even know what martial arts were all about? Wouldn't she rather be happy adorning the advertising billboards?

Sacha shook her head. *Someone must have misled me. Wait until he hears my side of the story.*

But as soon as Sacha took that delicate hand, she almost jolted. The hidden strength and power in that grip was something else. This was no ordinary girl!

"Shall we start?" Emerald pulled out her scarf and took off her jacket. "So, you had ninja training in Paris."

"How'd you know?"

"Because I have a nose to identify ninjas."

"And CIA training..."

Emerald cut her off in the middle of her sentence. "in Washington DC, I know. You even lived in Paris."

"And I should have never left it," Sacha spoke as she became aware of the pools of sweat under her armpits.

"Hey, Mumbai grows on you."

Sacha was baffled by that genuine smile and calm voice for a moment. Also, the way Emerald moved was something she had not seen before.

"Since you are here, why don't we start today?"

"Why not?" Sacha fixed her ponytail in a bun, getting prepared for the fight. She didn't even know when Emerald had discarded some of her ornaments.

By the time they came out of the locker room, the boys were gone, and they had the big room to themselves. Within minutes, they both got into position.

"Just try your best!" Emerald said, lowering her hand.

Suddenly, Emerald's leg raised, ripping out toward Sacha's face. Sacha blocked the blow with her hand, but then she tripped. Sacha's eyes widened as she felt herself falling. Emerald looked at her, waiting for her to get up. What was going on? She got up immediately but not fast enough to prevent another punch. Sacha's eyes widened, and her anger exploded as she fought to defend herself. But all her efforts to restrain Emerald failed.

"It's all in the mind," Emerald spoke slowly as she stopped. "I believe you will grasp my teaching faster than you imagined. Provided you can control your temper."

Sacha opened her mouth to speak, but Emerald had already turned her back by then. "I will see you tomorrow."

Not a single hair on her head looked out of place.

Not a single bead of sweat on her body.

Who was she?

Sacha pursed her lips and started to proceed towards the corridor's exit.

"Hey Sacheesmo!"

"Hi, Dad!"

"You are sweating!"

"No."

"Was it too tough?"

"Of course not, Dad." There was a slight irritation in Sacha's voice now. "Shall we go?"

Rebuffed by her sudden attitude, Isaac stared at her daughter.

"How about eating out?"

"All I want is a nice bath and some organic food."

"How was Emerald?"

They were on the stairs now. Sacha paused and lifted her head to see into her father's eyes.

"Where did you find her?"

"You mean Emerald? What do you mean?"

"Who recommended her?"

"Some of my friends. Why? Isn't she good?"

"The girl looks like a supermodel and punches like a pro. Have you ever seen someone like that before?"

"I forgot to tell you. Mr. Ghosh had called," Isaac said.

"Seems as if she has ascended from a different planet. Look at how she walks, talks… wait, what did he say?"

As the father-daughter duo descended the stairs and sat in the Padmini cab Isaac had arranged, elsewhere out of sight, Emerald tapped away at her comms device, unique on earth, smiling broadly.

"There, finally, I have met her." She typed some more. "I am so looking forward to teaching her."

Unaware of Emerald's extra-terrestrial conversation, Sacha slipped inside the cab and thought about the article she had published in Indian Express.

As if God was showing some mercy on her finally, the rain started to pelt at once. She stole a look at the overcast sky, then at her father.

"Mumbai already had 570 mm rain until now, said Isaac." "It has been lashing the city continuously."

"Imagine what would happen to all these low-lying areas? The rising sea levels could turn cataclysmic for this city."

"Didn't you mention climate change dangers in your last article?" Isaac spoke and then guided the cab to their building.

"We still have time." Sacha took a deep breath. "The eyes of all future generations are upon us. If we choose to fail them, they will never forgive us. Unless we don't treat climate change as a crisis, nothing will happen."

Lost in her thoughts, she didn't even realize when she had entered the house.

The sound of their telephone vibrated loudly in the peaceful house. She ran to fetch it, hoping to catch up with the newspaper editor this time.

"Hello?"

An unnatural silence greeted her.

"Mr. Ghosh? I just came home."

There was no sound at the other end.

Hungry, tired, and now irritated, Sacha repeated her greeting.

Although no one spoke, she could hear heavy breathing at the other end. It was evident that this was not Mr. Ghosh. Who then? A prank call? But she hardly got any.

"Who is it?" Isaac asked.

She shrugged and was almost ready to hang up when a raspy voice spoke.

"Keep your ideology about climate change to yourself, Sacha. Or get ready to disappear from this earth."

Before she could grasp or comprehend it, the call disconnected.

As Isaac went to the kitchen, Sacha sat in the living room, still recalling the chilly words and the threatening tone of the caller. Who was it, and how did he know about her column? She fought hard to shake off the jitters and proceeded with the rest of the night's events. But she couldn't shake off the feeling of being watched over.

Chapter 24:
Dowsing for Mehra

"Isaac, you there?"

Nancy's calm and gentle voice echoed through the walls, and Isaac Jr. jumped to his feet immediately. A Y-shaped tree branch then fell on the floor near his feet. He picked it up before going towards the door. This willow twig with a fork of branches of equal length on both sides was his favorite tool. It felt light in his hand as if it was an extension of his body.

Yes, he was into dowsing. Using it, he could find water wells, metals, gemstones, and even missing people and unmarked graves. A large house plant sat in a corner, a succulent on a bedside. The wooden bookshelf on the other side showcased a few of his pride possessions, like a rabbit's foot, a Porsche Panamera, and an astrolabe used aboard the US nuclear submarine Nautilus. His mom's degree certificate from Duke University with a major in Psychic Research hung on the top. The other wall was covered with black and white prints, and photos were displayed in simple frames.

"Isaac?" Nancy's voice was a little impatient now. "Are you in the shower? I need to leave in half an hour."

As Isaac heard this, he kept his weapon on the light brown wooden side table and opened the door. He had to get to her now. He rushed towards the door, hitting his leg on the bed, but he didn't care. When he opened the door, he found his mom standing there with an enchanting smile. She looked beautiful at this age, too, and he hugged her.

At 6 ft 1 inch, he towered over her feminine frame.

As he enveloped her in his arms, she sighed softly and rested her head on his chest.

"Soon, you will be seventeen."

"Yeah."

"Time flies. I am proud of the boy you are becoming."

"And yet you don't trust me enough." His voice was filled with sorrow now.

When Nancy heard these words, she immediately came out of his embrace. "Look, Isaac…"

"Yeah, this is not the time or place to discuss." He threw his hands in frustration. "I know, Mom, but why don't you get it? I need to know about my father."

"Listen, I made your breakfast. Your favorite vegetable juice and...."

"Mom. We need to talk."

"Later."

Isaac smiled sadly as he watched his mom go through her daily routine while evading him. He knew that when it came to his questions, she would still not answer them, no matter his age.

"My client will be here in an hour," Isaac advised.

He quickly brought out the magazines from his room. He didn't know when his mom left, and after an hour, when the doorbell rang, his head was still lowered in the papers, reading about the latest archeological investigations.

"Hello Sylvia," he welcomed the middle-aged woman standing at the door. "Please, come in."

"Thanks," the woman hesitated and followed him to the drawing room. "I have heard about your work. I heard how you help emotional, physical, or mental healing. I have been feeling exhausted for a couple of months. All medical tests revealed nothing, but I knew something is wrong with me. I am not my usual self."

"Please stand there," Isaac pointed at a place approximately eight to ten feet away from him. As Sylvia did so, he grabbed his dowsing tool and held it loosely, keeping it parallel to the floor.

He then took a deep breath and 'cleared 'himself. So that he could focus on Sylvia's questions, first of all, he wanted to check her energy level.

He slowly whispered to himself. "Show me the physical energy of Sylvia." His eyes were slightly closed. His breathing turned calm, and he started to walk towards her. Sylvia stood like a statue, holding her breath, curiosity written on her face.

Somewhere two feet away from her, Isaac's tool began to swing slowly, and he started searching for the energy field.

A few minutes passed as he concentrated on finding the concentric rings of energy emanating from her body. Then he stopped. His tool had yet to open up the way it usually did.

"There is no wonder you feel exhausted. There is a complete lack of energy. It is as if someone is blocking you."

Then he led her to the table and sat in front of her.

"Were there any changes in your personal life recently?"

At first, she moved her head in denial. But as Isaac sat there patiently waiting for her to open up, she finally gathered her courage and started to speak.

"Yes, there is. My father-in-law moved in with us."

"I see. And how is his behavior towards you?"

She pursed her lips. "We were never on the same page. I tried hard to understand him, but I don't know why he keeps finding faults with whatever I do."

"And you don't like him?"

"It is not that. I understand that he is old. And my husband is a good son, believing in old values, taking care of his family…I do support him, but…"

"But this is too much to take into your stride. You are not alone." Isaac's voice was serious. "Sometimes we all go through rough patches. But that doesn't mean that life is over. This, too, shall pass. I can see that these thoughts have taken over your aura. And you need to regain the power by taking control of your mind and life. Have you ever meditated?"

She looked at him. "No."

"Then you can start learning. It will create a shield around your aura, preventing energy loss."

She nodded and, after some small talk, thanked him and left.

He got ready as he also had to go.... to college.

After thirty minutes, Isaac started walking on the footpath to catch a bus.

Two men in safari suits appeared from nowhere.

"Come with us." One of them whispered.

"Who are you?"

"You don't have to know." the second suit spoke.

"I am not going anywhere." Isaac looked around. Usually, this part of the road was crowded. But somehow, today, there were many fewer people around.

"Looks like he won't listen this way," the first man talked to the other. When he nodded, the man took a small gun from his pocket and pressed it at Isaac's side. "If you don't do as we say, nobody will stop me from killing you."

Isaac had no choice.

They led him to an expensive car parked near the bus stop. As soon as they were near, the car door opened from inside, and one of the men pushed him towards the seat.

The man closed the door as Isaac slipped inside, albeit not by his choice. And his breathing stopped when Isaac saw who was sitting in the back seat near him. He knew Mr. Mehra, a well-known politician. Ruthless but otherwise humble regarding humanity, Isaac often read how he worked to help the poor, especially the children.

"Surprised to see me, Isaac?"

He couldn't speak immediately. Isaac bit his lips.

"Look, Isaac, you are a mature boy so I will come straight to the point. You must know me." There was a hint of arrogance in Mr. Mehra's voice.

"Yes, sir. Who doesn't?" Isaac had found his voice now. He was sure this was a mistake because Mr. Mehra had no reason to abduct him like this.

"You are thinking I got you here by mistake. But it is not!"

Was he also a mind reader?

"I need your help."

Isaac's taut muscles relaxed a bit now. Mr. Mehra was like a lotus in a pond full of dirty politicians.

"It would be my great honor, sir."

The politician took out his expensive rimmed glasses and started to wipe them. Once done, he put it back and then looked at Isaac.

"I have heard you are a dowser."

"Well,..." Isaac started to speak when the man raised his hand and stopped him. "Saudi Arabia has the second-largest fossil fuel reserves but somehow, my company cannot find it."

Isaac's posture became rigid at the mention of the fossil fuel. "We want you to find it with your dowsing knowledge."

"Earth is our only home for now." Isaac folded his hands at his chest as he looked into Mr. Mehra's eyes. "Fossil fuels harm mother nature and all creatures residing on it."

"Who cares about such bullshit?" Mr. Mehra's lips widened into a sly smile now. He kept a hand on Isaac's shoulder. "Don't worry; you will get your commission once the job is done. And yes, don't worry about the expense. We will fly you there."

Isaac ground his teeth as he understood why he was in the car now. But Mr. Mehra was not like others.

"The fossil fuels add to the global warming." He tried again. "Earth is getting a little too warm, and if we don't stop now…"

The man cut the sentence once again. "I am not here to listen to your lecture. Leave that global warming to the activists and environmentalists." Then his voice turned softer as he slipped near Isaac. "Trust me, this is a golden opportunity. You will be rich beyond your imagination."

"And what if I don't agree?"

"You are wise enough to know, isn't it?" Mr. Mehra's voice was slow and yet threatening. "Not only you, but your entire family will have to pay for the consequences. Including your father."

Isaac drew in a sharp breath. "My father? Do you know him?"

"Of course. And trust me, you will be the reason behind his destruction." Mr. Mehra then turned his head. "Driver, stop the car."

As the vehicle braked deliberately at the same place they had picked up Isaac, Mr. Mehra opened the door. "Take a day or two. But not more than that. And yes, if you ever shared this with anyone, you already know what will happen."

And the shocked, sad Isaac started walking towards his home.

Chapter 25:
Holi Moly

"I realized managing a teenage boy of such brilliance can be tough." Isaac Sr. spoke on the phone.

"Trust me, you have no idea." Nancy rubbed her forehead as she sat down on the nearest couch. "He is after me all the time."

"Being a stranger to my son feels ridiculous and I wonder why I tolerate it. Was it a good decision to separate them?"

"Isaac, stop." Nancy drew in a deep breath. "We are not going back there. There is no point. Remember, we had no choice?"

There was no sound from the other end.

"Isaac, we have got to get our day going. What did you think about tomorrow?"

"It's the Holi celebration in my neighborhood. Why don't we bring the two kids to that location? A public place lets us see what happens when they're near each other, but they'll remain strangers to each other."

"Sounds like a plan," said Nancy.

"Then 11 o'clock tomorrow?"

"I'll be there with Isaac Jr." Nancy put the phone down when Isaac Jr. entered the room.

"Isaac? You are home early."

One look at his face and Nancy got up at once. "What's wrong?"

Her son ran a hand through his hair. "Nothing."

"Why don't I believe it?" Nancy's expert eyes caught up with the hidden worry without much effort. "Is there anything I should know?"

Isaac didn't reply. Instead, he went to the fridge and fetched a water bottle. "Who was on the call?"

"Call?" She was caught unaware. "Aah, you are talking about that call. Nobody. Umm, I mean my friend. Asking to join me for the Holi celebration tomorrow."

Isaac took a sip from the bottle. "Well, good for you, mom. You hardly go anywhere."

"I meant us, Isaac," Nancy spoke slowly in a firm tone.

Isaac shrugged. "What would I do out on the street there?"

"Well, I am new to this place. Take it as your duty, sweetheart."

"Come on, Mom, you don't need me around...." Isaac's words echoed in the empty room as Nancy had already left.

§§§§§§§§§§

It was a scorching March day in Mumbai the next morning when Isaac got up.

Nancy was already ready. She looked radiant in a white kurta, while Isaac looked the opposite. Dark circles were under his eyes, and he had a sad look.

"Are you sure we should go down?"

"Didn't you sleep well?" Nancy asked. And then she opened her mouth to add more when someone down the street started to play Bollywood Holi songs on the loudspeaker.

"Well, this is insane. I mean, I hardly know anyone there." Isaac had to raise his voice as he pleaded for the last time.

Nancy brought him freshly squeezed orange juice. "Stop protesting. By the way, Sylvia called to thank you. She has been thinking about what you found yesterday, and it makes sense."

Nancy continued, "She is an empath, struggling to set her boundaries with others. Deeply feeling other people's feelings, and she needs to learn to set boundaries."

"I am so glad you could help," his mom continued. "You have the perfect gift."

Isaac Jr. hadn't spoken a single word.

§§§§§§§§§§

When they both went down the street after half an hour, the loudspeaker played popular Hindi songs at maximum volume. Children ran up and down the street, coloring each other with various colored powders. Partiers staying on the upper floors threw water balloons from their high-rise porches. Although Isaac did know some of his neighbors behind colored faces, it was difficult to recognize them.

A man stood on a bench, holding a giant garden hose, drenching many with colored water. "Happy Holi," screamed he and soaked Isaac as well.

"What the hell," Isaac cursed. He didn't even know this man. *"What kind of festival is this!"* He talked to himself. *"People even colorize passers-by!"*

"Don't feel bad, it's Holi."

When had this man left his water hose and slipped near him? Isaac was so lost in his thoughts that he didn't even realize it. He peered at the stranger, suddenly feeling uncomfortable.

"Excuse me," Isaac muttered and started to walk away, searching for his mom in the crowd. But she was nowhere to be seen.

But as soon as he started walking, the stranger limped behind him with the sound of a grating bone, and Isaac moved his head in astonishment. The March heat was enough to make anyone moan. As the man walked, a shadow seemed to envelop him, temporarily creating darkness under the noon sun.

"Are you following me?"

The man smiled, briefly showing his crooked teeth.

It was Saturday, and most of the people were on the street. Isaac started walking fast, small steps towards his house. His body throbbed with adrenaline, his muscles taut, and his ears focused on the footsteps next to him. He couldn't wait to get back to safety. Doubt and suspicion crept up his spine as the man seemed hellbent on coming after him. Isaac's skin prickled with newfound sensations, and he tackled the threat before it got out of hand.

They were in the parking lot behind the building now. The place was deserted, except for a single watchman who was busy taking a nap when no one was watching.

The man was wearing strange clothes which hung loosely over his relatively short body. Isaac wondered if the man had borrowed someone else's clothes for the occasion of the festival, but it didn't make sense.

As he kept looking, the man stepped near. Gosh, his left hand, although colored with the tapestry of dry Holi powders, was cut and dark; it oozed near-black liquid, drenching his ill-fitting clothes.

"Hey, who are you? Why are you after me?" Isaac asked him as his stomach rumbled.

There was no answer. Instead, his cut hand got extended, which Isaac had never seen before, and wrapped itself around Isaac's throat, squeezing his life out. Isaac's hands went to his throat, trying to remove that iron-like grip as he struggled to breathe and fought to save his dear life.

The man's deadly features were becoming more prominent as he drew near. Wait, this was no man, instead, a creature. And right now, there was no time to think who it was or why it was trying to kill him. He had to save his skin first.

The wind started blowing with a powerful passion unheard of in Marsch. The doors banged, leaves began scattering, and suddenly, the sun hid behind dark, gloomy clouds. Isaac swore the sun was at its most brilliant, beautiful self just a minute before, with not a single dark cloud in the sky.

But he didn't have much time to think. The graphite sky showcased the lightning, a powerful stroke of white light against the gloomy atmosphere, accompanying a thunderous boom. The zig-zag electrical charge stroked the man-creature immediately, and he started screaming. The man was in flames before Isaac could understand what was happening; his hand loosened and hung lifelessly at his side. Then, the sky opened up, drenching everything on site.

Isaac filled his lungs with much-needed air as he breathed hard, trying to understand what had just happened. The loudspeaker had stopped now that rain poured from the sky. Isaac stepped back to check on the man-creature, but all he could see was burned ashes mixed with the soil.

And then, just as it had started suddenly, the rain stopped. Dark clouds parted like they were making way for the sun, and the brilliant afternoon came again. The sky looked as if nothing had happened a minute before.

As Isaac ran a hand through his wet hair, ensuring he was not dreaming, his eyes went to a girl leaving the parking area, almost his age. A girl with a look of power, strength, and serenity. Who was she? Why did he feel he had seen her somewhere?

Chapter 26:

Eyes on Emerald

"Hey, Emerald, long time no see," Isaac Jr. lifted his head in surprise when Emerald stood at his doorstep one morning.

"Just busy with stuff, you know," she followed him inside. "So, how's life, cousin?"

Isaac Jr. shrugged his shoulder. "Going on, with college and my hobbies and mom's traveling…"

"Life is pretty complex," she completed his sentence in a single breath and then grinned. "I know."

"Mom just left a few minutes ago to run a few errands," Isaac Jr. opened the fridge. "What would you like? The usual?"

"Of course," she removed her scarf and stretched her lithe body onto the living room couch. "Most of my time is invested in my classes."

"And the rest is in gadgets," Isaac handed her a juice can. "Why do you love technology so much? Don't you use your intuition at all?"

Emerald took a swig. "It's a long story. But everybody has some hobby. Anyway, I find most human tools are still too primitive."

"You want elegance? I should show you how my dowsing works. It uncovers fears, traumas, and emotions hidden inside the human mind. Anyway, I need to go. Mom will be home soon."

"Yeah, see you." They exchanged five, and then Isaac Jr. left the house.

Emerald finished her drink and smiled. She switched on the TV but found nothing interesting. Luckily, she didn't have to wait long because Nancy arrived home in ten minutes.

"How you have been?" Nancy enveloped Emerald in her arms, although it was getting difficult with her daughter's tall and robust frame. Once Emerald emerged from her embrace, Nancy looked at her with a mother's eyes. "Look at you, and you have grown so much."

While Emerald smiled radiantly at her, Nancy realized that if Emerald was growing, so was she. The thought brought her back to the reality. They had to do so much.

Nancy sat down and asked. "Did you meet Isaac?"

"Yes," she nodded. "He went out."

"I hope he suspects nothing."

"Of course not. As the Nordics told you, he can't know my true identity," said Emerald.

Nancy sighed. Her voice was low. "I know, and yet sometimes it saddens me. You have frequently visited this place and shared many memories with my son, yet he only knows you as his cousin."

"And that's how it is supposed to work now," Emerald replied.

And then suddenly, as if she realized she couldn't let her emotions run the show, Nancy looked at Emerald and spoke. This time, her voice was devoid of any regrets or feelings.

"How is Sacha holding up?"

"Oh, she is a great kid," Emerald spoke as if she was not Sacha's age, making Nancy smile. "There is just one thing about her that upsets me. She misses you so much."

The smile disappeared once again. "I know. I was never a part of her growing-up years, which disturbs me."

None of them spoke for a minute, and then Emerald got up and went to Nancy. "Aundrid wanted to talk with you."

"It has been days since I got any messages."

Emerald took out a small rectangular device from her jacket. It had a small screen and multiple buttons. As soon as she tapped in a few numbers, the screen came alive, and Aundrid's face appeared. Once the initial exchange ended, Aundrid's clear, machine-like voice echoed in the room.

"The thralls are keeping an eye on each of you. On the surface, it might look as if they are lying low. But as per our Nordic intelligence report, they are motivated to attack any of you, so beware."

Nancy and Emerald nodded.

"Nancy," Aundrid's voice was grave now. "The thralls are succeeding in spreading fear among humankind. And I am afraid the Earth will face the biggest climate change anyone has ever seen. It's time to plan our next step."

"Please guide us." Nancy looked at him. "The children still don't know anything about their power."

"There will come a time when they will realize their potential," Aundrid added. "I can see shortly; they will meet influential people who will change how they think."

And before Nancy could reply, the screen went back.

Emerald switched off the device and stood up. "Someone called me regarding the class. I need to go."

"You be careful," said Nancy

"Yes, Mom," Emerald picked up her scarf, wrapped it again, and walked towards the door.

And as Nancy watched her back, she couldn't stop thinking. Even though she had two wonderful daughters, she could not live with either. The thought saddened her again.

§§§§§§§§§

After an hour, Emerald was sitting at her desk.

"Hello," she smiled. "How can I help you?"

The stranger standing in front of her was abnormally short and stout. Emerald had an uncomfortable feeling at once. But the girl had come for a query, and it was Emerald's job to help her.

"Can I meet Emerald?" She asked, and Emerald blinked. Although the girl's voice might sound ordinary to others, Emerald felt it was off-beat.

At first, Emerald wrapped her scarf closer to her body and stretched her bejeweled hand to her. "I am Emerald. How can I help you?"

The girl's dark face became even darker as she squinted at her.

"I would like to join your martial arts class."

"Um," Emerald held back her suspicions, "Sure. Did you have any training before?"

"Not much, but that's why I came to you, right?"

Was she being straightforward or sarcastic? Emerald couldn't gauge.

"Why don't you sit down? I will give you more information, and you will also need to fill out a form."

"Of course," the girl grinned, showing her ugly yellow teeth this time, and a warning bell rang again in Emerald's mind. Maybe she was wrong and was overcautious due to Aundrid's warning. Ignoring her gut feeling, she bent down to open the drawer and took out some forms.

Her eyes were still watching the girl in front. But what was this? Someone attacked her head from the back with a metal rod!

Emerald felt dizzy and turned her head to see who was there. Except for the girl and herself, nobody else was in the room.

Huh, the same girl was standing at the back, grinning like a fool, holding the rod, ready to bang her once again.

Wait, how was it possible? Emerald mumbled. Perhaps she was too giddy and imagining things. She rubbed her eyes, but no, she was not dreaming. She quickly got up at once, and to her utmost disbelief, the girl had a similar clone standing behind her. Nancy turned to face the one at the back and forcefully punched her.

This blow surprised the girl, and her eyes widened as her nose started to bleed.

However, Emerald had forgotten she was dealing with two people.

The one behind her laughed hysterically now and held a handkerchief against Emerald's nose. Emerald struggled to remove it, but it was of no use. Within seconds,

Emerald was lying unconscious on the floor, thanks to the chloroform.

And the girls clapped. The room was filled with two thralls, who tied a black ribbon around Emerald's eyes and lifted her.

Chapter 27

Saving Emerald

All Emerald could think of was how that strange creature had managed to clone itself in front of her eyes. Once her lithe body hit the floor, she remembered nothing else. Not even traveling to another place. Not even recalling how two ugly thralls had laughed as they had dragged her unconscious body to their vehicle.

"She is so heavy," complained one as he barely managed to lift Emerald.

"Who would have imagined such a tiny body could be so strong!" Said another named Qeekan.

"I am sweating all over," the first spoke again as he wiped his wrinkly forehead. "The earth somehow increases my metabolic rate."

"And I am craving sunlight. My energy level is so low after completing this task."

"Huda would be pleased. Don't you think so?" The first thrall grinned and then winced when his head almost hit their spaceship, and the small jewel on his forehead started to glow at once.

"Quiet! Can't you see where you are going?" said the second alien as he pushed Emerald's body further into the soccer-like ship. "We don't want to attract any attention."

And as he had predicted, the whole shuttle attracted attention when it suddenly vibrated loudly. Huda's chilling voice echoed.

"Daffass, where are you?"

The first alien appeared to fumble with the control while the second attached a small device like a blood pressure cuff to her body.

"Boss, all done. We will be there in an hour."

"Make sure she doesn't awake. Otherwise, you two would be no match for her..." With that, Huda's voice slowly faded, and Daffass breathed in relief.

§§§§§§§§§

It was night when Daffass and Qeekan managed to land their spaceship at the base.

"I need to rest," Daffass murmured, and Qeekan clapped. Four thralls appeared with a stretcher and carried Emerald's cold body inside the earth-base.

The center was busy even at this hour of the night. A couple of thralls were busy running errands while some were out in the field to access wind turbines and generate energy for the spaceship.

"Huda has asked to see both of you." A short, stout thrall with dark skin and glistening eyes like marble looked at Daffass and Qeekan.

They both nodded and then followed the thralls carrying Emerald.

"We had issues with the turbines last night," Qeekan whispered. "Huda was unhinged. We lost two babies just in ten minutes."

"If that happens frequently, no one will elect Huda again as the leader," Daffass added. "Lately, many are talking against him."

"I hope that the ship functioned properly in my short absence. Being an only engineer is not a joke."

The base was shaped like a maze, like a child's puzzle. They crossed many walls in a zigzag. The air turned cold as they made their way. They went deep inside the building, where even a bird couldn't reach.

When they reached the destination, Huda was pacing the room like a caged lion. The jewel in his head shined bright red.

"He is angry," nudged Daffass to Qeekan. "Be careful."

Once the drone thralls put the stretcher down, they disappeared as if even they could sense their chief's nasty mood.

"Did anyone follow you?" Huda asked Daffass.

"Of course not." Daffass pursed his lips. He was already sweating despite the chill in the air.

"Why can't you train more people?" Now, Huda turned to Qeekan. "Winds are erratic in this part of the earth. We need a stable system."

Qeekan nodded and opened his mouth to speak when Emerald made a whimpering sound.

"Where am I?" She rubbed her forehead. "Why is it hurting?" And then she sat down.

"Don't stress your pretty head too much…" Huda stepped in her direction. "Now tell us who is Sacha and how is she related to Isaac?"

Emerald's eyes widened as she heard these words and looked at her surroundings.

"Who are you?"

"Your enemy," Huda said in a very calm voice. "Now answer my question."

"I don't know any Sacha."

Huda's eyes turned to one of the drone thralls at the far side. The drone pressed a lever, and a thick metal neckband came out from the ceiling, clutching Emerald's neck firmly.

"Will it be comfortable to talk now?" Huda laughed.

Emerald's hands went to her neck at once, fighting hard to remove it, but it was useless. She was sure she would suffocate in no time.

§§§§§§§§§

Sacha entered the passage leading to Emerald's Ninja class. It was one o'clock, and her dad had tried frantically to stop her. But she wouldn't listen. Something was out of place. When she didn't listen to him, Isaac Sr. agreed to accompany her to her martial arts class. As she took one more step toward Emerald's classroom, Sacha recalled the stranger who had asked her about Emerald and her class.

Sacha bit her lip. She couldn't deny that the short girl looked very strange. But she didn't mind. She looked strong and capable of beating Emerald. And that's all Sacha needed. Emerald had been outperforming her since they met, and it was time to teach her a lesson.

She switched on the lights, gestured to her dad to wait, and then ran to her locker room.

Nothing was out of place, and yet nothing seemed right.

There was a strange smell in the locker room, and Emerald was nowhere to be seen.

"Chloroform," Sacha spoke to herself. She sat down at the table, closed her eyes, and imagined....

§§§§§§§§§

The ear-piercing crash was something the thralls had never heard before.

When the spaceship's outer door was broken, the thrall watching over the entrance stretched his thick hand to press a warning buzzer. But unfortunately, he didn't have that much time. Two strong hands wrapped around his neck, and his eyes turned upwards as he fell to the ground, dead!

She looked around. Time was of the essence, and she had to work quickly. She narrowed her eyes, observing the numerous levers on one of the walls at the entrance. They all looked the same, and nothing was written on any of them. She had to rely on her gut intuition.

She could hear the approaching footsteps.

She zeroed in on the last lever. "Let's do it," she cried as she pulled it down.

She had not imagined it would be so heavy. Sacha concentrated on the task at hand and tried one more time. With a creaky loud noise, it finally lowered as she wanted.

"Who is there?" Someone shouted.

"Agghh, who cut off the electricity?" Huda's outrageous voice echoed in the whole maze. "Qeekan, go and have a look," he shouted at him.

Qeekan breathed heavily and lifted his leg to make his way to the entrance when a tremor took him by surprise. He turned his head and looked at Daffass.

BOOM! The wires were short-circuited, the room turned dark, and the explosion was loud. It didn't take Qeekan long to understand that someone had fiddled with the wind energy, and the thralls around him started to breathe heavily, including Huda.

The red light on Huda's head had also dimmed to his utter frustration.

"Qeekan, go!" He shouted again, but in the dark, Huda couldn't see that his alien engineer friend was fighting hard to get a dose of oxygen.

A foul smell permeated the chamber, and everyone struggled except Emerald. Luckily, she didn't depend on oxygen like them. But the metal collar around her neck was bothering her. And the hold was too strong, even for her. She whimpered in pain when a strong hand pulled the lever and freed her.

"Emerald, quick," Sacha spoke in a low voice. "We don't have much time."

"Sacha?" Emerald looked at her in disbelief. "How in god's name...?"

"Shh, we can talk later; just hold my hand."

And without hesitation, Emerald clutched her hand, trusting her wholeheartedly.

Sacha smiled even though Emerald was not able to see the smile. Actual power was not in belittling others. She led Emerald to the entrance, passing through a few dying thralls, and teleported safely.

This was one of the most struggle-filled days Sacha would ever remember, yet oddly satisfying.

Chapter 28

Real Archaeology

Isaac Jr. looked at his surroundings.

"This is heaven," he whispered as his eyes went to the snow-covered peaks.

He was standing atop the rocky surface, surrounded by the magical Himalayas. A wind whipped across his beaming face, and his eyes started to water. But for once, Isaac didn't care. Clouds floated around the mountaintops and swirled around him in an icy welcome he loved.

"No wonder the world's greatest archeological mysteries are hidden here." He spoke aloud again.

"We are late, Mr. Isaac," a voice made him turn his head. His guide was standing behind, waiting for him.

"Yes, yes. Just guide me towards Mustang Mountain, and then you can leave."

The man dressed in a simple shirt and trousers nodded, and within a few minutes, Isaac was on his way to unearth hidden relics of the ancient structures.

"The climb is quite dangerous." The guy offered him a butter tea and hard-dried Yak cheese when they stopped for a break after a couple of minutes again.

The steep climb and cold air had made the quest more difficult than Isaac had imagined. But he didn't mind.

"Many have suffered broken bones."

"Ever imagined how the original dwellers journeyed to these caves or even lived there?" Isaac Jr. smiled as he spoke.

He was here to learn more about the caves, following the footsteps of researchers. Two shelters were already discovered from nine, revealing much about the past. Sleeping rooms, grain storage bins, hearths, and domestic rooms were already found. But archeologists were still wondering what was hidden behind the giant sandcastles, and Isaac Jr. couldn't stop himself.

Once the refreshment was over, the guide gestured at the watch, and Isaac Jr. got ready again.

They walked in compatible silence for thirty minutes and finally reached the site.

The guide pointed towards the caves situated above ground from afar.

This is where he was supposed to leave Isaac Jr.

But this is where the actual journey began.

This is where only a few people have been able to go until now.

"Thank you very much," Isaac Jr. shook his hand and then paid him.

"Be careful." The tourist guide warned Isaac Jr. again, and then they parted ways.

Isaac Jr. started to walk towards his destination. While his mind remembered the guide's cautious words, his heart was enthusiastic, and his walk was energetic even after such a long journey. He was a passionate young man, and in his heart, he knew he would find a gem this time.

Was he right?

Only time could tell.

The sun rose to the sky.

Why is the sky bluer here than in other places? It looked like the blue duvet his mom used to wrap around him during winter months.

And the thought made Isaac Jr. pause.

He had not informed her. And although it was normal for him to travel alone, somehow Isaac felt he should have mentioned this trip to his mom.

It's okay, he gave solace to himself. I will be home tomorrow. But in some way, the thought of not informing her about his whereabouts this time stayed with Isaac Jr. as he walked and climbed toward the destination.

He was so near and yet so far. By the time Isaac Jr. entered the first cave through a large hole, he was tired but exhilarated at the same time, if that was possible for a human being.

It was the most enormous chamber he had seen. It was terrific to find large timbers and flagstones inside. He had not expected it. The wooden parts seemed to belong to shelves. Isaac stood near one and started to examine it when he heard a footstep behind.

Feeling a little surprised, he turned his head and was surprised when he saw a middle-aged man standing behind him.

"Hey, looks like I startled you." The man said. The cave was not lit very well at this hour of the day. Therefore, Isaac Jr. couldn't see much. But from what he could see, the man looked 50-55. Maybe a couple of years older than his mom.

His eyes were hidden behind spectacles, but it didn't hide his intelligence. He ran his fingers over the swirls in the wood. "2000 years old, at least." And then he turned to Isaac Jr. "I am Dr. Kashyap."

"Isaac Newfield." Isaac Jr. stretched his hand. "Pleased to meet you."

"So, what brings you here, young man," Dr. Kashyap smiled.

"The beauty, the mystery, the past of those who lived before us…" Isaac Newfield paused and then added. "I am studying archeology."

"That's very interesting," Kashyap replied. "The marriage of science and exploration and religion drew me to these caves."

It was getting darker now, and they both started to walk towards the door when Kashyap stopped. "An archeologist should also have some intuition or psychic power."

And these words stopped Isaac Newfield in his track as well.

"How could you know that I ..."

Kashyap raised his hand. "That question can wait. I can only say that this meeting has a purpose and will be revealed someday."

"I don't get you, sir."

"Well, as a psychic, it must be a challenge to interpret intuition as real versus unreal until one has developed a stable level of consciousness," Kashyap added. "Sooner or later, you will need to develop a skill that accelerates the growth of silence. So that you can see which thoughts are 'real 'and which are 'noise."

"And how do I do that?" Isaac Newfield asked.

"By special meditation and by practicing the siddhis. Patanjali's Yoga Sutras mention that if you sit quietly, pay close attention to your mind, and practice the sutras, you will gain superpowers."

"But, everyone can't learn that, said Isaac Jr. You need a yogi or a guru for that."

"And that's why I am here." Kashyap led Isaac to the exit. "Some people can never escape their destiny, no matter what, and you are one of them, Isaac Newfield."

Isaac's eyes widened, and he opened his mouth to speak. But in his heart, he knew that whatever was happening was predestined, and he should trust Dr. Kashyap.

Soon, both of them left the caves, and after dinner, Dr. Kashyap started to teach what he had learned himself many years prior.

§§§§§§§§§§

Nancy called Isaac Oldfield at once. "Isaac?"

He picked up immediately. "What's wrong, Nancy? Why do you sound upset?"

"I was able to follow our son until now. I knew where he had gone."

"Then what's the problem?"

"Suddenly, it is as if he has disappeared. I cannot follow him with my intuition, which worries me."

"I am sure he'll be safe."

"I want to believe it, too, but why does my heart refuse to trust that?" And with that, Nancy cut off the call and closed her eyes again in an attempt to track her son.

Chapter 29:

Weather, or Not?

Isaac Jr. opened his eyes and looked around. He bore the facial expression of one who had received a great gift. And imagine, he was not even expecting it.

The world around him was calm and peaceful, and he breathed. When he decided to explore these caves, he had not even imagined in his wild dreams that he would meet a yogi. And his life would be changed forever.

Isaac Jr. didn't know how that fateful evening had turned into another day; it was pretty late now. He had to return home. His mom would be worried otherwise.

With a blissful heart, Isaac Jr. turned to Dr. Kashyap. "I am never going to forget these two days."

In response, the man smiled. "Yes, and never forget who you are. Someday, you will need what I just taught you."

Isaac Jr. bent down to touch the feet of his mentor as he had seen many Indians doing that. "Now, please grant me the permission to leave."

Dr. Kashyap didn't let him bend. Instead, he embraced Isaac Jr. in a sportsman-like hug. "If you ever need help, now you know where to find me."

He paused and then looked at the sky. "Although it is a fine day, you can never trust this region. Weather can take a worse turn at any time. You'd better be on your way."

With that, Dr. Kashyap let Isaac Jr. step back. Isaac Jr.'s eyes went to his magnetic, serene face, and he thanked his lucky stars again.

"If ever I get pushed around by life, I'll use these lessons I just learned."

With that, he took a step and started his journey once again. The mountain path was steep and narrow with rocks, each footstep challenging his progress. Sometimes the track was not even visible. But Isaac didn't mind. He was quiet within, full of joy and calm.

For him, the path was the least challenging of his obstacles. Adjusting his backpack, Isaac Jr. braced himself and continued to descend slowly. Thick, dark green boughs arched over the place, sometimes blocking the sunlight. While they muted the harshness of the midday sun, that didn't make his journey easy.

Given his high spirit, Isaac Jr. hardly missed civilization in this part of the mountain. Due to his elevated mood, he failed to notice the changes other humans might have seen. The blue sky became grayer with each passing minute, and a fierce wind started to howl on the horizon.

He steadily made his way, putting each foot carefully, one after another. He slipped a little every few steps but soon got the hang of it and righted himself before he ended up on the rocky, unforgiving ground. Soon, he would reach the base and then find transportation. Little did he know he was not the only one treading on this mountain.

§§§§§§§§§§

Gravak sniffed hard. Keeping up with this human was relatively easy. He didn't understand why Zaud had been so restless. As Isaac Jr. paused to take out the water bottle from his backpack, Gravak stopped, too. His golden-brown eyes glistened like topaz under the pale sun. But nobody could see him except his leader, Zaud, watching him from the space shuttle at the far end.

"You remember what you are supposed to do?" Zaud repeated, and Gravak almost lost it.

"I know why you sent me here, boss!"

"Then why are you taking so much time? If you delay any further, we might lose him."

"I can concentrate only if you let me be," murmured Gravak, wishing to cut off the connection and get rid of his supervisor immediately. Zaud was a good man but impatient. Gravak knew patience was the key when dealing with people like Isaac Jr. He was not taking any chances.

Gravak unhurriedly raised his hands, and then the dust and smog started to line the atmosphere. As the wind continued its whipping, Isaac stopped.

"Dust storm?" He narrowed his eyes, observing the horizon. Although it was not evening, the daylight had dwindled to almost nothing.

"I never heard of this," Isaac Jr. whispered. Then he recalled Dr. Kashyap's words that the weather could take the worst turn at any time. "I wonder if he knew what I was getting into." Isaac Jr. braced himself and began to climb down again.

He was at a level where the base was visible yet far from his position.

Perhaps I underestimated this mountain spoke Isaac Jr. to no one.

"Or overestimated your capacity, you fool!" Gravak, who was walking just a couple of steps behind him, spat.

"Now, enough of this. I need to get back home." He added again and then started to wave his hands rhythmically as if he were a band conductor, summoning the orchestra.

He was indeed!

The only difference was that his orchestra was designed to play the music of din and discord.

As if following the gesture of his hands, Earth began to shake, resulting in unheard-of tremors in this region.

Isaac Jr. took one more step and then halted. The wind storm had already made it difficult to watch his steps. Grey ash and dust drifted around him, almost blinding him, and then the ground beneath his feet gave way, making Isaac Jr. fumble for stability.

Isaac Jr. scratched his head. Perhaps he was imagining things. He closed his eyes, and big rocks fell quickly and dangerously from the top when he opened them. His perception distorted as the ground under his feet trembled again, making him fumble for support.

But there was no support.

The vibrations coming from below were strong and scary. The noise rose like an extended thunder. What was he supposed to do? He had never heard such a roar before.

He fought hard to balance, but what happened after that was like a slow-motion movie. Everything was a blur: the world around him, the mountain rushing by, and he knew he was falling, and there was nothing to stop him from getting hurt now. He was hurtling, tumbling down at a speed he didn't like. If he continued to move at this speed, his end was inevitable.

Why had he not seen this coming?

He had the gift of psychokinesis under certain conditions of great danger. And it had failed him completely today.

Isaac Jr.'s mouth went dry as blood started to drip from his body, and a groan escaped his throat. His body twirled and jerked, hitting hard rocks and plants. The wind made it impossible to see where he would land, and Isaac Jr. knew he would be lucky to survive.

He closed his eyes, praying for a miracle, and then a substantial body stood like a boulder in his way and stopped his slide. This sudden change of events caused him to open his eyes again. And what did he see? A ninja-like female, dressed in all black, tall, and muscular, stood midway, protecting him. Her legs remained firmly planted on the hill despite the tremors. Her white hair framed her beautiful face, and he blinked.

Hadn't he seen her before?

But where?

"Now listen carefully!" Her clear voice was not loud; it was hardly audible. "Each of us has strength, but if you don't believe in yourself, you can't save yourself, forget about saving the world."

Isaac Jr.'s eyes widened.

The woman continued. "This is not a normal earthquake. But we don't have time to think. Just trust me, okay?"

Isaac Jr. hardly had the energy to nod.

The girl extended her hand, helping him stand up and supported him. "Close your eyes and do as I tell you."

Chapter 30:
Real Visions

She had not slept well the whole night. After tossing and turning for a long time, Nancy had given up on catching any sleep. It was common for Isaac Jr. to go on expeditions for a day or two near Mumbai. He was not like other teenagers of his age. Being mature and responsible, her son had given no reason to be restless. This trip was also the same. And yet here she was, at the end of her wits, frustrated and worried about being unable to track him.

And the weather didn't give any solace as well. Since dawn, ominous dark clouds gathered above, mimicking her state of mind. When one more attempt to trace Isaac Jr. failed, Nancy started making coffee. Maybe her mind was agitated right now, and things would straighten out if she tried later.

The muggy day and the leaden sky made her gloomy, and she opened the window to remove the suffocating stale air.

What was this?

The window swayed and banged as an unforgiving wind shook and swirled everything around. Nancy squinted at the gray sky. Suddenly, the world felt so small and close. The air was thick with humidity, and she had no doubt it would rain.

On any other day, she would have welcomed the rain to give some relief from the scorching summer heat.

But not today.

Because in her heart, everything about today felt wrong. Especially in this weather.

There was hardly anything she could do.

Picking up her cup and newspapers, Nancy returned to the living room window and sat on her favorite chair. She had picked it up so lovingly at a prestigious store. But the lush fabric and soothing colors did not comfort her today. The wind suddenly picked up, baying like a lone dog. And within minutes, a low crackle of thunder rose, disturbing the stillness of her street.

There was still no news from Isaac Jr.

Soon, the heavy rainfall dragged down the blackened clouds, and they filled the street. At once, it cast the world in a somber mood.

It was not the rain that disturbed Nancy. Instead, the heavy cloudburst behaved unnaturally to her expert eyes.

Moving from the window, Nancy switched on the television.

"People residing in Mumbai woke up to heavy rains. After months of scorching summer heat, the rains are a huge relief sign." The newsreader paused and then continued. "The India Meteorological Department (IMD) has predicted 'heavy to very heavy rainfall' at a few places. We are already getting reports of water-logging on the streets causing massive traffic congestion. Heavy downpours and water-logging have hit train services as well. Mumbaikars are advised not to come out of their homes unless necessary. Some areas badly hit by water-logging include Borivali, Sion, Santacruz, and King Circle. Due to the constant rain, schools and colleges will remain closed today. Power cuts are likely to occur in some areas while the rain has forced even the courts to declare a holiday today."

The news was not encouraging at all. Nancy sighed and switched off the TV. Outside, the rain lashed out mercilessly, beating on the earth in heavy sheets. For the first monsoon rain, this was unnatural. Letting her intuition take the lead, Nancy closed her eyes and concentrated on her thoughts. Five minutes passed, but she could not track Isaac Jr. Was this storm in any way associated with her missing son? The idea was scary and one she didn't want to imagine.

Nancy drew a calm breath, urging her mind to show her what she had felt since this morning. Overwhelming anxiety and nervousness overtook her as she picked up the outside energy and focused on the task.

At first, nothing came to her.

And then visions in little clips flashed in front of her eyes.

"Good thing, we are inhuman, isn't it, Erutav?" The strange creature's harsh voice sounded rusty and cruel. His bark-like skin had shades of gray and black, glistening in the darkness. He didn't care about the planet Earth. All he wanted was an earth without humans. One look at him and Nancy understood that it was delusional to even think that they could be like humans.

Another one, apparently Erutav, bobbed his egg-shaped head to the leader. "Nobody will even realize what is happening."

Nancy rasped as she heard the conversation. So, she was right. This storm was not natural. But how? Was it possible for thralls to even create such calamities?

The boss, Rynyk, stretched out his antennae as if he were tuning into a television channel. After a minute or so, he spoke. "Flood the city so much that not a single human dare to venture out today."

Erutav disappeared as a cloud of dark smoke.

And Nancy's eyes widened in horror. She felt she was not able to breathe.

Was destroying lives as easy as ordering a pizza for these beings?

She concentrated on Rynyk but couldn't understand what was going on. He turned to a desktop-like device kept on a bureau and started tapping it with the stub of mass attached to his hand-like structure.

Was he dictating which parts should be flooded?

"One day, we will submerge the entire planet," Rynyk spoke. "These fools don't know that by increasing global warming, they are helping us…"

Nancy couldn't believe her eyes. As Rynyk increased his speed frantically, Nancy knew she had to do something.

Somehow, she had to stop thralls and not let them destroy Mother Earth. This vision had made her desperate to take action. She didn't care if she was grasping at straws. Quickly opening her eyes, Nancy went to fetch the water bottle and called Isaac Sr. She narrated the whole story to him.

"I am not sure I've experienced anything like this." She spoke.

"And that's our signal to work hard to stop them," added Isaac Sr. from the other end. "You are right. Thralls might be behind our son's disappearance."

"What are we going to do now?" Nancy said at once. "I am scared. Because the truth is when I close my eyes and think how destructive those aliens can be, my heart stops…"

"I see our children defeating them, Nan." Isaac Sr.'s voice was peaceful. "The one thing I can't live without is our kids. But I somehow trust their abilities."

"And what if something happens to them…." Nancy's voice lashed out with untold emotions. "The thralls are too powerful."

Suddenly, the doorbell rang, announcing someone was at the door. Nancy ran to the entrance, forgetting about the phone. A flicker of hope burned high as she eagerly opened the door. When her eyes went to her son's face, she hugged him and sobbed into his chest.

Chapter 31

Asuras vs. Adityas = Rakshashas?

Being a successful university professor or psychologist was one thing.

And being a good father was another!

Isaac Sr. touched one of the artifacts from the Roswell UFO given to him by Army engineers. They had been assigned to move the spaceship from Roswell to Hanger 18 at Wright-Patterson Air Force Base. Many things flashed before Isaac's eyes: his job, meeting Nancy, going on the Nautilus, the birth of his children, and the many events that showed the kids were extraordinary. Then, the anxiety started to block his memories.

Was he right in separating his children?

Didn't they deserve to be with each other? After all, they were twins and hardly recalled anything about the other.

While he had the pleasure of having Sacha with him, he had never been a part of his son's life. There were so many things he wanted to teach him, so many things he wanted to tell him.

Yes, he badly wanted them to be a part of his life. And yet, Isaac Sr. knew he could never have that.

Who does he tell that he missed his boy like crazy?

Isaac returned the artifact to its case and sat down, thinking about Nancy's call. Although the rain had stopped now, Mumbai was still full of chaos. Luckily, Isaac Jr. was back, and Isaac Sr. could learn the full story from Nancy. Thralls were powerful and dangerous. If they decide to cause havoc, nothing can stop them.

Isaac had been trying to understand their methodology when the phone rang. It was one of the officers from the US military.

After the initial formalities, he asked about Isaac's progress in finding non-lethal defense techniques. Isaac Sr. had been assigned to India to research practical uses of Patanjali's Yoga Sutras and Ninja techniques for special ops forces.

"The rising sea levels will cause mass displacements of people," the officer added. "Did you know that right now, global warming is identified as a major threat to international security?" His voice was grave.

Isaac Sr. listened while the man spoke. "We're afraid that civil unrest can be the greatest threat. As nations scramble to find safe land for their citizens, it may also trigger mass migration and military threats."

"So, what do we do? How do we protect our people?" Isaac interjected.

"We just know the man who can be helpful to us." The major added. "His name is Dr. Kashyap."

"How do I find him?" Isaac spoke as he took one more sip of tea." Where does he live?"

But there was no reply. The line went dead.

"Perfect! Finding a man in this city is like finding a needle in a haystack," he murmured sarcastically. The telephone rang again as if the captain had heard Isaac's comment.

"So, where do I find that Dr. Kashyap?"

"Mr. Isaac?" The voice at the other end was calm, collected, and not of the officer. "Which Dr. Kashyap are you talking about?"

"Umm, who is this?" Isaac had enough experience not to trust strangers.

"Can I please speak to Sacha?"

With unknown forces around, Isaac was not taking any chance. "I am Sacha's father."

"I am Dr. Kashyap. Perhaps the man for whom you were searching!" Was the stranger smiling at the other end?

"Your daughter is very talented. I read her article in the newspaper and thought of congratulating her."

The tea cup slipped from Isaac's lips and fell to the ground. Who knew how his lucky stars worked? He was agitated a few minutes earlier about finding this man, and now the man had called for Sacha.

Somehow, Isaac found his voice. "Sure, umm, Dr. Kashyap, I mean the famous Dr. Kashyap?"

There was a slight laughter. "Fame is man-given." Dr. Kashyap paused and then continued. "I was a common man and will always remain a common man."

The man was genuine.

Isaac needed help with how to continue the conversation.

"Sacha has done her research well. She is brave and has an eye for detail. Scientists have been warning about global warming for decades." Kashyap said.

"Yeah. We are consuming fossil fuel at an alarming rate."

"It's scary. What kind of planet are we going to leave for our future generations? And yet we take everything for granted." The disappointment was evident in Dr. Kashyap's voice now. "It's our responsibility to leave this planet in better shape for our children."

"You are right. Global warming is real, and it is here. Even the Vedas mention that if the polar ice caps melted, civilization living on the coasts of continents would be threatened." Isaac spoke at once and then stopped.

Perhaps he shouldn't have said that.

Dr. Kashyap might think that he was trying to flaunt.

But instead, he heard, "Interesting. It seems like you have studied the Vedas too."

"Well," Isaac hesitated. "Not much, but I am very interested in yogic powers." There was no way to mention that Isaac was researching non-lethal defense techniques for the US military. "I am studying the Yoga Sutras." He paused and then added. "I have always wondered how this Vedic knowledge can be used for the benefit of mankind against the most dangerous threat faced by mankind to date?"

"That's wonderful. Global warming is a big issue and will get out of hand if we don't do anything about it. But that was not the only threat to humanity during those times, as mentioned in the Vedas." Dr. Kashyap stopped and then added. "I usually don't have a habit of chatting like this on the phone, but as you seem to be a learned man, I couldn't stop myself."

Isaac Sr. smiled. "I perfectly understand it. Please continue."

"During that period, humanity also faced attacks from the Asuras and the Rakshasas. Asuras were a class of power-seeking super-beings and fought regularly with the devas, a more benevolent group of super-beings. According to Hindu mythology, Rakshasas were man-eater humanoids. Then there were the Adityas, a distinct class of benevolent gods, protectors of all beings, guarding the world."

As Dr. Kashyap added more, Isaac Sr. wondered if the thralls could be the Asuras wanting to gain power on the earth since olden times and the Nordics could be the Aditya protecting the planet. And who were the Rakshasas? Did the thralls empower humans who became known as Rakshasas? Did the Vedas also show how the past civilizations protected themselves against this threat? He had to meet Dr. Kashyap.

Chapter 32:

Brave 16-Year Old

Look around. If you can't see what I am, you are either blind or too full of yourself. All around, politicians and influential people are ignoring the fact that we are responsible for our planet. We will regret it if we continue exploiting natural resources and not curb carbon emissions.

Isaac stopped reading the newspaper. His daughter didn't have a filter when it came to expressing herself. The way she had taken up the challenge to make people aware of global warming was admirable. But at times, as a parent, it worried him.

"Sacha, where are you?" Isaac Sr. audibly searched for his daughter. At sixteen, his girl had admirable traits and a multi-dimensional personality, while other girls her age might still struggle with hormones or find boyfriends.

She exited her room, her hair wrapped in a towel, fresh from the bath.

"Look, dad," her voice was filled with excitement. "I received a letter from a lady."

Isaac started reading it.

Dear Sacha, I am as passionate about global warming as you. But I never had the nerve to come forward and raise my voice. Alas, everyone is not courageous like you. Whenever I read your articles, I see hope. All is not lost yet if we take the required actions. Thanks for kindling that flicker of optimism in our lives, dear girl. Don't give up.

"You are creating quite a buzz!" He smiled at her. "Dr. Kashyap called me to congratulate you."

"Oh, yeah, I've heard about him." She removed the towel from her head and started to dry her hair.

"We had a chat. He seems to be a nice person. Anyway, where are you headed?"

"I'm going to a seminar arranged by one NGO that works with the climate and the environment. There will be journalists, climate activists, and possibly some influential people who can take the right steps."

Isaac Sr. was proud of his girl at the moment. He never imagined how easily doors opened for her and how she found her way around in the things she believed in.

"I am coming with you. What time do we leave?"

§§§§§§§§§§

Sacha stole a look at the people sitting in the front. She could recognize some faces. But the hall was packed to a capacity as she had seen before. People took Mother Nature for granted and never gave her the respect she deserved.

Not the one to feel intimidated, she spoke with authority at her appointed time, thanking everyone for the opportunity she was given to express her point of view.

"We are facing a disaster of unspoken sufferings for many people. We see floods, death from heat, fires of unimaginable extent, and yet we ignore the issue. We tell ourselves it is happening somewhere else in the world, not to us. Why do we fail to understand the clear connection between the increased extreme weather events, natural calamities, and the increasing climate crisis? Why has no politician come forward and take responsibility for action? If we don't take steps to stop this crisis, who else will? We can't sit peacefully hoping that the solution will emerge out of nowhere." She paused and checked the audience for reaction. While some nodded in agreement, other faces looked as if they were in deep thought.

She continued. "Even as a child, I understood one thing clearly. We must stop the emissions of greenhouse gases. If not, it might set off that irreversible chain reaction beyond human control. The bigger our carbon footprint is, the bigger issues we will face in the coming years, and the right time is NOW!" She emphasized the last word. Her speech was clear, confident, and up to the mark. "I request all of you people present and people with public responsibility to treat this as a climate emergency and take the required steps before it is too late."

Flashes of light emanated from photographers placed around the room.

As she thanked them and sat down, the room filled with clapping. Sacha sat down on the dais at her designated place.

§§§§§§§§§§

Isaac left when Sacha finished her speech.

When the entire seminar ended, and Sacha was about to leave, someone called her. "Miss Oldfield, wait a minute."

She turned her head and stopped in her tracks.

It was Mr. Mathur, a well-known journalist, writer, and TV personality.

"Hello," Sacha spoke at once.

"That was some speech!" He spoke at once. "Well done! How do you do this?"

"Do what?"

"Speak so clearly, without any fear? Even adults would be shaking if they were at your place."

She smiled. "Those who are right don't have to fear, isn't that true?"

"I admire your spirit. But just writing about climate change or speaking in such seminars will not take you any further."

"Then what should I do?"

"I know the man who can help you." Mr. Mathur whispered, and Sacha was super thrilled. It was one thing to be admired and another to be supported. And she was not so naïve as to miss the difference between those two concepts.

When she didn't reply, Mr. Mathur insisted. "Come with me."

To appease her curiosity, Sacha followed him. When Mr. Mathur led her to a man, she couldn't believe her luck. It was Mr. Mehra, the ruthless businessman, but when it came to helping the downtrodden of humanity, he became a humble politician.

Sacha had often read in the newspapers about how he was always ready to help poor, less fortunate people.

And a surge of hope took over her. Mr. Mathur was right. He was the go-to man. He had power, money, and authority. She thought things might take a better turn if he supported her.

"Your parents must be proud of you." Mr. Mehra spoke as he looked at her from his expensive rimless glasses. He was wearing an impeccable suit. "You are quite brave for a sixteen-year-old, aren't you?"

Although he had said these words calmly, smiling slightly, nobody could understand whether he was complimenting or threatening her.

Chapter 33:

Meeting Amrita

Isaac Jr. looked at his favorite library's regal Victorian and fabulous brick structure.

This was his go-to place to hide and mull about everything – from finding the correct information about a new topic to calming his mind when things became turbulent.

And today, he was here for both – he wanted to know about Dr. Kashyap and the Yoga Sutras he spoke about.

Also, things could not have been more askew on the home front. He knew he had worried his mom, and there was no excuse.

He should have shared every event of this trip, how he had met that remarkable man, how an unknown force was bent to kill him, and how a strange yet familiar girl had saved him from death.

And yet he didn't open up. He kept everything bottled up inside as usual.

Becoming a teenager made it challenging to be as close to his mom as he used to be.

The thought was disturbing, and Isaac almost tripped when climbing the library stairs. Balancing himself at the last minute, he took two steps at one time now. He then thought things would have been different if his father had been around.

Berating himself for such thoughts one more time, Isaac Jr. entered the quiet room filled with soft blues, whites, and grays and pulled out an inky treasure from the ornate bookcase. The sense of easy solitude relaxed him. Isaac Jr. looked around. Except for a few boys studying quietly, the room was empty. He selected a far corner where no one could disturb him and sat down.

Why was he like this?

Despite being gifted, why did he still feel like he didn't belong?

Will he ever become what he had dreamed of?

The thoughts kept creeping, but today, Isaac Jr. was in no mood to let his mind master him.

§§§§§§§§§

By the time he left, it was five. The Mumbai heat was terrible once he was out. Squinting at the sun, Isaac Jr. started to walk. It was not as if he had found solutions to his troubles, but yes, he had covered a lot of ground on Dr. Kashyap for a day. His home was far, and he would either need to take a city bus or an auto rickshaw.

He was about to call out and stop one when someone shouted," Isaac,"

He turned his head and smiled wide when he discovered it was Emerald. "Hey cousin, what are you doing here?" Then, turning towards her completely, he walked toward her.

But then, another figure came into the periphery of his vision and almost stopped him dead in his tracks.

The young woman was willowy, not overly tall, dressed in an all-white classic kurta and churidar. She looked flawless. Her white lace dupatta fluttered slightly in the wind, and his heart missed a beat.

Who was this girl?

"Isaac, meet Amrita, my friend." Emerald took a step and introduced the young woman.

"Hi," said Isaac, still in awe of her beauty.

"Hello, Isaac," Amrita replied in a soft voice.

"She is a journalist, by the way," Emerald added. "She needed to visit the library for her work."

Once again, Isaac was at a loss of words.

He didn't know what happened when he stood in front of girls. He was not as muscular or well-built as other boys his age. And that didn't help either when it came to confidence.

"That's interesting." But he had an uncanny desire to know more about Amrita. Somehow, Isaac found the courage. "So, what do you write about?"

"Mostly the dangers of global warming and death by rising sea levels," she replied immediately.

"Wow!" He smiled, trying hard to hide his glee.

"Are you in a hurry?" Emerald looked at him. Was his liking of Amrita so evident on his face?

"Of course not!" He had to know what his cousin was getting at.

"Great, I know where to grab sandwiches while you both talk shop."

Could Emerald read his mind?

Isaac hoped not!

As he nodded, Emerald winked when Amrita was not watching. Isaac smiled as the three began walking towards the small restaurant at the end of the road.

Once they sat, Emerald began placing the order.

"We need to deal with the global warming on an urgent basis." Isaac continued his talk with Amrita.

"It is a fact. No matter what anyone says." Amrita added. As her eyes met his, Isaac could see she was beautiful and intelligent.

"On top of that, the rising sea levels could have devastating effects," Amrita added. "especially on coastal cities farther inland affected by the tides." She informed. "Anyway, enough about me. Emerald tells me you study archeology."

"Yes, and he is a dowser too." Emerald didn't let Isaac reply. Her enthusiasm was apparent. "He can find water wells, metals, gemstones, or even missing people using it." She paused and then added in a confidential whisper. "He doesn't like to brag about it."

Before Amrita could reply, the waiter brought their food.

Once the food was served, Emerald asked," You are also into yoga. Is it really possible to attain psychic yogic powers like telepathy or clairvoyance?"

"Isn't it explained in Patanjali's Yoga Sutras?" Amrita took a small bite and spoke.

"Stories of enlightened yogis having psychic or physical superpowers are often heard of in India." Isaac poured a ketchup on his plate. "These abilities are described in Patanjali's Yoga Sutras, as Amrita mentioned."

"Amrita's dad is well-versed in Vedic knowledge," said Emerald as she sipped the cold drink. According to him, the powers that seem otherworldly to us are available to all humans."

"And they can be accessed with the proper discipline." Amrita completed the thought.

"He seems like a special man. I hope someday I can meet your father."

"And do you know who he is?" Emerald inquired. "Dr. Kashyap. Have you heard the name?"

Issac's mouth remained open. First, Dr. Kashyap and now his daughter – were these meetings pointing to new hopes?

Chapter 34:

Destiny's Children

Staring at the pristine white walls of her apartment, Nancy opened the file of the case she was working on. The girl had disappeared a week ago. No one had a clue about her whereabouts. She had been working on finding her for the last three days and could not lead the police anywhere. She poured a hefty dose of caffeine into her cup and looked at the missing girl's picture once more.

Her innocent face stared back at her.

According to her parents, the girl was depressed for a few months due to poor academic performance.

In her own age and time, Nancy had not heard about anyone becoming depressed at such a young age.

What was wrong with today's children?

Oh god, the missing girl was almost her children's age. The thought made her restless, and her mind wandered. Although she lived with Isaac Jr., there was a side to him that he always kept hidden from her.

Contacting Sacha or forming any bond with her was out of the question for Nancy. She had to rely on whatever information her husband gave her.

What if the kids were also facing the issues faced by other teens? As if being a teenager was insufficient, her children had unusual, possibly frightening abilities.

But she didn't know its history or how they should handle it. She and Isaac Sr. tried their best to equip their two children, but they still didn't know what happens in their inner worlds.

Managing such power was a gigantic responsibility; her children were still young and unaware of the deceit in the world.

What if someone made them pawns and planned to hurt them? The thought sent a shiver through her body and filled her with dread.

Her children won't even know what went wrong.

After returning from his trip, Isaac Jr. had been in his room most of the time. Despite his mother asking him repeatedly, he had kept to himself, which worried her now.

Her boy never used to keep things to himself.

Perhaps she was overthinking or might not be equipped to handle a teenage boy.

Either thought was not comforting at all.

And the current police case of a missing depressed teen girl stressed Nancy. She knew herself well and her limitations, too.

She was a worrier when it came to her children. And once her mind started circling to negative thoughts, there was no looking back.

But all was not lost. Still, there was somebody who could tell her what was happening in her children's lives.

Not wasting a minute now, Nancy bent and pulled out the bottom drawer of her table. She lifted an old ornate box the size of a large TV remote and kept it on the table. The box had a lock that opened only when you inserted a proper number combination.

Sliding the wheels carefully, she struck the correct combination on the first try and gently opened the box.

Lying in, there was the lock of hair from the Nordic male who had contributed DNA to Emerald: Aundrid, the chief of the Nordics.

Although he had suggested she shouldn't use this tool unless necessary, Nancy knew it was about time she talked with Aundrid.

She quickly cleared her desk, putting the papers and files inside the drawers, lying on the top. Most of the desk was devoid of any papers, giving a fair view of the empty white wall behind.

And that was all she needed now.

Lifting the thick bunch of Aundrid's hair, she closed her eyes and sent him a psychic message stating she needed to talk with him.

And true to his words, after exactly two minutes, as he had stated, Aundrid's face got projected on the empty wall behind the desk.

Nancy still didn't know what kind of system it was.

She still needed to find out what technology the Nordics used. But right now, she didn't want to know about it.

After the initial exchange, she looked at the friendly alien worriedly.

"I am at such a juncture in life where I don't even know what's happening in my children's lives. Are they happy?"

The kind alien's eyes stared at her with understanding as if he knew how difficult it was to hide things from your children.

Nancy added. "Are they able to comprehend the circumstances that surround them? Are they able to handle the powers they are gifted with?"

Aundrid nodded first and then spoke. "Don't worry so much. The children are following their destiny, and there is hardly anything we both can do."

The happy images of her past as a complete family flickered before her eyes, and Nancy gasped. It was silly to want or even think about the things she would never have.

"Why are you still judging yourself for separating them?" Aundrid's calm voice was like a balm to her wounds. "You did what you had to do. And if it makes you happy, I can tell you a little about both."

Nancy slipped closer.

"Sacha is a strong girl, mature, confident, and with a stable head on those iron shoulders. She doesn't know her destiny yet is powerful enough to find her way. Not being with you has impacted her in some ways but also made her more determined.

Isaac is still lost at times. But in the recent past, he has met some influential people who are ultimately going to show him what his destiny is. No wonder you cannot track him, as he is learning some powerful mental techniques to equip him to face the fate he was born to face. He is learning the yogic methods that date back some 12,000 years. Both have encountered problems, yet they are more determined than ever."

Wrinkles in Nancy's forehead disappeared, and the corner of her lips rose to a smile.

All was well in her world if her children were getting prepared for their destiny.

Chapter 35:

Blood Money, Flood Money

"Under the project 'Smiling Buddha, 'India successfully detonates its first nuclear weapon, becoming the sixth nation to do so." Sacha read the headline loudly.

"Did you receive any hate mail after that seminar?" Isaac Sr., who was reading another newspaper, asked her.

They both were in the living room. Being Sunday, they didn't have to hurry today.

"Dad," her voice was a little impatient now. "Did you hear what I said? India's first atomic bomb exploded!"

Noticing he was squeezing and straining his eyes, she got up and fetched his spectacles from the sideboard.

"Aren't you supposed to wear them when you read?"

After putting his glasses on, he noticed she was still standing and had not returned to her reading. He sensed Sacha wanted to talk. He could never be around for his son. And so, he would do whatever he could for his daughter!

He took off the spectacles and put them aside. Then he turned to her. "Yes, it is indeed a big step for the country."

Sacha pulled the chair near her father.

"Here's the truth: after my articles, I received several letters mentioning people getting nervous, fretful, and anxious about climate change. I think they have an unrealistic fear of something bad happening to them."

Isaac turned the page of another newspaper now. "The papers also echo the same sentiment. People are getting fearful, and more people report stress issues."

"I wonder what is wrong with them," Sacha asked. "Oh, I'm going to meet Emerald."

"Anything urgent?" He quickly scanned her face. "It's Sunday! Our time!"

She smiled now. "I'll be back for lunch."

So far, his daughter had not given him any reason to doubt or question her living arrangements.

He hoped that was going to stay the same.

"Want to go out?" He smiled back at her.

"I won't miss it for anything." With that, Sacha went to her room, and they both left the house in an hour.

§§§§§§§§§

However, Isaac's mind was restless.

He didn't want to reveal his suspicions in front of his daughter, but while reading the newspapers, he felt something was out of place.

The world didn't seem the way it should. And that was worrying.

There were a few people he could call to find the answers.

Instead of calling his military friend or the new friend Dr. Kashyap, Isaac Sr. contacted the Nordic chief. He wanted a different angle on the issue: while the previous ones are from the earth, the latter could offer another view.

Nancy didn't know that Isaac was in touch with Aundrid. And she didn't need to know it, either, because sometimes the news he shared with Isaac was not very optimistic. And Nancy was already over-worried.

Isaac pressed the red button on the little device given to him by the Nordics, and true to his words, Aundrid's face appeared on the screen, saying, "Have you heard about the Schumann Resonance?"

The smart Nordic was able to read Isaac's mind. He didn't waste any time. "Unlike other planets, Earth has its rhythm. You must know that you don't live on the Earth but inside it."

"Yes, in the atmospheric cavity formed between the Earth's surface and ionosphere," Isaac spoke.

"Now, do you know that all humans swim in an absolute sea of invisible energies and oscillating fields?"

"You mean the Earth Pulse?" Isaac quickly added. "The heartbeat of the Earth?"

"Exactly. Named after German physicist and Professor W. O. Schumann, the Schumann Resonance is not unheard of. It has been there for thousands of years. Many ancient civilizations also had some knowledge about it."

"But what is its relation with people?"

"Scientists have identified a relation between the Schumann Resonance and human well-being. They suspect that this earth pulse impacts human consciousness. If the Schumann Resonance is somehow blocked or filtered, people don't feel well." Aundrid sighed. "It modifies your physical, mental, and psychological well-being. And when it is reduced in strength, it can make people anxious, fearful and restless."

"I see," Isaac said. "And who can have power sufficiently enormous to change the Schumann Resonance of the Earth?"

"I can think of only one group capable of doing it," Aundrid spoke.

"Thralls?"

"Exactly. By making people more fearful, they easily gain control over them."

"So they can destroy human beings and then possess the earth?" Isaac spoke. "Who would have ever thought about it? What will happen to us if thralls have such unimaginable powers?"

"And we have Sacha and Isaac Jr. Don't forget that," Aundrid said. "You must have read about the project Smiling Buddha as well."

"Sacha and I were discussing it this morning."

Aundrid said. "It is straightforward to see that the government is increasing fear in people. They are sensing the mood of the population…"

"And they want to capitalize on that, increasing the popularity of the politician in charge?" Isaac asked.

"Absolutely. I won't be wrong if I say that some politicians might be under the influence of the thralls. For instance, Mr. Mehra."

Isaac's forehead wrinkled. "I don't get it."

"Look here," Aundrid spoke, and then a large bedroom came into focus on the screen. Sitting on the bed was a man about 50 with a young woman. Isaac Sr. had never seen such a beautiful lady before. Large eyes, porcelain skin, and voluptuous body. However, there was something in those eyes, a kind of magic that could hypnotize anyone.

She looked into the man's eyes intensely.

"Tammana," the man sounded irritated as he pushed her hand away from his body. "This is not a time to play."

She pouted in response but didn't budge from her position.

"You are my finance advisor, too. I'm concerned that climate change and rising sea levels could destroy my properties and wealth." The man spoke again.

"You don't have to worry at all, sweetheart!" She soothed him and put her hand on his face. "You're a powerful man. Why don't you run a public relations campaign against climate change?"

This time, he didn't remove her hand. "But that is wrong. The climate changes are happening, and it's about time we, especially me, took a step as a responsible government servant."

She slipped near and put her head on his chest. "And lose it all? Those sea-facing bungalows? Farmhouses? Are you ready to give up on these comforts?"

And this time, Mr. Mehra raised her hand and kissed it. "I love your thinking. Every day, I fall in love with you more and more."

Smiling slyly, Tammana touched the black cross around her neck.

§§§§§§§§§

"She has succeeded, hurray!" Somewhere far on a different planet, an ugly-looking thrall captured the signal.

And the screen went blank.

§§§§§§§§§

Isaac Sr. clenched his teeth. The thralls were powerful and reaching out to people by any means. He had to do something. But what?

Chapter 36:
Corporate Decisions

Isaac Sr. stood patiently before the trip to his office. Sacha was getting ready, and he waited for her to join him. At times, both of them went together.

Suddenly, the landline started to ring. It was Nancy.

"Switch on the TV at once!" She spoke with excited breath.

"Why, what happened?"

"You need to take care of Sacha." That was all Nancy said before completing the conversation. Feeling jittery now due to her nervousness, Isaac turned on the television. When he found the channel where Mr. Mathur spoke, he stood, unable to take his eyes off the screen.

"What are your views on Sacha Oldfield's speech on global warming?"

"Sacha, who?" Mr. Mathur narrowed his eyes. Sacha, who had come out of her room ready to leave, rushed to be near her father.

"He doesn't remember me?" She almost shouted. "How could he? He promised he would help me."

Isaac took her daughter's hand.

As if he was enjoying this game, Mr. Mathur took his sweet time before replying to the program host.

"Oh, the girl with the glorious thoughts..." Mr. Mathur smiled now. "I am confused. If I have forgotten, please remind me, what was her age?"

"Sixteen!"

Sacha swore under her breath. "Why is he acting like this? Mr. Mathur was the one who introduced me to Mr. Mehra."

And then she turned to Isaac. "Look at his face. I can see he is lying even with his smirky smile."

"I know. But right now, we have nothing to prove that. Let's listen to what he has to say," Isaac suggested as he held his daughter's hand.

"After Miss Oldfield studies more deeply the relevant subjects, she can return and advise us." Mr. Mathur added.

Then he opened a magazine in front of him on the coffee table. "Here is the Time magazine, which mentions that the atmosphere has grown warmer in the distant past before humans existed in numbers. I say forget about fossil fuels causing climate warming; we're moving towards another warm period anyway. It's not the fault of humans. And that teenager has no clue about it."

Sacha started to cry now. Her body shivered as sobs escaped her throat, and Isaac Sr. sighed. He now knew why Nancy sounded severe. Getting condemned on national television was a blow, even for an adult like him. Sacha was just a child.

He ran a hand on his daughter's back, letting her cry. Pain poured out with every tear as Sacha's tears fell fast and thick.

After a while, with red and puffy eyes, she accepted the tissue from Isaac and wiped her face. After a glass of water, she was ready to talk.

By then, Isaac had canceled all his appointments for the day.

"I am tired," she spoke in a low and sad voice. The world is not what it looks from the outside. People are not what they pretend to be."

Isaac just nodded, letting her speak her heart.

"Why would leaders like that lie?" Sacha's voice was raised a bit now. "Why can't they accept the seriousness of the issue? They want to hide like an ostrich when a real problem comes. Well, Mr. Mathur is not the first one. I have seen others, too. It's awful to see so much lying by people in power. They discredit and demean important ways to reduce climate warming."

"So, what have you decided to do about it?"

Sacha looked into her father's eyes. "Isn't it clear, Dad? I can take only so much hate. My reason for journalism was to bring out the facts. But apparently, people don't want to hear that."

Then she got up. "I am giving up writing for the press."

Isaac's face wrinkled. "What would you do then?"

This time, she laughed a little. "Don't worry, Dad. I won't get married and settle down early, like my Indian friends. I am so surprised at the limited options Indian girls get regarding career options."

They were treading on a challenging part now. Usually, discussing such delicate issues was a mother's job, but Sacha didn't know about her mom. And Isaac had to face the music all alone.

He cleared his throat in preparation for the odd conversation he would have now. He tried to make light of it. "I am relieved to hear that you don't have plans to settle down like other girls your age in this country. I assume no boyfriend is waiting on the horizon with a ring."

"Of course not, Dad," she immediately replied. "If so, won't I tell you?"

Isaac's face broke in a smile now. "Of course, you will. We share everything under the sun, right?"

She nodded and then looked at the far horizon. After a minute or so, she spoke again. "I don't know how I can reply to Mr. Mathur. He has power and authority both. Maybe I should leave journalism, complete my studies, and join a corporation."

"It's good that you think practically. But the idea of leaving what is close to your heart and joining a corporation?"

"Why, dad, what's wrong with that?"

"So much." He tugged at her hand now. "Sit down, Sacha. We need to talk." Isaac's voice was serious now.

"These companies are not what they seem to you." He took a breath and then continued. "I tell you from my own experience. Many big corporations are beholden to defense contracts. You haven't heard about corporate greed yet. Many companies...."

"Right now, Dad, I feel so isolated from the world." Her voice was sad yet clear. Yes, some of those big corporations might be to blame. But not all the companies are alike." She waited a bit, made eye contact with her dad, and then proceeded to talk again. "I've had enough. Nothing is going to change my mind now."

Isaac feigned nonchalance as his girl left the room. But to say he was unaffected by her decision was like denying the truth for which he was alive.

Chapter 37:

Isaac Jr.'s Refusal

"Listen to me," Isaac Oldfield, her father, had urged Sacha as the last retort. "Before you finalize anything, meet Mr. Ghosh, your editor."

"Meeting him is not going to change anything." Sacha had spoken at once in response. "But okay, if it gives you peace…"

"Thanks," her father looked at her with hope.

And that was the reason Sacha was at the small office, which had become her second home. The place was done tastefully in mahogany and white. She was sitting in front of the editor and stole a look around.

"I will not stop you from resigning if you want this." Mr. Ghosh's glasses had slipped to his nose, and from above them, he peered at her kindly. His voice was gentle. The man might be her father's age. Medium built, simple yet sophisticated.

She didn't know what to say. It was Mr. Ghosh who had given her the first break. After climbing the steps of numerous newspaper offices, she finally came to him with very little hope in her heart. Sacha had assumed that like other employers, even he wouldn't trust her words because of her young age.

But she was wrong!

Mr. Ghosh had listened to her patiently and read what she had previously written. After an hour or so, he had happily agreed to publish her articles in his newspapers.

Her heart grew heavy as the fond memories of this place came back to her. "Thanks, Mr. Ghosh; I knew you would understand me."

"I wanted to show you something." He picked up a couple of envelopes on his table and passed them to her. "These are fan letters."

She opened one impatiently. Her readers always came first, and she always wanted to know their views on her writing.

"It's upsetting to know the animals we love are in danger." Wrote an eleven-year-old from Mumbai. "It is heartening to know someone also cares for them."

"Dear Sacha, I love reading your column. And I am very proud of you. We are both of the same age, almost. And yet, I don't dare to raise my voice like you." This was another letter from a boy her age. "If we don't act now, then we are doomed."

Sacha took a deep breath and started reading the rest of the letters. All had the same voice. They admired her courage and agreed with her. They also thanked her for spreading the awareness and hoped that Sacha would be able to do something. Those letters reminded her who she was and what she fought for.

Once she was done, Mr. Ghosh asked. "What are they writing this time?"

A warm smile spread on her face. "The usual stuff! How I am doing the noble work of spreading awareness about this big issue."

"And do you want to leave it because someone said something uncomplimentary about you?" He paused as he chose his words carefully. "There will be many who choose to work in corporations, but only one Sacha who feels responsible for the world."

She didn't speak anything. Those letters and Mr. Ghosh's words had hit her hard. She got up and murmured, "Thanks!"

And then, she was on her way to her house to tell her dad that she was not leaving her beloved profession.

§§§§§§§§§

It was late, yet Isaac Jr. was not able to sleep. The incidents of the past few days kept him awake. He recalled how he had met Dr. Kashyap at the cave, and then they had gone to his place, where Dr. Kashyap had equipped him with yoga and meditation techniques.

What gratitude he felt as he left that place.

How great he felt as if he was prepared to tackle anything now.

And yet, when the crisis came, Isaac Jr. couldn't do anything. He didn't have the confidence or knowledge to deal with it.

A feeling of doom took over.

He was sure he would have died that day if that girl had not saved him. But who was she? She had a look of power, strength, and serenity. Although she looked his age, she was not anything like him. But why and how had she found out he was in trouble, and why had she helped him?

Isaac Jr. started pacing the room now. It was sure that he had seen her before. But where?

§§§§§§§§§§

Sacha is not going to leave her passion.

Isaac Sr.'s words still echoed in Nancy's head as she smiled. She knew her daughter. She knew how powerful she was. And how they needed her.

When she heard footsteps in her son's room, Nancy was about to go to her own room. Why was he up now? Over the last few days, Nancy noticed Isaac Jr. was almost lost and hardly spoke to her. She had no idea what was going on in his mind. Feeling determined to talk with her son, Nancy knocked and then slowly opened the door of his room.

What did she see?

A large gray aura had enveloped her son, which surprised her. Was it an aura of gloom and despair?

If yes, she had to find out the reason behind that.

"Isaac, I forgot to tell you Sylvia's friend wanted your consultation. Will you be free this weekend?"

"No, Mom, I am not interested in dowsing anymore!"

She froze at hearing the unexpected. "What?"

"Yes, Mom," Isaac spoke with determination now. "I've realized it's not for me, I don't want to fight any climate change or find any 'hidden resources.' "

Nancy couldn't believe her ears. Her son loved these things and talked about leaving everything he believed in!

But by looking at Isaac Jr.'s demeanor, she knew he wouldn't listen to a single word she said. Nancy left the room silently. Once in her room, she closed her eyes and tried to read her son's mind. A barrier prevented her from entering. Although she couldn't read much, she saw a beautiful young girl called Amrita.

Who was she, and was she the reason behind Isaac's latest change? Nancy had to find out.

Chapter 38:

Emerald's Protest

Isaac Sr. had already messaged his U.S. supervisors regarding the latest status. Everything needed to be fixed now. He had started doubting his abilities. However, he didn't know whom to consult. Aundrid had given him solace regarding his children. But Sacha had already disappeared, and he was unsure about his son either. How was he supposed to believe that Nordic?

He waited for Emerald, who had messaged him about meeting him. Emerald rarely turned to him; when she did, it was something of utter importance. He hoped she would bring some news on Sacha.

"I wondered if you know why Sacha left the house?" He asked the minute Emerald entered his house.

Her pale Nordic skin glistened in the morning rays, and her green eyes danced in amusement. "And good morning to you too, Mr. Isaac."

She followed him inside. "I knew you would ask this! She is safe. It's good that she has this time to think. Meanwhile, if you request, her principal will take her back. And yes, Sacha will return soon."

Isaac Sr. opened his mouth, but she gestured for him to stop. "I am sorry, I don't have the liberty to tell more. But trust me."

He offered her refreshments, and then he asked. "Did you happen to meet Isaac recently? Although I get updates from Nancy, I still worry about him. Can you tell me what is happening in his life now?"

"Have you heard about Dr. Kashyap?"

He ran a hand on his head. "Of course, I have. I thought he was the one who had called Sacha to congratulate her for her news article."

"Yes, the same man. Fortunately, he is involved in the lives of both twins. Especially Isaac Jr." She said, sounding pleasant and warm. "By the way, I had led Dr. Kashyap to Isaac. As the Nordics had predicted, he will be very influential in Isaac's life."

"Tell me more, please!"

"I have no idea." Then she shrugged and got up. "Thanks for the breakfast. I'm sorry, but I need to leave."

"Wait, have some juice," Isaac spoke, but Emerald had already left by then.

§§§§§§§§§§

270

"Mom?"

"Sacha?" Nancy's voice was full of surprise... "How did you find me?"

But when Nancy went to the door, her smile left. It was not Sacha but Emerald.

"Hey,"

"Hi, Mom, were you expecting someone else?"

"Stop addressing me like that. Isaac Jr. might hear you."

Emerald's face had a shadow now. "He is out, and why can't I address you like that?"

"You know very well," Nancy spoke in an irritated manner now. Right now, her mind was focused on Sacha.

"So, all you can think about is just Sacha! Am I also not your daughter?"

"Emmy," Nancy's voice rose now. "What has gotten into you? Of course, you are!"

"No, Mom," despite being told by Nancy not to address her that way, Emerald still stuck with it. "I was just created as an experiment, and I am the property of my handlers. I can't do anything on my own. I have to follow their orders. I can't even address you as my mother."

271

Nancy got up and went to the other end of the room near the window. Turning her back to Emerald, she stared outside and then spoke. "Stop it, Emerald. We both know why you can't. But I do love and care for you. However, you must remember that you are not a two-year-old child anymore. Stop throwing such tantrums," Nancy turned towards Emerald.

"Why lie to me?" Emerald sounded as though she was going through an enormous pain. Love and care for me, huh?" And before Emerald could think, the words just left her mouth. "Forget about me; you can't even take care of your son!"

Nancy turned to her at once. "What happened to Isaac?"

Emerald never spoke without thinking; today was the first time she had revealed and said something she should not have said.

"Nothing, Mom," she lowered her head. But Nancy didn't buy it.

"Are you hiding something, Emmi?"

"I wonder that myself. Why do you ask me about him despite our more-or-less staying under the same roof? Anyway, Mr. Mehra, a well-known politician…"

Nancy raised her hand and stopped Emerald. "I know who he is; what did he do to Isaac?"

"He wanted Isaac's help to find the hidden oil—fossil fuel…"

"And?"

"And when Isaac refused, Mr. Mehra threatened him!"

"Oh my god," Nancy's hand stilled the slight quiver of her mouth. "I swear, Isaac never told me."

"That's not all!" Emerald said in a serious tone now. "When Isaac went to the Kondana caves a few days before, the thralls tried to kill him!"

Nancy walked towards Emerald now. "What are you saying? Was that the reason Isaac didn't return on time?"

Emerald nodded her head. "If not for Sacha, Isaac would have had a tough time beating that thrall with his beginner's superpower."

Nancy sat down on the couch. "I must tell his father."

"I won't take your time." Emerald got up. "I had just come to say that, just like the twins, I want to live on my terms. I am not going to support you either."

With that, she started walking…

"Wait, Emerald." Nancy stopped her. "How could you say that? You are not a human. You are a humanoid."

"A humanoid created to meet your needs. I am a humanoid, but you have forgotten I have your genes. Who said I don't have feelings?

You have worried about Sacha from the beginning. Because she doesn't stay with you. Have you ever worried about me?" She pointed a finger towards herself. "Do you think I am just a machine?"

Nancy couldn't believe her ears. Such an outburst from Emerald was unexpected, and as Emerald stormed out of the drawing room, Nancy realized Emerald was speaking the truth. She had indeed never worried about Emerald. And the pain of that truth hurt her like a sharp arrow. If Emerald backed out, then they were doomed for sure.

"It is not what you think, Emmy, it's not what you think…" Nancy kept repeating these words, but Emerald was nowhere near to hear them.

Chapter 39:
Sachas's Departure

Sacha was happy now. It was evident from the way she hummed. She was glad she had made the right decision after meeting Mr. Ghosh. Even her dad said the same. But, she refused to listen to him then. So, if there were a next time, she told herself to approach her dad before taking any drastic steps.

While humming at her desk, she writes her article to send to the office by tomorrow.

"The inequalities of climate change can make rich countries richer and poor countries poorer." She stopped humming and spoke her words to check their rhythm. "Warming weather and rising seas can create a sobering patchwork of economic imbalance. Hmm," she stopped writing and thought to herself. *Perhaps it can create a drop in prosperity levels as well. What actions are we going to take against this? Wait, I need to check my notes.*

Sacha got up and went to the bookshelf at the other end of her room, near her bed. She habitually made notes when she read something interesting or valuable. She fumbled through several arrays of books lined up neatly, and then, when she fetched the brown leather-bound diary, a small book dropped from the upper shelf.

She bent down and smiled when she noticed the colorful book was titled 'Hungry Caterpillar.'

She thought *silly me, still keeping the childhood memories* as she picked up the book. As she was about to put it back, memory took over her. A beautiful young woman with blonde hair and blue eyes kneeled before Sacha as she served breakfast.

A small, chubby boy also sat in a high chair before her.

"The Very Hungry Caterpillar went deep in the forest..." the woman's soothing sound echoed in Sacha's ears.

Was she her mom? If not, then who was she?

And who was that boy adamant about wanting the book that Sacha had liked so much?

Feeling uncomfortable now, Sacha sat on the edge of her bed and tried to clear her mind. But those images wouldn't go.

Who were those people?

What was her relationship with them?

Determined to find out, she rose quickly and went to her dad.

He was reading something; was it another a journal? As her footsteps came near, Isaac Sr. lifted his head and smiled at his daughter.

"I am so glad that you changed your..." His voice was enthusiastic, but she didn't let him complete his sentence.

"If I ask you something, will you answer me, Dad?"

Isaac Sr., noticing her grave voice and pale face, put the journal aside. "what's wrong, Sacha?"

"Where is my Mom, Dad?"

Her words hit Isaac like a bullet. He was unprepared for this question, and right now, he didn't know what to tell her because Sacha had never asked about her mother in detail.

"I have told you before. Your mom died in an accident after giving birth to you."

"If so, then who was the woman feeding me breakfast when I was young?" she asked at once. "She had blue eyes, blond hair..."

"It must be one of the caretakers." Isaac didn't know how to reply otherwise.

"That can't be!" This time, Sacha's voice was clear yet firm. "Because her love for me was visible on her face and smile," Sacha stated. "Are you hiding something from me, Dad?"

"Of course, not my baby. How can I?" Isaac replied and then handed her an unopened letter. "It came this morning. Must be one of your fan mails."

"This is from my college." She read the address and replied, "Oh, it must be about the coming exams. I am glad our principal is concerned about students doing well."

Apart from that, Isaac was happy that he had turned the conversation in another direction.

"I have to submit my article tomorrow and I can't concentrate. I was thinking of going to the office and completing it there."

"Okay," said Isaac as he picked up his journal again. And as Sacha went to her room, he sighed in relief. He had to discuss this with Nancy and would call her once Sacha left. Ignorant of the impending doom, Isaac again began reading his journal.

§§§§§§§§§§

It was clear that he was hiding something.

If not, why was there a hesitation in her dad's voice?

She didn't ask about her mom much, but she was a grown-up now. And she had full right to know what had happened to her.

Did her father still see her as a small child?

The thought was enough to disturb her.

Deciding to leave for Mr. Ghosh's office after a bath, Sacha sat on the bed and tore apart the envelope from her college.

Her eyes went to the typed letter, calculating how many days were left before the next exam.

But what was this?

It was not an exam schedule. But a letter to inform her that the college had decided to expel her.

```
Dear Sacha,

     We regretfully inform you that
given  your  actions  during  Mr.
Mathur's interview on TV about your
seminar   speech,    the   college
reviewed  its  policies  and  is
required  to  drop  you  from  this
```

academic year. As a reputable
university, we hope you understand
that the trustees must disavow
involvement in any controversy that
can harm the institute's reputation
or ability to attract donations.

"What the hell!" She muttered and rechecked the letter. The principal signed it.

No, what she read was correct. The college had indeed decided they wanted nothing to do with Sacha anymore.

She squashed the paper and threw it on the ground. Then she lowered her head, and silent tears started to drop from her eyes.

Nobody understood her.

Her father hid things.

This world didn't deserve her.

The thoughts kept coming one by one, making her resolve firmer with each passing second.

She had enough.

With a quick touch of her fingers, she wiped her tears and pulled down a small backpack from her wardrobe.

Chapter 40:

Generation Gap?

Isaac's belief that if he guided his children, they would save the world was shattered. He had made it his lifelong goal to raise the twins according to their destiny. And despite trying hard, he still failed at it.

His mind told him that Isaac Jr. and Sacha would return and discover their life purpose. But his heart had lost all hope by now. How and what was he going to tell Aundrid? That one of his children had run away while the other had been too scared to fight back? Since the day he had known his children had superpowers, Isaac had imagined them as superheroes.

"Again, blaming yourself?" Nancy's voice made Isaac Sr. lift his head. He tried to smile in response. But couldn't.

She pulled a chair up to the table and sat. This restaurant was usually not crowded in the afternoon, so she had asked him to this place.

She ordered beverages and lunch plates for each and then looked at her husband.

"Any news of Sacha?"

He took a deep breath. "No, not yet."

Their eyes met and she could see the pain, the helplessness in her husband's eyes. "Should we call the police?"

He raised his brow. "Umm, it just has been a day. I have already talked with Emerald. She vaguely indicated Sacha might be staying with one of her friends and will return once she realizes her mistake."

Nancy could see how undone he was, and her heart went to her husband. "You are not at fault. You have raised her very well." Nancy added and then sighed. "We can't be just sitting here idly until she returns to her senses. I wonder if things might have been different if I was around."

Isaac Sr. kept his hand on his wife's. "Don't talk like that. We did what we had to." And then he looked up at her. "She found one of her old storybooks and she remembered you!"

"Oh god, poor child. I can't imagine what she must have gone through! Did she come to you after that?"

He looked at her with a serious expression. "Of course she did." Isaac Sr. didn't mention that after Sacha's inquiry about Nancy that day, he had spent much time regaining his composure.

Isaac spoke quietly. "But then they are grown up now. You can't expect to hide things from them forever."

A waiter came back with their food. She had requested simple South Indian meals. But none of them had an appetite to eat much.

"I thought she had gone to the office, as she mentioned." Isaac took a spoonful of Sambhar (Indian lentil). "But when she didn't return at her usual time, I went to her room and found this letter."

Nancy stopped eating and read the letter at once. She looked stunned now. "This can't be happening to our child."

"I have no idea what to do now."

"We can't have her feel this vulnerable due to something deeply dear to her heart. That Mr. Mathur made a public scandal out of nothing."

Had Mr. Mathur been present at this table, Nancy would have given him something to regret. "And I thought he was helping her," she said.

"Sacha is still a child. Doesn't know who to trust. But I see this as my failure. I am a grown-up man. I should have known and protected my daughter…" His voice trailed.

"Stop beating yourself up, Isaac. We can't allow this to happen." Nancy pushed her plate away, rapidly ordering a coffee. "I am going to meet the principal tomorrow. Let me see if I can convince him to take her back."

"I am deeply concerned about our son as well. Did you know we crossed paths last week?"

Her eyebrows scrunched. "When? No, that boy doesn't tell me a single thing!"

"Mr. Shah's dog died under mysterious circumstances."

"Who? Your neighbor?"

He nodded. "Yes, the pet was healthy and not sick. Somehow, Mr. Shah found burn marks on his body and…"

Nancy almost stood up. "Burn marks?"

"Yes, do you recall what I remembered only now?"

"Of course, Isaac, how couldn't I? Someone was trying to kill me on Nautilus…" She paused and then drew in a sharp breath. "Oh my God, that means THEY know where you live!"

He tried to lighten the situation with a small laugh. But it didn't work. "Yes, they do, and Isaac had also seen the dog with burn marks."

"Did he recognize you?"

"I don't think so."

"Thank god for such small mercies. We can't have more issues now."

He took a sip of his coffee. "I know what you mean. What are we going to do about the twins?"

Nancy said. "We have been waiting for this moment for so many years. And we raised our children according to the Nordic's guidance, so that makes a difference."

"But suddenly, everything looks bleak. Yes, we put so much faith in their support. But, if the twins don't fight together, we will not win this war against the thralls and save mankind."

Then he went silent. He felt the pain of his damaged heart. Looking at his fallen face, Nancy didn't know what to say. "I believed in Emerald, but even she has issues with me."

"Is it us or them? Is it a generation gap, or have we failed as parents?" Isaac finally revealed what he had been thinking for days.

He continued, "Things have not worked as we wanted. Perhaps we overestimated our children or didn't prepare them enough. I wish I could tell my children who they are fighting! I feel so guilty about hiding things from them."

"Isaac…listen," she tried to reassure him. "Everything will be okay."

His voice was grave now. "What if something bad happens to any of them? I don't want to lose them, Nan. I don't want to fight with bad aliens anymore. Let's leave Mumbai and go back. At least we will be able to live as one family."

Chapter 41:

Mesmerizing Crystals

Although it was a bright Saturday morning, it did nothing to lift Isaac Jr.'s spirit. He was sick, sick of his life, sick of his college, his passion, and his family. Everything that his mom did or didn't irritate him nowadays. She asked him too much about his life or didn't take any interest. And that angered him further.

Once or twice, she had caught him talking to Dr. Kashyap. But luckily, Isaac Jr. evaded Nancy's inquiries about the caller. Thank God Amrita was not like that. She gave him space when he was lost in thoughts. And yet, reminded him that she was around if he ever needed her help. How lucky he was to find her.

Isaac Jr. was lost in thoughts when the doorbell buzzed. It was a courier for him.

"What is it?" Looking at the size of the packet, Nancy couldn't stop being curious.

"I don't know," he shrugged. "I was not expecting anything."

"Well, open it then!" Nancy said.

He nodded and tore open the package. His eyes widened when he saw a brand new expensive dowsing rod.

"Didn't you say you were not ready to take more cases?"

"Yeah," hiding his amusement from his mom, Isaac silently checked the attached card. When he read the name, he couldn't believe it. Dr. Kashyap had sent this dowsing rod to him.

"Who has sent it?"

"Umm, what, yeah, one of my old clients.."

How nice of Dr. Kashyap to send him what he wanted for a long time. How did he know his heart's desire?

She peered at him from her glasses. "Does he or she have a name?"

"Oh!" he laughed artificially now. "You won't know him, Mom." Then, he added without giving her any chance to question him more," Emerald and I are going to a birthday party this evening."

Before she could ask the name, he had already fled from the room.

"Don't I know the name of that friend?" She talked to the silent walls.

§§§§§§§§§§

It was late when Isaac Jr. returned home, and Nancy had already eaten.

Isaac Jr. went to his room after meeting and wishing her good night. He was floating in the air right now. Little did he know that the birthday party was Emerald's ploy to get him some quality time with Amrita.

Isaac Jr.'s heart skipped a beat and jumped wildly as Amrita entered the birthday party of 'not-so-common friends.' How was she invited there? Isaac had no clue; frankly, he didn't want care either.

Will he be able to sleep tonight? Isaac Jr. wondered as he tossed and turned on the bed for the night's hundredth time.

Isaac, Isaac...., Someone called him. It was Dr. Kashyap.

"Hello," he smiled at Dr. Kashyap.

Did you like my gift?

"Of course, um, thanks!"

No problem. Why don't we taste it? There is a small town situated at the junction of Asia and Europe. This was once considered an essential region in forming a complex

Aryan society. I am searching for some evidence of a lost
Neolithic civilization and need your help.

"What exactly should I do, Dr.?"

I want you to use your psychic levitation and travel
through the air, reach the place, and find what I am
looking for!

Isaac nodded slightly and then concentrated on the
details his spiritual guru gave.

He could feel his body lifting off the ground, and he
left the house through the large window of his room. He
didn't have time to think about how he could slide through
the window grid. Soon, he was soaring higher and higher.

The night got darker as he ascended towards his
destination. Isaac didn't know how long it was going to take
him. He didn't know the place or how he was supposed to
reach there and find what Dr. Kashyap was looking for. All
he had with him was his intuition.

The dark blanket of the hallowed night sky had
adorned itself with the pool of subtle light from the crescent
moon. He had never imagined exploring the world this way,
and it was funny.

The air grew thick and heavy as he crossed lands, farms, towns, cities, oceans, and continents.

Isaac Jr. was breathing heavily. He didn't know how much time had passed. All he could think of was about the ancient town Dr. Kashyap had talked about.

At last, he was there.

Finally landing on the deserted land, Isaac Jr. wiped the thin layer of sweat from his forehead and focused on the task.

He had the new dowsing rod with him. Closing his eyes, Isaac Jr. recalled what Dr. Kashyap had told him about the place.

After some time, he opened his eyes and started to walk slowly. The night was cold and scary in this part of the world. There was not a single soul visible in this part of the town. Isaac wondered if anyone lived here at some other point in time.

After roaming around, he was almost ready to give up when his rod pointed in a specific direction. Smiling in relief, Isaac walked until suddenly, his rod pointed down. He dug in the dirt.

He didn't have to try harder.

A small basket with mesmerizing crystals appeared under the soil, and he blinked.

Was this the treasure Dr. Kashyap was looking for?

Dr. Kashyap, Dr. Kashyap, look what I've got here! Isaac shouted in the silent night, knowing his mentor was nowhere around.

Those jewels brought an air of calm around him, and as he picked them up, Isaac Jr. felt as if all was well in his world. All his worries and woes had vanished in the thin air.

Give it to me! Dr. Kashyap's commanding voice shook him. How did he even manage to…

But before Isaac Jr. could inquire, Dr. Kashyap smiled and pointed a finger at a distant place.

Have you seen that?

Not knowing where he was leading him, Isaac Jr. walked to the place and felt his heart would explode in his body. Beads of sweat trickled down his brow, and fear sparked in his belly.

Lying alone on the sand was Isaac Jr.'s dead body!

And with a scream, he lost consciousness.

Chapter 42:

The Kashyap Question

His body wanted to run faster, yet he could not do so. Instead, he just stayed put where he was. He didn't have any weapons. And couldn't figure out what to do about what he was experiencing.

He reminded his brain that now was not the time to surrender—throw in the towel. But his excellent decision ability seemed offline, and fear clenched its deadly jaws around him.

Isaac Jr. thought he might die from the pain submerging his brain.

Was this a nightmare? It seemed more like a night terror to him.

Looking at Dr. Kashyap, he desperately screamed for help, but no one was near.

Isaac Jr. took a step back, not knowing what to do.

But yes, he had to go back; he had to go back to the place from where he had come.

He closed his eyes and concentrated heavily. Oddly, Dr. Kashyap's face didn't go away. Isaac kept waiting, but nothing happened.

"Isaac, Isaac…." someone was calling him.

"Wake up," this time he could hear it. It was his mom. Isaac Jr. opened his eyes.

"Why were you screaming?" She asked immediately.

"Nothing, Mom," he replied with zero emotion, wanting to hide the nightmare from her.

But his faltering voice and sweating forehead couldn't be hidden.

"Look at you; you are scared." Nancy went near her son now and touched his head. "Is everything alright? Would you like to talk?"

Isaac Jr. grew pale but decided not to disclose anything to his mom. He knew she might panic. Getting a hold of the situation, he sat on the bed. His calm demeanor surprised him. Just a few moments before, he was shouting for help.

Was he dreaming?

If it was a dream, why did it feel so real?

No, he could feel the wind, the travel, the different atmosphere, and the location.

It was not a dream.

But if it was not a dream, did that mean he had somehow managed to travel back safely?

And Dr. Kashyap? Hadn't he seen him in the dream?

Isaac Jr. got up from the bed and went to the room's far corner to get his dowsing rod.

It was still standing at the place he had left it last night.

And yet, oddly, he remembered fetching it from this very corner.

Luckily, Nancy had returned to the kitchen, most probably to get him breakfast, and Isaac Jr. sighed in relief.

Running his hand on the stick, Isaac Jr. noticed the emotions it generated in himself. It was as if he had traveled in a black hole, and there was no coming back. Something was off, and he had to get to the root of the problem.

He still didn't remember how he had come back from the desert. All he could remember was standing like a statue before his dry skeleton.

Did this mean he was going to die?

Or that someone was going to kill him?

But who?

The big question mark loomed before him, and Isaac Jr. started to take deep breaths after trying to calm himself.

Damn, it was Dr. Kashyap who had taught him the meditation.

Dr. Kashyap had appeared in his dream and asked for help. To locate those crystals.

Did those crystals hold any significance? They must; otherwise, why would Dr. Kashyap want his help to find them?

Dr. Kashyap was his mentor, the one he trusted unquestioningly. But was he hiding something from him?

Isaac Jr. recalled how and under what circumstances he had met Dr. Kashyap for the first time.

He banged his hand on the bed. He realized he had never thought how someone else could suddenly appear at that particular place, a historical site almost deserted.

Did this mean that someone was keeping an eye on him?

Did this mean that somebody knew he was alone in the caves?

That someone could be Dr. Kashyap himself!

The thought jolted Isaac Jr. He had never thought this way. Dr. Kashyap probably planned the whole thing because he wanted to use him.

Until now, Dr. Kashyap was pretending to be his guru. He needed Isaac's help; he was planning to kill him once he was done.

Many instances of his past lives danced in front of Isaac's eyes. He had stared at death numerous times.

Was Dr. Kashyap his enemy, and he couldn't even see that?

He was a fool who trusted people unquestioningly.

Was it just because he was young?

If yes, Dr. Kashyap didn't know what he had got himself into. Isaac Jr. might be young, but he had resources…

Cursing his naivety, Isaac went to the dresser and opened it. He was sure he had kept it there. But after going through the cupboard again, he needed more time.

"Damn," he muttered as he frantically rechecked the shelves. It had been a few months, but he recalled he had not tossed out the calling card.

Then where could it be?

Swearing again, he stopped checking his shelves methodically and lifted a pile of clothes. A rectangular card fell.

As Isaac Jr. lifted it, a big smile spread on his lips. There! He had found a way to deal with Dr. Kashyap.

§§§§§§§§§

"He has been behaving strangely," Nancy spoke the whole sentence in one breath. "No, I could feel something wrong with him."

There was some reply at the other end.

"No, I don't think we can wait so long. Please come now. I need help!"

She set the telephone down without waiting for the person at the other end to answer. Her son was already troubled. She didn't want to add to his doubts. But one thing was sure: nobody would touch her son while she was alive.

With this resolve, she smiled brightly and knocked on Isaac's door with the breakfast.

Chapter 43:

Take Care of Kashyap

He had been miserable, and food was the last thing on his mind. But Isaac Jr. let his mom put the tray on the table.

As he turned his back, she asked. "Are you not going to college?"

"Yeah, in a while." He replied in an instant. "I'm not attending the first lecture because the professor will be absent!"

"Okay," she took a step and turned her back, starting to walk. Then she turned towards him again. "And who did you say sent the dowsing rod?"

"Oh, Mom, did you join the Covert Ops Force overnight?" He always teased her out of uncomfortable questions.

"Well, inquiring about their children is every parent's birthright, and you will…."

"Only understand when you become a parent yourself!" He completed her sentence, stopping her midway, and smiled, hoping he successfully hid his crummy mood from her.

And as he wished, Nancy smiled and left the room.

He couldn't read what was going on in her mind, though!

Once she was gone, Isaac closed the door and removed the card from his pocket. Then he silently went to the telephone and started dialing the number.

The call was answered on the first ring.

"Mr. Mehra's office," a polite yet stern voice replied at the other end.

"Can I speak to Mr. Mehra? I am Isaac."

As if he had spoken a magical word, the line was passed to Mr. Mehra immediately. Isaac Jr. had little time to consider how the famous politician could take his call.

"Hello, Isaac," he greeted him. "So you have thought about my proposal."

It was not a question but rather an affirmative statement, an assumptive close on a deal.

Isaac Jr. was taken aback for a moment. He gulped when Mr. Mehra added. "So, do you agree to help me?"

"Only on one condition," Isaac spoke quietly.

"I can give you anything you want!" Mr. Mehra's voice was almost gleeful now. "Let's meet. My chauffeur will pick you up in half an hour."

"No, no," Isaac hesitated as he stared outside through his window.

All hell would break loose if his mom watched him sitting in Mr. Mehra's luxurious car.

He swore that this was the last time he was helping Mr. Mehra. It was the last time he was ever going to call him again.

Somewhere deep inside his soul, a voice stirred.

What are you going to do, Isaac? Stop right now!

But today, Isaac Jr. was not in the mood to hear the words of his conscience.

"But we need to discuss the matter." Mr. Mehra sounded impatient now. "Look, Isaac, you might not know, but I am a busy man, and I hope you are not playing games with me."

"Of course not, Mr. Mehra," Isaac interjected but then took time to continue as his mind protested the whole thing.

Ignoring it, Isaac spoke. "I just need to know the details of the place."

"That's it?" Mr. Mehra's voice sounded exclamatory now. "What else do you need?"

Taking one look at his dowsing rod, Isaac said. "Nothing; I have everything I need."

"Very good, then when can you start?"

"How about now?" The words left Isaac's mouth even before he could think about them.

"You won't change your mind, right?"

"How can I? Of course not. You can trust me."

"Good. Then my secretary will explain everything to you. Are you sure you don't need to travel anywhere?"

"No, Mr. Mehra, just give me an hour, and I'm sure I'll get back with the results."

"I like your confidence." Mr. Mehra added. "Remember, if you failed to deliver…"

"There is no chance of that!" Isaac cut him short. He was in a hurry.

"And how am I supposed to pay you?"

Isaac was flustered at the question. He knew what he wanted, and yet, he didn't speak.

A few moments passed.

"Isaac, are you there?" Mr. Mehra's impatient voice had risen a little.

Was he crazy to think this way?

But he wasn't the only person who wanted to harm his enemy.

He coughed. It had not taken him long to solve his dilemma.

"I want you to take care of a man."

"What's his name?"

"Dr. Kashyap."

"Consider it done."

"Remember, I should not be involved, anyway."

There was a laugh at the other end.

"You don't know me, Isaac. You have no reason to worry."

Then Mr. Mehra gave the phone to his subordinate, who gave the needed instructions to Isaac.

Had he done the right thing?

Was he misusing his power to help a man like Mr. Mehra?

But it was done. Isaac would not take back his words.

He opened his encyclopedia and started to read about the given location. Knowing the place helped him.

After an hour, Isaac was ready to use his dowsing rod.

He was so lost in his work that he didn't realize someone was knocking. When he didn't get up to open the door, the sound got louder. The person was in a hurry to meet him.

Not able to neglect it anymore, Isaac reluctantly stopped working. He put his dowsing rod aside and opened the door.

Emerald was standing with a man he had not seen before.

"What are you doing here?"

"Isaac, listen," she was looking for words. "You have to come with me."

"Where?" His eyes widened. "And who is this man?"

"Amrita is not well; she is in the hospital."

"What? But we talked last night. How? What happened to her?"

"I can answer all your questions. But we need to leave right now."

"Where?" Isaac was unable to think straight. He still had to give the locations of oil fields to Mr. Mehra.

"Isaac, can we talk on the way?" Emerald was irritated now. "Come on now, my uncle will drive us there!"

"Your uncle?"

"Yes, he came from the U.S. this morning. I thought he might help," she threw her hands up. "You know, with hospital and all those formalities…"

"Okay, okay. Let me inform Mom."

"I have already told her. Now hurry up, Isaac. You don't want to lose a single minute."

Isaac stole a look at his dowsing rod while his mind was a whirlpool of thinking about Mr. Mehra, his words, Dr. Kashyap, and Amrita.

As he followed them outside, one more thought struck. He had seen this man somewhere. But where?

As he slipped into the backseat of the car, Isaac remembered this man was around when his neighbor's dog had died under mysterious circumstances. But then Emerald said he was her uncle and had just come from the U.S.

Was she lying?

Who was this man?

What had happened to Amrita?

And how was he going to complete his work in an hour now?

Isaac's mind worked even faster than the car's turning wheels as he sat silently, looking outside the rear-view window.

Chapter 44:
The Truth

The evening sky enchanted the earth with beautiful hues of oranges and purples.

But they did nothing to lessen the anxiety Isaac had been feeling now. Emerald's uncle was driving with utter serenity as if nothing had happened. If they had to hurry, then why was he not going faster?

"Can we go faster" Isaac bristled under his breath, and Emerald's uncle nodded, although he didn't speed up.

Muttering a curse, Isaac started to think about the events that had happened this morning. Looking at how the day had turned for him, Isaac Jr. could now see it was unlike any other.

Was this event related to his dream? Or rather, the reality-like invention? He didn't know.

And there was even less chance that Emerald or anyone else knew what had happened to Amrita.

Isaac Jr. couldn't understand why they failed to talk with his mom just because Emerald mentioned she had already informed her. And by listening to Emerald's tone of voice, Isaac figured Amrita must be diagnosed with some dangerous disease.

"Can we talk now?" He turned his head and looked at Emerald sitting in the backseat.

"What did you want to know?"

"How about telling me where Amrita was admitted for a starter?"

"Why are you so worried? I am taking you there."

Isaac Jr. noticed that the car turned off the highway near Lonavala as the evening grew darker. He started to ask where they were going when his eyes caught the truth. Emerald's uncle was driving towards Kondana, the small village near the Kondana Caves where Dr. Kashyap lived.

Was Amrita being treated here? He couldn't believe it!

The suspense mounted with each passing moment, and Isaac finally breathed when the car stopped at Dr. Kashyap's residence. He would get all the answers he needed now.

But the dogged Isaac Jr. needed to prepare for what he saw now. Dressed in her usual white Salwar and Kameez, Amrita opened the gate with a big smile as if she knew he was supposed to come!

She didn't look sick at all!

"What's going on Emerald?" Isaac recalled his anxiety and stress in these past few hours and wanted to take it out on his cousin.

He stepped towards Amrita when Emerald said, "Follow me!" Her tone was not commanding yet profound. Then she gestured for Amrita to take her uncle inside.

Not knowing what else to do, Isaac Jr. followed Emerald, who had easily entered the house, belying she was not a visitor.

They entered the room where Dr. Kashyap was sitting. As soon as he saw them, he got up.

"Hi Isaac, how are you?"

Remembering last night's incident, Isaac's body stiffened as he smiled at his mentor.

Can anyone even know there was a murderer hidden behind his welcoming face?

But why would he want to kill me? His brain asked one more time.

Isaac sat on the couch sighing, and Dr. Kashyap cleared his throat. "Nothing is wrong with Amrita; she is good, as you saw, and yes, I know you have many questions, and that's why Emerald has brought you here."

"But why this lie? Emerald could have told me face to face that you wanted to meet me."

"She could have, but I am afraid you might not have trusted her after last night's incident."

Isaac Jr. got up from his chair. "What are you talking about?"

"Isaac, please sit down!" Dr. Kashyap instructed him in a clear voice. "Don't look so surprised! I think people who know the powers of yoga shouldn't be so shocked at how deep minds can go!"

Why was Dr. Kashyap talking in riddles? Isaac Jr. shifted uncomfortably in his chair when Emerald added," Dr. Kashyap had not gifted that dowsing rod to you, Isaac."

Isaac almost failed to manage his shock once more. "He didn't?"

"Nope!"

"Then who? *Oh my God!*" He jerked his hand to his forehead in despair.

Could Mr. Mehra himself have deceived him with his Guru's name?

Possible!

What a fool he was! One trick and he had fallen for that cunning politician's trap.

Things were not what he had imagined them to be. With regret, he told Dr. Kashyap how he had received it. Isaac Jr. was quite ashamed when he remembered his talk with Mr. Mehra.

He was about to tell Mr. Mehra to kill Dr. Kashyap, and thank God, he didn't. How foolish he was. Where was his common sense?

"I didn't call you here so you can self-sabotage yourself, Isaac." Dr. Kashyap's voice brought him back to reality. "I had an intuition that someone was trying to kill me."

"I won't let anything happen to you," the words fell out of Isaac's mouth.

Smiling as he shrugged off Isaac's comment, Dr. Kashyap added, "Nobody can stop destiny; never forget it, Isaac. That's why I have had you here; I need to tell you some secrets that will be safe with you if I am no more!"

Isaac thought for a minute. Things were happening so fast that even he could not grasp them.

"We don't have much time." Dr. Kashyap added.

"I don't know what you are talking about, Dr." Isaac Jr. sounded panicked as he glanced at the Doctor, noticing that Emerald had entered with her uncle.

When had she disappeared?

Isaac could easily imagine he was lost and confused, still praying it would all go away when Dr. Kashyap gestured toward Emerald's uncle. "Isaac, meet my friend, Ian; if I am gone, you can trust him. I have known him for a long time, and he would help you."

Isaac stood up and shook his hand with Ian, still dazed at the events' turn.

Still, things were not adding up; how could Emerald's uncle be Dr. Kashyap's friend?

"Promise me, you will not hesitate to go to him," Dr. Kashyap insisted.

Not knowing what else to do, with a choked voice, Isaac Jr. said, 'Yes".

For the hundredth time that day, he couldn't understand why he felt he was not meeting Ian for the first time.

And, Isaac Jr. remembered: *I must call Mr. Mehra immediately; otherwise, he'll be furious for not getting the dowsing locations he wanted.....*

"Let's eat and then sleep; we have a big day tomorrow." Dr. Kashyap spoke as if nothing had happened. "I want to take you to a special place."

Chapter 45:
Under One Roof

"We have brought them both under one roof," Ian spoke. "I don't know how long they will stay like this?"

He waited a few moments to hear what the person at the other end was saying. "Yes, but while our son knows, Sacha doesn't know anything. Will their minds work in the same way, in perfect synchronization?"

It was not good to eavesdrop on somebody, but he didn't do it intentionally, Isaac Jr. thought after getting up to fetch a glass of water, and hearing Ian's conversation on the phone. He returned to his room and stretched his tired body. The night was heavy, filled with secrets.

Unaware of Isaac Jr.'s presence, Ian had continued talking. Later, Isaac Jr. processed what he heard.

What was he talking about? Ian sounded strange. Anyway, it was none of his business.

Why was Dr. Kashyap saying that he had an inkling of his death? Did Amrita know that?

And what did he want to share with me? Why was there such an urgency that Dr. Kashyap had to call me on a false pretext here?

The questions kept Isaac Jr. awake. This was the longest night of his life. With so many people around, it was difficult to contact Mr. Mehra, and this troubled Isaac Jr. He wished the night would end so he could get the answers he needed.

But somehow, sleep eluded him. He was sure he had to play some role in Dr. Kashyap's destiny. But what?

§§§§§§§§§§

"Isaac, Isaac…" Amrita woke him the following day. "Get up, it's already eight."

Rubbing his eyes, he sat up. "Couldn't sleep last night!"

"Everyone is waiting for you at the breakfast table," she smiled.

Did she know about her dad's intuition?

What would happen to her if… no, he must not think like that. If someone were trying to kill his mentor, he wouldn't let them.

When he went down, Emerald and Ian were already having their coffee.

"Where is Dr. Kashyap?" He asked Amrita as he fetched a cup.

"Dad gets up early when he is here," she replied. "He loves to take a walk near the caves."

Isaac Jr. frowned. This must be a routine for Dr. Kashyap, but Isaac Jr. started to feel uneasy at the thought of Dr. Kashyap all alone near that deserted area.

"What time did he leave?"

"Over an hour ago. He'll be back any time now." Amrita informed him.

But Isaac's mind was already on another track.

If he left now, it would be too late. No, he will have to use another method to reach Dr. K.

"Excuse me," he stood up. "I had some urgent work."

"At least finish your coffee..." Emerald suddenly spoke. But those words were useless as her cousin had already left the room.

§§§§§§§§§

It gave him solace to know the place; otherwise, teleportation wouldn't have been possible.

This effort was going to take a toll on his mental energy. But right now, there was no other way.

Isaac Jr. wiped his brow. He was not comfortable using his power. Pushing his fear away, he closed his eyes and remembered the place with all the minute details where he had met Dr. Kashyap for the first time.

Beads of sweat appeared on his forehead, and his body grew hot, but there was no looking back now. His body felt so heavy, but he still wouldn't give up. Isaac Jr. imagined walking on the rocky terrain and was there before he knew what was happening!

However, the scene he faced took his breath away. Dangerous, fiery smoke and dust had settled in, and the ground beneath him shook.

It didn't take long to understand that the mines someone set in the mountains were exploding now, and Dr. Kashyap was somewhere there.

"Dr. Kashyap," Isaac Jr. shouted," Where are you?"

There was no reply.

He felt jittery and robbed of energy, but where was his mentor?

Isaac Jr. took one more step when new flashes lit up the sky where the mines exploded!

He could smell the incandescent radioactive gasses and the threatening fire. He had to wet it down.

Isaac Jr. summoned his power and energy to bring rain. When a single drop hit his face, he smiled a little, hoping to get rid of the fire soon.

But his hope turned into despair when a heavy storm came out of nowhere. Dust whipped up into the air, almost blinding him. The wind howled like some horror movie opening scene, and Isaac cursed.

Even nature was against him today.

Visibility went to zero, and he could still hear the explosions nearby. He coughed when he inhaled the suffocating smoke and glanced ahead, determined to walk no matter what.

He shook as the temperature rose. Amid the scorching, unfettered flames, he saw lifeless charcoaled trees that were lush green a few minutes before.

And there, lying on the ground, he saw what he never wanted to see!

The explosion had taken what was alive, and all he had was regret for that life taken.

"Dr. Kashyap," he ran towards the body now.

As he looked at the remains of his mentor, Isaac crashed to the ground, holding his head in his hands.

He was a terrible and worthless person.

Dr. Kashyap had already warned him about his death, and now Isaac was so near. And yet, he couldn't do anything to save him.

Yes, he couldn't be trusted with responsibility; he could only see the disaster, not stop it!

And Dr. Kashyap wanted to talk with him.

Many secrets had died with Dr. Kashyap.

The thoughts invaded Isaac Jr. as he cried.

Why had nobody informed them about the high-powered explosive detonating near the mountains?

Was it an accident or a murder?

The mere thought was enough to chill his bones as Isaac Jr. felt weak and helpless, half due to the efforts of teleportation and half due to his failure to arrive on time.

Chapter 46:
Schumann Resonance

Isaac couldn't be blamed for his current mental state after what happened to his mentor. Echoing his present mood, a storm started to rage. And it was still going strong, unlike himself.

In the aftermath of Dr. Kashyap's untimely death, or rather a murder, Isaac Jr.'s perspective on the world changed entirely.

It was as if he had fully matured overnight.

Will he ever forget the lifeless body of his guru, lying on the ground, before he could reach him?

Or the tear-stricken face of Amrita, who was inconsolable?

No, he had to find out who was responsible for Dr. Kashyap's death. Until then, his anguished heart would never know peace.

Dr. Kashyap's last words to him still echoed in his ears, *"Nobody can stop destiny; never forget it, Isaac. That's why I have had you here; I need to tell you some secrets that will be safe with you if I am no more!"*

He was already late. Late in saving Dr. Kashyap, late in placing his trust in him. Late in not letting Amrita have her beloved father around. Time was already running out, and he knew nothing. He shouldn't waste more time now. He had to take action, but what?

While he was still lost in thoughts, Nancy entered the room. "I have been thinking about Amrita. My heart goes to that poor girl."

He turned to her. "She is a strong girl."

"I suppose. But she is too young." Her face fell. "Agreed, she doesn't have a choice. But losing her only parent is tough to endure."

"Maybe Emerald can invite her to stay with her." Isaac Jr. added, hoping this would solace his Mom.

"I can do it, yeah," Emerald nodded as she offered a cup of coffee to her cousin. "But I still can't believe Dr. Kashyap is gone." She spoke in a low voice.

"Thanks, Em." Isaac Jr. sighed. "Imagine, he already knew about the future."

"Have you thought about what things he wanted to share with you?" Emerald asked him.

"Many times," he added. "And yet I don't have a single clue."

"Why don't we ask Amrita?" Emerald stirred her coffee as she looked at Isaac Jr. "What if Dr. Kashyap kept a diary, journal, or something like that?"

Isaac Jr. pursed his lips. "I don't know Em. That looks like a far-fetched idea."

"But there is no harm in trying, right?" She placed her coffee cup on the side table. "Wait, I am going to call her right now."

"There is no need," Amrita's somber sound filled the room. Isaac Jr. cast his eyes toward her, and his heart broke again at what he saw.

Amrita was leaning against the door frame, her fingertips gripping the edge as if she feared falling, and Isaac Jr.'s heart missed a beat. Emotional pain flowed out of every pore of his being when he looked at her sad face.

Taking a slow step in his direction, Amrita extended a small black diary to Isaac Jr. "I also thought that Papa might have left some clues. Ian and I started to go through the books in the library, and he found this."

Ian, who was standing behind Amrita, stepped in now. "Dr. Kashyap has some fascinating theory about the Schumann Resonance, and I want you to go through it."

"Thanks, Ian." Isaac Jr. murmured. "Why don't we meet tomorrow morning? I can go through the content, and we can discuss the next step."

"Of course," Ian declared his agreement. "Good night." And he proceeded to exit the room. Nancy followed him, leaving her son, Emerald, and Amrita alone.

Once they were far from them, Nancy spoke in a low voice.

"Are you sure you want our son to know about Dr. Kashyap's secret?"

"I don't have a choice, Nancy. Strengthening the 7.87 Hertz Schumann Resonance is the key to saving humanity. It supports the brain's alpha rhythm. Less alpha means more fear. And as Dr. Kashyap discovered, the enhanced fear among humans creates greed that results in denial of obviously human-created global warming."

They were in the sitting room now. The sky, gray, like a coal miner's handkerchief, loomed low, closing in on the world.

"If what you and Dr. Kashyap say is true, our planet is in great danger." Nancy looked at her husband with worrisome eyes. "But how do we make the Schumann Resonance stronger?" She rubbed her forehead. "I mean, who is going to believe us? Moreover, we don't have more information."

"We don't, but others can help us out. Research in Japan shows that as the Schumann Resonance fluctuates weaker, blood pressure increases. Pretty strong evidence."

Her eyes shined for a couple of seconds. "There are others?"

Isaac Sr.'s face broke into a slight smile now. "I already spoke with Aundrid."

"Dear god, how did I forget he might have the solution!"

"Indeed, he has. That guy is amazing if I say so." Isaac Sr. looked at his wife now. "According to him, an important crystal field near the North Pole was neutralized by altering the electromagnetic field that arises from the liquid iron core of the earth."

"North Pole? The liquid iron core of the earth?" She repeated. "Who can touch and play around with something like that?"

"Who else?" He added. "Our old enemy."

"Oh my god, thralls!" She almost got up. "What are we going to do now?"

"Aundrid was also working on that. I suppose he has solved the riddle by now."

Chapter 47:
Aundrid's Plan

"Are you sure this is safe? What if Isaac catches us?" Nancy looked at her husband with concern. "Calling Aundrid right now could reveal what we hid from our son."

"Hold on, Nan. Given Dr. Kashyap's death, you might be overreacting. Don't worry, I already spoke to Emerald."

Isaac Sr. reassured her," Emerald knows we need time to chat with Aundrid. She and Amrita will keep him occupied for a couple of minutes."

Nancy nodded half-heartedly. The last few days were stressful for all of them. No one saw this coming, and despite trying her psychic best, she could not envision any solution to fixing the crystal field and upping the Schumann Resonance energy level.

On the other hand, she did see the denialism and political backsliding if the thralls' strategy weakened more people worldwide.

"Do you think Aundrid knows what to do?"

"I'm sure he has some trick up his sleeve." Isaac Sr. told her. "Let's call and find out."

Nancy didn't have much choice. She followed Isaac Sr. to a vacant room far from where the children discussed their next steps.

It was good that she had the foresight to carry the special ornate box with her.

Not wasting any time, she took out the hairlock, and as if he was waiting for their call, Aundrid's sad face appeared on one of the empty walls.

"Aundrid," she greeted him.

"Hello, Nancy, how are you doing?"

"Not great, somehow holding on." she quickly replied. "I am puzzled by what my husband just said."

"Yes, the thralls managed to diminish the Schumann Resonance."

I bet they did, she spoke to herself. "I'm unsure if we still know how powerful they are."

"Yes, well, you already know that they did some attacks on us."

Nancy sighed as she looked at Aundrid. "I don't doubt it after the recent tragedy."

"But don't forget we have Sacha and Isaac Jr. on our side."

"I believe they have powers. But I have no idea how they will fight against them."

"They are the only people who can save the planet," Aundrid added. "But even they will need some help."

"What kind of help, Aundrid?" Nancy turned to her husband. "We are here for them, right? But I'm worried about the Schumann Resonance being throttled down. If we don't neutralize the thrall controls soon, our civilization will be crippled by irrational, fearful human actions."

"What would you guys say if I told you the answer to that riddle lies with you."

"Me? I don't get you, Aundrid."

"Remember your North Pole journey?"

Nancy took a step in Aundrid's direction. "Well…I.. Yes, we did. Wait, you mean…But it can't be that!"

"Why not? You are right. I am talking about the UFO lying on the floor of the Arctic Ocean."

"I never thought about it," Nancy spoke in haste. "But how can that help us?"

Aundrid flicked a switch, and the screen went black for a few seconds. And then it filled up with the picture of the UFO resting on the sea floor.

It had been a lifetime since the Nautilus had deposited it there. What a journey. Her eyebrows scrunched as she observed it. So many memories came flooding at once.

The UFO disappeared, and Aundrid's face appeared on the screen again. "You remember how you had triggered the MayDay signal?"

"Yeah."

"My team worked on it. They calculated that on a day when the moon eclipses the sun, simply triggering the MayDay signal solves the problem.

The UFO MayDay event sends out transponder energy that re-invigorates the Arctic crystal field. The crystal field then normalizes, allowing the Earth's magnetic liquid iron core to return the Schumann Resonance to the higher levels needed for reduced-fear living."

Her mouth opened in awe as she stared at Aundrid. "Gosh, how did they reach that conclusion?"

A small laugh escaped Aundrid's lips. "That's a big story. They were pretty sure about it, and I am proud of them."

"I guess the weight on my shoulders feels lighter after hearing this." She spoke at once. Then halted. "So, you are saying that all I have to do is send a MayDay signal to save our planet."

"Luckily, the moon eclipse comes in just four days, so we don't have to wait long."

"Then what's the problem? I can start reaching for the UFO at once."

"Nancy, are you sure you can do that?" Isaac Sr. came forward this time.

"Why not? Wait, let me show you." With that, Nancy sat on the nearby chair and closed her eyes. Aundrid and Isaac Sr. were silent as she focused on the image Aundrid had shown a few minutes before.

Seconds turned into minutes, and heat rushed in her limbs as she fought harder to access the UFO. Sweat appeared on her forehead, but nothing happened.

After a couple of minutes, she opened her eyes. "Sorry guys, something is not working. I tried very hard. But there is a wall between the UFO and me that I can't penetrate."

"It's not a riddle," said Aundrid. "Your teleportation powers can't extend from your location to the North Pole."

"Oh my god, yes, you are right. The North Pole is quite far; I didn't think of that." Nancy bit her lower lip. "What would we do? The moon eclipse is just four days away, and we are running out of time."

"And that's where I suggest we involve the children in this," Aundrid said. "I realize that is the only way."

A few worry lines appeared on Nancy's forehead now. "No, Aundrid. I don't think that's a good idea. The twins don't know our past, our history. Until now, we have never told them the story of their birth."

"Or the circumstances under which they were born." Isaac Sr. spoke now. "Even though Sacha has tried several times, I haven't told her anything."

Nancy nodded to her husband.

"But we don't have a choice. Don't you see?" Aundrid threw his tiny hands in the air as a gesture.

." We don't have to tell Isaac Jr. everything," Isaac said. "After reading Dr. Kashyap's diary, I am sure he would know about the reduced power of the Schumann Resonance. Just ask him to teleport there with his dowsing rod, find the UFO...."

"And follow my instructions to trigger the MayDay signal during the moon eclipse?" Nancy couldn't stop herself. "I know, Isaac. I don't think he will take my request at face value without wanting to know the truth first. What if he asks who lowered the Schumann Resonance? What am I supposed to tell him?"

Aundrid spoke. "We can find a way to ensure our secrets remain safe."

"Are you sure?" Nancy asked him. "Do you think my son could teleport to the North Pole?"

Aundrid sighed. "Don't you know about the special powers he has? And if needed, we can get Sacha and Emerald involved, too."

"Hmm, but there is still one problem. "What if he, too, can't access it and fails like me?" She asked. "You are sure that triggering a MayDay signal from the UFO during the moon eclipse has no consequences?"

"Isaac did have a couple of experiences in the past." Aundrid reminded her. "Don't forget that he was born to do this."

"Teleporting to the North Pole is a big thing." Nancy narrowed her eyes. "Even for him. But he would do it if we told him the truth. Just tell me one thing. What are you going to do to keep the secrets safe?"

"If you wish, I can make him forget about the whole event afterward," Aundrid told her.

"Oh, I forgot about your technologies. Well, then, it is settled. I am ready to answer his questions." Nancy took a deep breath. "I hope your scientists haven't messed up the calculations."

"Don't worry." With that, Aundrid waved his bluish hand as a gesture of goodbye, and the screen went blank.

Chapter 48:

When Do We Start, Mom?

"We shouldn't waste more time." As soon as Aundrid left, Nancy turned to her husband.

"Yes, but how do we bring this entire thing up to Isaac?" Isaac Sr. revealed his uncertainty.

"What thing?" This sudden statement caught the duo unaware. When they turned to the voice, they froze in place. Their son stood before them, along with Emerald.

"Umm, Isaac…" Nancy frowned, not knowing how to handle the situation. One thing was for sure: her son would not accept a fake explanation. She smiled and led him to the chair, buying more time. "I need to talk with you."

"Why don't I get us some coffee?" Emerald quipped.

"Great idea," Ian spoke. "I'll help." As they left, Isaac Sr. gestured to his wife to put the show on the road.

Slightly nodding, Nancy sat in before her son. "Did you have time to go through Dr. Kashyap's diary?"

"Not much, but I just now read a couple of pages where he talked about the Schumann Resonance."

"It is connected to all humans, and someone out there wants to kill the human race," Nancy added.

"Don't talk in riddles. Please, Mom. I am not a kid anymore."

Looking at her son's face, she knew he was right, and he had a right to know.

"Isaac," her voice filled with concern. "Someone, consider them our enemy, has neutralized the Schumann Resonance, and if we don't get it up to the normal range…"

"We are done." He cut her in the middle and completed the sentence. "My question is, who has the power to reach the core of the Earth?"

Nancy hesitated, watched the door, and as if on the clue, Emerald entered with the tray.

"Thrills!" she added. "Bad aliens who want to rule the Mother Earth."

As soon as she had finished the sentence, a hearty laugh escaped Isaac Jr.'s throat. "Stop joking around, cousin, and by the way, it was quite lame. I have seen aliens only in movies and books."

"Unfortunately, some among us won't think twice before destroying what belongs to everyone." Nancy's voice was grave. "They are ruthless and devoid of any kind of feelings."

"And do you want me to believe that? Come on, Mom, give me some credit for seeing right versus wrong." Isaac Jr.'s eyes met Nancy's, conveying his disbelief.

Standing at the door, Isaac Senior, AKA Ian, interjected, "Don't you recall the attack on you during Holi?" And after saying it, he immediately winced.

"Wait," Isaac Jr. took a step in his direction. "How do you know that?"

Nancy sighed silently as she rubbed her forehead, and then she came up with a reply. "Why, Emerald must have spoken about it to Ian."

Then she looked at her daughter.

"Of course." Emerald caught on quickly. "I found the event funny. I couldn't help telling my uncle."

"I see," Isaac Jr. rubbed his forehead, as well, and Nancy looked at her husband helplessly. "So you mean to say that the bad aliens, the **thrills**, wanted to kill me?"

"Exactly!"

"Why, Mom? I am not their enemy…"

And knowing full well that she didn't have a choice, Nancy took his hand. "Yes, you are my child; yes, you are."

Not mincing the truth this time, she took a deep breath. "You were born on a submarine called 'Nautilus 'at the North Pole … under the influence of the Pole Star and a UFO."

Her son opened his mouth to say something when she stopped him. "And due to the special circumstances, you were born with special powers…"

Issac Jr. got up. "Submarine? Pole Star. What are you talking about?"

She gulped. "At your birth, I knew nothing about those powers. But as you grew up, I realized you were unlike other children your age."

"What were you doing on the submarine, Mom?" Isaac Jr.'s voice was low as his eyes met hers, demanding answers. "Where is my father? And why did you hide these events?"

A sob escaped Nancy's voice as she instinctively understood how her son was hurting. "Trust me, I had my reasons…trust me, please." As she pleaded, her eyes were wet.

But this did nothing to calm her son, who was on the verge of cracking up. "It sounds like you and I were a part of some conspiracy theory. I didn't expect this from you, Mom."

Nancy started to cry now. She knew the skeleton in her closet would only generate pain for her son. But she had no choice. She had to do this. If her son started to hate her for keeping this a secret, she would have to deal with it.

She wiped her eyes and cleared her throat. "I agree. I have hidden things from you for your good—you and your sister." She clutched his hand and made him sit again. "Yes, your father was with me then, and trust me, we were so happy to have you."

With that, Nancy narrated her past to her son, leaving out details like her husband and her other daughter.

She didn't even know when Ian and Emerald had left them. This was her moment, and she had to reveal things that weighed on her chest for many years.

"I am sorry, I couldn't speak about this when you were growing up. Seeing your special powers scared me, and I wanted to protect you at all costs. I hope you get that."

When there was no reply, she added. "I just want to tell you this is not about me or you or your father. But it's even bigger than that. And the time has come when we must repay the planet."

"What are you hinting at?"

"Listen," she slipped near. "If I can somehow send a MayDay signal from the UFO lying on the floor of the Arctic Ocean right at the North Pole, the Schumann Resonance can be restored. But unfortunately, I can't do it by myself, I need your help. Are you with me?"

She extended her hand to him. He didn't reply as he stared far at the horizon and even as her heart went to him. Her son was still a child, and he had to deal with so much in a single night.

She waited patiently, watching him as his face reflected the dilemmas he was facing. At the same time, she prayed that although she had not told him about his birth before tonight, she wouldn't have to pay so much for that. She hoped that her son would understand her circumstances and see beyond the temporary anger that he felt right now.

Her heart was in her mouth as she closed her eyes and prayed—praying to God that she wouldn't lose her son.

She was praying to God to show him the proper direction and praying to God for the well-being of others.

After what seemed like hours, a robust and masculine hand clutched her soft, warm palms, enveloping her in his warmth. "So when do we start, Mom?"

Nancy's eyes opened immediately, and she started to cry again, thanking God. Not able to see her breaking up like this, Isaac Sr., who had returned, wrapped her in his arms, and she sobbed and sobbed...

If they were together, nobody had the power to harm the Earth.

Chapter 49:
Off to the Caves

"What did you say your name was?" Amrita spoke to the man standing at her doorstep.

"Chopra," the man smiled, revealing his crooked teeth, colored by overeating paan (betel leaves prepared and used as a stimulant.). "Your father was my boss's best friend."

Looking at his outrageous clothes, she doubted it. Her father would never befriend someone like this fellow. But then he was talking about his boss. Not himself.

Isaac Jr. and Nancy two days ago. Although Emerald and Ian were around, she was alone at the house right now.

"I am sorry, I am getting a little forgetful." She made way for the man to enter. "Please, come inside. Have a seat."

The man followed her, sat, and when she started to ask more questions, he took out an old yellowed black and white photograph from his bag. "See, this is your father, and here is my boss, Mr. Mehra."

Mehra. She had not heard that name before. But she still extended her hand to check the picture. Standing beside a man in a suit, it was indeed her father.

When she didn't say anything, the man spoke. "Dr. Kashyap and Mr. Mehra were in talks to do something about the global warming issues. I am sorry your father is not here anymore. But who can fight destiny? Mr. Mehra wanted to meet Mr. Isaac, as Dr. Kashyap had often mentioned his name."

"Yeah, Dad was very close to Isaac." Amrita agreed. "And he usually shared everything with him."

"We thought so," muttered the man as he patted his mustache.

"Did you say something?" She asked the guy.

"No, no, um, where can I find Isaac?"

"He is at the Kondana caves near..."

The man stood up abruptly, stopping her with a hand gesture. "I know the place." He walked to the door and opened it.

"Should I give any message to Isaac?" she asked his fleeing figure.

"Why trouble you? I will deliver whatever I am sent to do!" The man exited the home with these words, leaving her with thoughts.

And then, after a minute or so, she kept thinking about his last words while standing at the same place. They sounded more like a threat. Damn! What had she done? She shouldn't have opened her mouth. Instead, she told him Isaac's whereabouts.

Wincing in pain and embarrassment, Amrita didn't know what to do. She had no choice but to wait until Emerald or Ian came back.

Her legs were tired from pacing the room, and her heart heavy when, after an hour, they both returned.

One look at Amrita's pale face, and Emerald spoke at once, "What's wrong?"

Amrita lowered her head. They were already in trouble, and she added more to it. No hiding that fact now. They had to deal with it.

"Isaac is in trouble." Amrita took Emerald's hand and then told them the whole incident.

"Mehra," Ian gritted, repeating the name. Then he looked at Amrita. "You're right. He's a conman and doesn't have good intentions."

"What do we do now?" Amrita's voice was full of nervousness and fear. "I am sorry; I trusted him after he showed me an old picture of Dad."

Looking at her pale face, Ian came near. "Don't worry. We'll find a way. When did he come?"

"About an hour ago."

"Hmm, he will take around two hours to reach the caves." Ian looked at the wall clock. "That means he won't reach there before ten."

"How will we contact Isaac?" Amrita spoke in a troubled voice. "He would already be meditating."

"I can leave for the caves right now." Emerald's eager voice echoed in the room. "I'll reach Mehra in no time." She folded her hands in front and stood determinedly, waiting for Ian to respond.

"Wait, Em, let me think." Isaac Sr. replied.

As Amrita went to see about their dinner, Isaac Sr. looked outside. He knew the man might not be alone and could have associates. Isaac Sr. didn't understand why

Mehra's men were chasing his son. But one thing was sure. Issac Jr. would miss triggering the MayDAy signal if they stopped his meditation. There was only a single night left before the total moon eclipse.

Yes, Emerald could prevent those men from hurting Isaac. But his intuition warned that Emerald would not be available for something even more significant.

At this moment, he didn't know what else was happening.

And it was not good to disturb Nancy when she and Isaac Jr. were hellbent on reaching the North Pole and sending the signal. Ian decided to go with his gut.

"I am contacting Sacha, Em. Somehow, I feel that I might need you for even something more important than this. Something only you can carry out."

"You are worried about thralls, aren't you?" She raised an eyebrow, questioning him.

"You got me. I don't know what they might be up to. But I want you around."

She nodded without questioning his curiosity, and Isaac Sr. immediately phoned his daughter.

"But who is that meditating man?" She inquired. "And why do I need to save him?"

"What if I told you that the guy is key to saving the planet?" Isaac Sr. replied.

"Don't talk in riddles, Dad."

"When can you leave?" He didn't give more clarification.

"In five minutes, not sooner. After all, I am staying at a hotel in Lonavala. And you won't even tell me why."

"Trust me, I would have brought you here if possible. Now, please do as I say."

"Hey world, here I come, to save you, yay!!"

Sacha's enthusiastic and little sarcastic voice brought a smile of hope to her dad's face. He hung up the phone. He knew his daughter very well.

Chapter 50:

Sacha AND Isaac

"Wait until I get my hands on that two-timer," crooned Chopra as he approached his destination.

"Mr. Mehra is never going to forgive him for cheating," said another goon wearing a black sleeveless T-shirt and jeans. His clothes let him hide in the night.

"The bastard doesn't know nobody plays games with our boss." The third man with the scar on his left cheek spoke.

"And that girl was so naïve." Chopra laughed heartily. "She thought I was telling the truth."

"Why did you leave her there, boss?" The man in black smiled. "We should have kidnapped her."

Chopra stopped walking and slapped him. "Do you think you are smarter than me?"

"No, no," the man put his hand to his cheek and stammered," I didn't mean that."

"Then keep quiet and do as I say." Mr. Chopra blurted.

"Boss, I found two men who were following us. I killed them."

There was tension in the air as Sacha, hiding under bushes farther up the path, strained to hear the conversation. She had gritted her teeth when the talk turned to abducting Amrita. She listened for more.

"You think I didn't think of that, you idiot!" Chopra barked again. "They might be innocent people. Don't you remember Mr. Mehra told us not to attract attention?"

"Sorry, but what is the plan now?" The guy was nervous.

"We are almost there, and you are asking about the plan now?" Mr. Chopra lost his temper one more time. But then he calmed down, realizing his mistake. "Didn't we discuss it already? We should be reaching the cave in five minutes now," Chopra spoke with utter nonchalance as if he was talking about something else, not violence. "I will take Isaac while you both lift his Mom."

Mom? So, there was someone else with that Isaac fellow in the cave. But Dad had not said anything about that.

Sacha waited for a minute, her ears tuned to the scene. From here, she kept watch. The leader, who called himself Chopra, was relaxed as if he was out for a walk. Nobody could tell from his smiling face what he would do next. His oiled hair sat flatly on his head as his white clothes flashed in the night light.

Sacha stared at those three men. She was hungry, exhausted, and a little angry with her dad because he wouldn't tell her the real reason for sending her here.

She wondered what kind of man Isaac was that he needed protection.

As they took more steps, her heart sped up in her ribcage. From here, she couldn't see if they carried any weapons. But she was running out of time. They were fast approaching. And while she wondered how to prevent their progress, she sneezed. And that drew attention in the quiet night. Harsh flashlights fell on the bush where she was hiding.

And then the sound. "Hey, who is hiding there?"

Stillness hit on both sides. If her anger were visible, the air would have been red. Then suddenly, she heard footsteps in her direction, and she rose.

The man in black didn't even know what hit him. Sacha's blow had so much force he fell and dripped blood.

Before the other two came to help, he stood up again and struck Sacha. His fist slammed into her face, and her stomach sank. Blood filled Sacha's mouth, and she stumbled briefly, noticing that Chopra and another guy had arrived.

Her eyes narrowed in determination as she punched blow after blow. The assailant's eyes widened before Sacha tilted her head and slammed it into his. She wanted to crush him to the ground.

"Who is this girl?" Chopra asked as the other man threw a punch that Sacha dodged and returned one of her own. In response, the man threw a sloppy kick, but it didn't work. He was no match for her.

Within a few minutes, she had both the guys on the ground, unconscious in a pool of their own his blood.

"I don't know who you are. But I don't want anyone in my way tonight." Chopra took a menacing step towards her. "Trust me, I take no pleasure in taking you down. But I'll kill you if you don't disappear right now. And anyway, everyone has to die someday."

She stepped back. Her instinct told her of danger. Run! It told her. But she was not a coward. She wouldn't go before she finished her task.

Her eyes observed each movement. When Chopra's shoulder relaxed a bit, she took a deep breath, and that was the moment Chopra needed.

She didn't see when he pulled out a gun, but a bullet spat out of his hand, hitting her forearm.

Sacha fell backward. She bled. Although she winced from the pain, instantly, she removed the scarf from her hair, tied it around the wound, and turned her eyes to her target.

Chopra waited as if he thought she would leave. He was analyzing her next move.

"Is that how you fight?" She gestured towards his gun as she crowed.

"Don't you taunt me," Chopra threw his gun to the ground. "You don't know how powerful I am."

And before he could move, she stepped in his direction. Her knuckles were bruised, and a deep scar bled from her arm, but she didn't care.

Growling, she threw herself at him with such force that Chopra could not avoid the attack. He looked down, and his eyes found a brick on the ground. He picked it up and threw it at her.

But he didn't know Sacha, neither her physical strength nor psychic powers. Her powerful chop broke the brick in half.

Regretting his decision to toss his weapon, Chopra scanned his surroundings, noticing the gun was lying at a small distance.

"You don't know who I am." He moved to grab his weapon when Sacha, like a thunderbolt, charged and swung her fist.

A rage-filled scream paralyzed the whole setting as Chopra's brain stopped working. Her second blow doubled up his abdomen. He fell to the ground into the fetal position to protect his vital organs.

Still wanting to kill her, he stretched his hand toward the gun. But Sacha's punch took his breath, stars danced before his eyes, and he lost all consciousness.

She picked up the gun.

The scarf around her wound had fallen away.

It was time to go back. Her work was finished.

But a magnetic pull stopped her when she turned away from the caves.

Why do I feel as if my work is still ongoing?

Did Dad send me only to stop Chopra?

There were so many questions that needed answers.

Sticking to her intuition, Sacha walked. She didn't have a clue about where and how she would spend the night. But staying near the caves was her destiny, which would show the way.

The silence turned eerie. She ventured out, following her instinct. Her footsteps echoed in the still air. After checking out her surroundings, she saw a faint silhouette of something resembling a building. She went near. Her eyes flickered as she looked at the ancient tower that had seen better days.

Luckily, she carried some water, food, and extra clothes in her rucksack as usual. That would sustain her for some time, at least.

She washed the wound and tied it again, not knowing what awaited her.

§§§§§§§§§§

While Sacha sat outside the cave and inside, Isaac and Nancy meditated, nature staged the majestic event they all needed. The Earth moved between the Moon and the Sun, casting nature's most immense shadow that moved quickly, plunging the Moon into night. Total. Darkness.

§§§§§§§§§§

Was it a gunshot? No, it can't be. Who can do it at such a time as now? At this quiet place?

But he was sure he had heard it and was not dreaming. Isaac almost got up.

Someone was in trouble, and he should go out and check it.

But he was running out of time and would fail in the mission if he didn't continue. The Sun, Earth, and Moon were in a straight line and would not remain like this for long.

From the depth of his being, Isaac knew that if he failed this time, there was no looking back. He would fail his mom, teacher, and the planet.

But at the same time, he couldn't stop his conscience.

He listened carefully. When things went quiet, he thought it must be something else and concentrated on the meditation again. But it was not easy sas his thoughts played ping-pong around his head.

355

He wouldn't be Isaac if he were not restless, would he? No.

But when Dr. Kashyap's face flashed before his eyes, grief sliced through his body.

Sitting in a padmasana (The Lotus pose), Isaac focused on his breathing as he chanted *Om So Hum*. The serene glow of a couple of his candles illuminated the small space.

Nancy was also sitting in the same position, on the floor, her eyes closed as she, too, used the mantra.

She also heard the shot, but she didn't say anything.

§§§§§§§§§

Nancy Newfield was not a totally relaxed and happy woman right now. Being here at the cave on the night of the moon eclipse was not something she did frequently.

Sitting without fidgeting didn't come quickly to her, unlike her son. She was trying her best, given the circumstances. She closed her eyes but lost focus after hearing the gunshot.

She shook her head, which suddenly filled with vivid images of her injured daughter. Did something happen to her? But Sacha didn't know her mother or Isaac. She didn't have any reason to be in Nancy's mind.

And then Nancy concentrated more on finding out the reason behind her restlessness.

Sitting on the smooth dirt in the folded leg position, she kept thinking about her husband and Sacha.

And like other times, her gift didn't disappoint her.

Like a movie, all the events flashed on the screen of her mind: how Mr. Mehra wanted to take revenge, how Chopra had fooled Amrita and found out Isaac's whereabouts. And how her husband had sent Sacha to protect her brother.

And then it dawned on her.

The task they were going to do was common to all of them.

But, unless both her children were united by intent, they would not win!

How come she had overlooked such an important aspect?

And how had her husband understood Sacha needed to be with them tonight?

She thanked him silently and then got back to her role. It was her duty to unite the twins.

With increased awareness and fiery breath, Nancy sent powerful thoughts into the universe. As Nancy wished, Sacha would know why her role was not over yet.

Once satisfied with her psychic work, Nancy returned to the meditation and joined her son.

After a couple of minutes, both of them opened their eyes.

"Are you ready?" She asked him quietly.

He nodded. He was the one who had protested and accused her of hiding things. And yet here he was. Calm and controlled.

Nancy wondered if it had to do anything with Sacha's presence outside.

She had done all she could to give Isaac a head start. She had talked about the UFO many times. She had even mentioned her own experience.

Yet, she wanted to join him in teleporting. *Remember, the UFO is at the bottom of the ocean, precisely at the North Pole,* she transmitted.

Yes.

You don't have any idea about what you are getting into. She recited again breathlessly. *Don't forget other aliens attacked the UFO.*

Mom, are you doubting my abilities or scaring me? This time, Isaac was a little irritated.

Thinking about the danger her children would face, yet another of the myriad concerns took over. Ignoring it, Nancy sighed and then spoke. "What time is it?"

Isaac stood up and looked at his watch.

"I should start preparing."

Her eyes went to his perspired forehead, and she almost opened her mouth to tell him about Sacha.

But instead, she too rose. "Can you connect with me from the North Pole?"

The extreme weather condition and their enemy flashed in front of her eyes.

"My guess is as good as yours, Mom."

Her breath quickened at the thought of what was lying ahead. She imagined him in the Arctic sea, all alone, searching for the UFO, and a fresh tear fell from her eye.

"Nothing will happen to me, Mom." Isaac then pressed his hand on hers. Was it his reassuring touch or some other influence, Nancy didn't know. But images of happy people living without fear filled her mind, and she smiled. She imagined her children restoring the Earth's Schumann Resonance.

"I'm sure we'll win," the words escaped her mouth, and then she knew it was time to let her son go and do what he was destined to do.

§§§§§§§§§§

"Did you hear that, Queekan?" Huda adjusted the headphone-like device worn over his large head. "The man doesn't even know what he is getting into. Does he think accessing a UFO at the North Pole is as easy as dowsing for water hidden under the earth?"

"Let him think so," Queekan crooned. "But don't worry, Huda. He won't succeed."

"Be careful," Huda whispered. "And don't forget to take Gravak."

"He is already here. You are worrying uselessly." Queekan added. "That man is too weak. Gravak had almost killed him last time near this same place. Remember how useless Isaac was at protecting himself?"

"And yet he didn't succeed." Huda's voice was filled with regret. "I don't want any mistakes this time. If you need, take more thralls."

"No, you are underestimating us. We are enough for this small task." Queekan boasted. "Within no time, we will send you a signal of victory."

And with that, Queekan disappeared.

Huda stared at the blank space where Queekan had been a few minutes before. He sighed in relief.

§§§§§§§§§

"Why are you pacing the room, Emerald?" Ian asked.

"Aundrid just contacted me." She stopped and then spoke. "He asked me to be ready."

Ian stole a look at the night sky. "Let's hope things work in our favor."

"It will. I am sure," said Emerald, and then she turned to him. "Just in case I need a cover…"

"I will handle Amrita if she asks for you." He cut her sentence in the middle.

"Alright."

"Did you hear from Sacha?"

"No, she should be returning anytime now." Ian, AKA Isaac Sr., sighed. "That girl is so strong-headed. Won't let me accompany her."

"Don't I know that?"

"But she doesn't know me," Isaac Sr. said. "I have arranged for my people to keep an eye on her. I hope they are doing their job."

"I won't bet on that!" Emerald smiled. "You should have let me go."

"No news is good news as of now. But I won't be able to rest until I hear from them." Anyway, all the best, Em. I know you won't let any harm come to the tweens."

And with that, Ian, also known as Isaac Sr., left the room. His work was done. Now, it was his children's time to take it from here.

Little did he know that Chopra's man had already killed the men he had sent after Sacha.

§§§§§§§§§

Isaac Jr. concentrated on the details given by his mom. He imagined himself teleporting to a distant place, and despite knowing everything, he found his thoughts drifting back to the times he had not succeeded.

A time when, during an India festival, someone had tried to kill him.

Or the time when Mr. Mehra's men had abducted him.

Or the time when he was almost killed near these caves.

His watch started buzzing. He had no more time to reminisce about events now. He had to summon his energies and think positively if he wanted to save the Earth.

But what if he failed?

Isaac was tired of his failures. He was not coming back if he failed.

It was surprising for him when the eerie silence turned peaceful. This was Isaac's thought as he closed his eyes and started to think about the journey north.

In no time after starting, he felt as light as a cotton fluff in the air. He could sense he had taken off, as his body weightlessly moved. And next, he flew out of the cave.

§§§§§§§§§

Not knowing what she was looking for, Sacha lifted her head, but she could only see the dark-pitched night sky.

Was she hallucinating?

Had pain made her dream now?

She was sure there was some movement from the cave.

She stretched her eyes and looked at it again. Nobody was there. Then why did she feel as if someone had come out?

She brushed off the feeling and broke the cookie in two, eating one part.

Had she imagined it, or was someone calling her? It was as if some invisible thread pulled her, and she didn't know where she was headed.

§§§§§§§§§

Isaac Jr. didn't have time to think about the mechanics of his skill. Isaac didn't know how long it was going to take him. All he knew was he had to reach the UFO.

He soared higher and higher, obviously unable to see the girl sitting all alone back at the cave. In the black night, he didn't feel any wind even as he speeded up.

His intuition and willpower were the wind beneath his wings right now.

And then suddenly, to indicate he was not alone, the blood-red moon ignited the whole sky, and he watched the coppery fiery magic in awe, temporarily forgetting why he was here. The magnificent moon took his breath away, literally hypnotizing him.

Isaac didn't know how long he had been staring at it; his focus wavered, and suddenly, the thoughts of failing at the mission overtook him.

He was like a scared, confused child who didn't know what he wanted to do.

Should he return?

He was not made to do this gigantic task.

He had no energy to do this.

And then, as if a strong belief had removed the cloud over his disbelief, his mind cleared.

It was as if an unknown hand was holding his hand, indicating he was not alone anymore.

He turned his head and looked around. There was nobody, and yet he sensed a powerful presence everywhere.

Who was it that pulled him like a magnetic bond?

Isaac didn't know anyone else who could teleport except for his mom.

And yet, he could not deny the presence of someone who had made him energetic, focused, and calm again.

Finally. There was no point wasting more time.

There was nothing to fear. He was in the right direction, and even nature was with him.

He had never imagined he would be watching the blood moon like this and feel something so deeply. Feeling ignited and recharged, he quickened his pace.

The air grew thick and heavy as he crossed lands, farms, towns, cities, oceans, and continents. And then, at last, the air was freezing.

Gravak sniffed and then raised his hand. A dense fog had erupted out of nowhere, turning visibility to almost zero.

Moaning, Isaac Jr. strained his eyes to see.

The visibility was almost zero, and he thought about nature being with him.

His gut felt that he had reached the destination.

The fog got denser now.

Fighting hard to see, he focused down and saw the vast Arctic Ocean.

Time to land.

Remember, the UFO is a saucer-like thing made of imitation wood, with a twenty to twenty-five feet diameter. The material can't be either broken or burned. There is not a single instrument or piece of electronic equipment or inside it. However, it has many small pieces of metal, like tin foil, on the bottom. Small beams with some hieroglyphics support it. Pink and purple symbols on the top look as if they are painted.

Nancy's words echoed in his mind, and he knew exactly what he was looking for.

Isaac slowly descended and dived under the water.

He was not ready for this.

He had thought his teleporting power would take him straight to the UFO if he focused enough.

Instead, he fell into the ocean itself.

Flapping his hands and legs, he started to swim. As his head bobbed beneath the waves, he was initially not very worried.

But after a few minutes, he wanted to change his opinion.

Panic started to take hold as he went deeper and deeper.

There was no one around, and he was not a good swimmer. What if he couldn't make it?

Every cell in his body screamed for oxygen; on top of that, he had to find the UFO.

Isaac started to think about his mother, hoping he would be able to connect with her psychically.

Like his childhood, he could maybe complete this difficult task with his mom's wise guidance and watchful eyes.

But his head pounded as if it would explode any minute.

And there was no way he could bring his mom onboard the sunken UFO.

Thrashing the water in frustration, he kept going.

The cold water had taken him by surprise. But he kept telling himself he would reach his destination.

The chill of the sea disappeared. Instead, a new type of paranoia took over. What if he could not survive finding the UFO?

And then, as if someone had waved a magic wand, he sensed the calm he was used to feeling before.

What had happened?

His crazy heartbeat had returned to its normal rhythm again.

And he was not struggling to swim anymore.

Instead, he floated in the water without a single care.

Air bubbles rose to the surface in clusters as he swam in the blue water, passing schools of bright-hued fish.

He didn't know oceans were so beautiful from the inside. Forgetting about all his worries, Isaac just concentrated on the task at hand.

He kept staring at an ever-changing panorama some five hundred feet beneath the surface. With the increasing pressure, he began to feel the water had become thicker, but there was no going back.

A lone fish passed him, and he stared at the marvel only a deep sea could bring. Isaac had trouble sensing it when someone pulled his leg. At first, he didn't realize, and then he was utterly shocked, totally unaware.

Isaac lowered his head in disbelief that someone else could be there. And what he saw was enough to chill his blood even more.

A dark-looking strange creature had captured him. He looked like a human, but Isaac could see he was not. The creature's golden-brown eyes glistened like topaz.

Isaac fumbled and tried to hit him, but it was agile at deep-sea depths.

It was getting difficult to hold his breath as the creature started to pull him towards the sea floor.

Something shone in the water, and Isaac realized he was near the UFO. All he had to do was free himself from this strange thing's clutch.

Isaac Jr. had started to swallow some water now and knew it was not good.

His limbs were tired before he even reached the UFO.

Isaac summoned all his force and tried one more time when a hand slipped around his mouth, and he almost screamed.

Another human-like strange creature had joined the previous one. And if they both pulled him down, he was no match for them, at least not under the water.

But no, he had to fight.

He had promised his mom.

He was here to save the planet.

Isaac Jr. gritted his teeth and struck his elbow to the creature's body.

The creature winced in pain. His grip loosened for a moment. And Isaac Jr. sighed in relief. But that joy was short-lived as the creature came back.

Were these the aliens his mom was talking about?

Well, Isaac didn't have much time to think.

If he didn't do something now, he would die.

Amrita and Nancy's faces flashed before his eyes, and Isaac winced.

Will he never see them?

Will he never know who his dad was?

What would happen to the promise he had given to Dr. Kashyap?

We each have strengths, but if you don't believe in yourself, you can't save yourself; forget about saving the world.

The words echoed in his mind, and he recalled the girl who had told this to him.

A new resolve filled him. He kicked hard, and this time, the creature holding his leg let out a painful cry.

But he wouldn't let go of Isaac's leg.

He was running out of time, and Isaac knew it very well.

Then, a rich mahogany handle and curved blade shone in the water as the girl moved swiftly under the water with her dagger, slicing both creatures within a minute.

The water turned grey as the black liquid oozed from the creatures.

Isaac's eyes widened. Wasn't she the same girl he had seen on Holi and near the Kondana caves? She was the one who had saved his life before.

How had she known he was in danger?

How did she reach here?

Suddenly, there was a storm as the wind howled, and the sky opened, bringing rain in heavy sheets, and the sea rose like a mountain, its water turning turbulent and unsettling. The wind rose, morphing the waves in angry chops, and Isaac couldn't understand what was happening.

But this storm reminded him of something.

He had faced such storms before. But when and where?

Isaac fought hard to remember but couldn't.

The girl still swam peacefully as if unaware or unaffected by the storm.

He wanted to thank her, but she pointed towards the shiny saucer and held his hand as they slowly swam.

It was challenging, but he had come so far.

It was indeed the UFO he was searching for. Isaac was tired now. And the girl didn't look any better.

His eyes went to the scarf that she had tied to her forearm.

Was she hurt?

He didn't have time to think much.

Isaac silently focused on the task at hand and closed his eyes.

MayDay! MayDay! MayDay! He repeated it three times and followed it with all the relevant information potential rescuers would need. As taught by Nancy.

His eyes were closed so that he couldn't see, but the storm disappeared immediately. And suddenly, as if someone carved out a road up there, a pink light rose upward through the water and then through the air, making way for a purple light before disappearing deep into the cosmos.

Then, a green curtain rose, igniting, swaying, stretching through the horizon in a beautiful carnal dance. An army of vivid shades marched through the entire sky, filling it in full glory.

Unaware of how the refreshed crystal field at the North Pole had amplified the Schumann Resonance, Isaac kept concentrating.

When he opened his eyes, he screamed.

The girl's scarf had shifted; she was bleeding and in too much pain.

Isaac didn't know what to do now.

How was he ever going to get help here?

He grabbed the girl's hand firmly but could sense he would not make it back.

His focus was diminishing, and he would need a lot of strength.

His eyes glazed under water as he drifted into the daze.

And then, someone pulled both of them.

Before sleeping in the dark pool, Isaac could see it was Emerald.

Isaac sighed.

He knew they both were in safe hands.

Epilogue:
The Awesome Part

After bringing the tweens back safely from the ocean, teary-eyed Emerald informed the parents that she was glad she had the opportunity to help them.

It was time for her to live with the Nordics. However, when the need arises, she would return quickly.

"We are sorry we could never inform the children who you are!" Nancy was barely able to speak.

"Mom, but at least I was a significant part of their lives. And that's enough for me."

"Promise me that you will keep in touch with us."

"Of course, who is going to stop me?" Emerald tried to smile. "There are many planets like Earth. Who knows? Maybe Aundrid will send me on another mission to Earth."

Nancy silently nodded as her daughter left.

Isaac Sr. had taken Sacha to her hotel room, and he stayed with her there.

Once Isaac Sr. was sure Sacha slept soundly, he called Nancy.

"How is she doing?"

"The doctor said, luckily, the wound was not very deep. The bullet had not penetrated the skin but touched it briefly. He treated the wound and gave her an injection. Don't worry, she is sleeping peacefully."

"Thank God, my heart had almost stopped when Emerald reported the twin's condition when she found them."

Isaac, a man of few words, spoke. "I'm going to miss that girl, Em."

"Do you think our children will remember anything once they get up?" She asked.

"I don't think so. Remember what Aundrid had mentioned."

"Yeah," her voice was low. "I talked with Aundrid. The tweens have strengthened the Schumann Resonance, and thralls 'power has been reduced significantly.

However, Aundrid warned that this didn't mean they wouldn't try to attack the crystal field and again reduce the Schumann Resonance.

For the time being, the planet is safe. Of course, it will take a couple of days to see how the stronger Schumann Resonance affects people," Nancy concluded.

"Yes, I should also report to the US military that yogic powers can be used for non-lethal defense. Those powers conquered alien monsters by activating the UFO transponder at the North Pole. We have come a long way, Nan," Isaac spoke.

"Yes," she sighed. "And look what a fabulous journey it was!"

"The only regret would be not staying together as a family." Isaac Sr. confessed. "Will you be ever able to forgive me for tearing apart our family?"

Nancy stood up and said on her phone," You did what you were supposed to do. And remember, it was not only your decision. Mine, too. Because we had to let our kids fulfill their destiny."

"What are you planning to do now?" Isaac asked.

"Maybe start a psychic archaeology business dowsing for ancient cities," she smiled. "I will just support our son in whatever he prefers to do now."

"I hope Mr. Mehra will leave him alone after this incident." He added.

"Yes, and what about you?"

"It all depends on Sacha. She told me she wanted to join the CIA. So perhaps I will go there with her."

"It's been a long night. You should go to sleep now." Nancy told her husband.

"A night which we are never going to forget."

"You are an incredible man, Isaac; I will miss you." And with that, Nancy hung up. She kept thinking about the past, how she and Isaac had met, their journey on Nautilus, the birth of their children, and their awe-inspiring destiny.

She didn't even know when she fell asleep on the couch.

Misty-eyed Amrita was sitting on Isaac Jr.'s bed when he opened his eyes. It was morning, and the early sun rays kissed the earth.

"Hey, good morning." He greeted her.

Amrita didn't reply. The tears preserved in her eyes started to fall at once.

He got up and sat on the bed. "Why are you crying?"

Wiping away her tears, she tried to smile. "Nothing. How do you feel?"

"Me?" Isaac Jr.'s lips flashed a smile. "Awesome, just exhausted, but nothing to worry about. Maybe I should stop reading so late."

Amrita's lips parted, but she couldn't speak when Isaac spread his arms towards her. And forgetting about all her worries, she snuggled in. His hug was more robust than anything she had ever known. And his strong arms told her everything that Amrita wanted to know.

About the Author

John Walter Sorflaten holds a Bachelor's Degree in Cinema Arts and Humanities, a Master's Degree in Education, and a PhD in Visual Studies. Born and brought up in Saint Cloud, Minnesota, John has many decades of experience as a usability engineer plus snow.

His friends and family consider him to be a classic INTJ personality. Moreover, John Sorflaten hails from Norwegian descent but has no accent. Even though his profession of making computer programs and web sits more user-friendly falls more on the technical/psychological side, his passion for writing insightful blogs on making human-computer interaction easier and enjoyable makes him a writer-to-be-dealt-with. Google him. Or Bing him. Or whatever.

John Sorflaten has a flair for both the technical and creative. He can be analytical and pursue artistic endeavors like making poems and films (documentaries). Moreover, John's day-to-day routine involves enjoying creation, meditating, and deriving profound conclusions about the nature of life before going to bed.

John recently visited his hometown of Saint Cloud, Minnesota, 67 years after leaving at age 13. He drove by the house where he lived in the 3rd to 8th grade. He examined the house his father built on the edge of town (at that time, next to the woods). He only recently realized that his father built this house so that his kids could play in that woody area and John could deliver newspapers near the edge of town. Or maybe the land was cheaper.

Besides the apparent nostalgia, John describes living in his childhood home as "A profound influence that set the tone for the rest of my life. I had the privilege of seeing nature's grandeur right next to my house. It was a blessing and overwhelming experience!"

Talking about his past, John left the Air Force as a motion picture officer in 1972. By the end of that year, he had traveled to California and Spain to complete his training as a teacher of Transcendental Meditation ™. In his words, life after that became "easier and more fulfilling." He still practices TM to this day and credits it as one of the most positive changes of his life, in addition to working at the National Security Agency for eight years, two marriages, two children, and five cats. And writing a novel or two with help.

Speaking more about the recent past, John recently discovered a book published in 2021 called "Radio

Psychics," by John Benedict Buescher. Because the subtitle said "mind reading" and the dates encompassed the career of his paternal grandmother who *was* a mind reader on the stage and radio, he looked in the Table of Contents.

Sure enough, *Signa Serene,* his dear grandma, has a chapter in the book. As the reviewer for *The Skeptic* published on its website 24 December, 2022, *"many performers cashed in on "Ladies Only" performances, Signa Serene specialized in this intimate advice format."*

Yes, that was so cool, he thought. He remembered his dad, Eugene, saying that as a recent high school graduate around 1928 or so, he traveled with his mom, playing the accordion during entertainment breaks on the Chautauqua. Yes, she had a few tricks up her sleeve (blouse), such as identifying the page and column of a newspaper for specific items that reporters tested her on. My dad said her manager used a word code to communicate the challenge through closed doors. For example, to start the question session, her manager would relay the question by saying "Um, Serene" to mean "page one." And "two reporters want to know if' ....as referring to Column 6 in the day's paper. You get the idea. She would rattle off the selected headline to wondrous applause and write in the local newspaper.

The idea of "Thrall Conspiracy Solar Conjunction" came to John's mind when he cognized a unique riddle. The riddle was that a hero was told by his dying mother that he was born out of time. After contemplating this riddle, John asked himself, What is the answer? How is that possible? Is it EVEN possible? Not long after that, the book took its overall shape.

In his contemplation, John realized that there were only two places on the Earth where all the time zones in the world flew together. *So, what time is it at the North (or*

South) pole? "Aha," he said. Eventually, John was able to answer this riddle and thought, *This answer is fantastic! The riddle and its answer should be a part of a book!*

He stumbled upon a historical instance that could support that riddle by remembering a particular August 23rd, 1958 event. The nuclear submarine "Nautilus" passed over the North Pole at 11:15 PM using an Eastern Standard Time clock. He then thought, What if I could write a novel based on the North Pole, The Nautilus, and someone being born? And the rest was, as they say, history.

The inspiration for the main character of *Thrall Conspiracy Solar Conjunction*, "Isaac Newfield," came from the Old Testament/Pentateuch (*Genesis*). In the legend of Genesis, God instructed Abraham to demonstrate his piety by sacrificing his son, not a customary animal.

Isaac's mother had given birth to him after menopause despite being infertile. As told an angel came down and informed Abraham and his wife that they would have a son. After hearing this, Abraham laughed, and before long, Isaac was born. Because of this, Abraham named his son "Isaac," which means "he laughs."

As the story goes, angels told Abraham to fulfill God's wish and sacrifice Isaac. But right before that critical moment, God instructed him not to sacrifice his son. Believe it or not, his story is discussed not only by theologians but also by very interesting people like Carl Jung, the renowned psychologist.

Carl Jung describes the commitment to sacrifice Isaac as symbolic of sacrificing selfish claims--a form of self-sacrifice. Apart from Jung, the illustrious 19th-century philosopher Søren Kierkegaard also wrote about this story in his book Fear and Trembling.

However, Kierkegaard defines the story in a completely different context to Jung. Kierkegaard described the event as a potential "murder" but also evidence that a bigger picture like Abraham's can work wonders. In other words, philosophically, the name Isaac has a lot of baggage, and his story has a special significance, especially concerning forces beyond our control.

This ends what John gave us about him. He said he'd put more stuff on the website, www.sorflaten.com, including source material for the book. He found cool articles about extra-terrestrials meeting President Eisenhower, medical studies about identical twins with different genders, plus other weird stuff.

www.ingramcontent.com/pod-product-compliance
Lightning Source LLC
Chambersburg PA
CBHW072109250626
47159CB00007B/2375

"SOVIET COMMANDER, THIS IS MAJOR CURT CARSON!"

Carson's voice, amplified by the loudspeaker, boomed out over the burning town.

"We are strong enough to win if we have to fight," he continued, "but we come under a flag of truce!"

Carson knew from experience that he needed a show of strength to convince the commander of the Spetsnaz battalion. At that precise instant, black holes appeared in the starry sky as the lightless Harpies, operating in stealth, topped the eastern ridge and ducked down into the gorge. The thunder of their passage shook the ground.

Carson stood up and pulled a white flag from his harness pack, a flag that signified not surrender but a willingness to negotiate before the killing.

He hoped to God the Soviet commander wouldn't fire the 73-millimeter that was aimed at him. He'd become meat if that happened. No way his body armor could stop that kind of incoming...